Border
Ambush

ANOTHER SAGEBRUSH LARGE PRINT WESTERN BY
WALKER A. TOMPKINS

Flaming Canyon

Border Ambush

WALKER A. TOMPKINS

Sagebrush
Large Print Westerns

Library of Congress Cataloging in Publication Data

Tompkins, Walker A.
    Border ambush / Walker A. Tompkins.
       p.   cm.
    ISBN 1-57490-201-6 (alk. paper)
    1. Large type books. I. Title.
[PS3539.03897B67   1999]
813'.54—dc21   99-30786
                                                           CIP

Cataloguing in Publication Data is available from
the British Library and the National Library of Australia.

An earlier, shorter version of this story appeared as "Gunhand from Mustang Mesa" in *Two Western Books* (Spring, 51).

Sagebrush Large Print Westerns are published in the United States and Canada by Thomas T. Beeler, Publisher, Box 659, Hampton Falls, New Hampshire 03844-0659. ISBN 1-57490-201-6

Published in the United Kingdom, Eire, and the Republic of South Africa by Isis Publishing Ltd, 7 Centremead, Osney Mead, Oxford OX2 0ES England. ISBN 0-7531-6014-5

Published in Australia and New Zealand by Australian Large Print Audio & Video Pty Ltd, 17 Mohr Street, Tullamarine, Victoria, 3043, Australia. ISBN 1-86442-247-5

Manufactured in the United States of America by Sheridan Books in Chelsea, Michigan.

FOR
CARYL, RUTH, and CARL SCHWEIZER
to whom I am indebted for
true Western hospitality

Border
Ambush

CHAPTER 1

BONES ON MUSTANG MESA

DOUG REDDING LEFT THE POKER GAME LONG ENOUGH to move his roan's picket pin to a fresh patch of grass. He tarried on his way back to the camp to roll a smoke, loath to face the others while this frustrated mood soured his temper.

Under the guise of a mustang hunter, Redding had scoured these Navajada wastelands all summer, without coming any closer to solving the mystery of a man's disappearance in these very hills. Tomorrow they would be back in Fort Paloverde with the herd, and Redding would be back where he started.

A setting moon threw the high peaks into stark relief, sinister and lonely, its silver shine failing to penetrate the piñon thickets above the wash where Jace Blackwine had camped.

Beyond the fence of lass ropes strung across the box end of the barranca, fifty-odd head of *oreana* mustangs were bedded down, the fruits of their summer-long hunt here on the edge of the Mexican border, fuzztails, that would fetch a handsome price from the remount officer down at the cavalry post.

Redding returned to the glare of the flaming pitch knot stuck in a split rock above the spread-out blanket where the stud game was in progress. He was reluctant to get back in the game, indifferent to the stake he had in the pot.

Half the crew were already rolled up in their blankets beyond the scarlet dance of the torchlight. Bull McArdle

1

growled a cranky admonition for Redding to quit delaying the game. A moose of a man who, in common with certain others of the crew, had joined Blackwine's horse hunt as a convenient method of eluding a posse that had driven him west out of Texas, McArdle was dealing the greasy deck of cards.

Redding fired his smoke from the pine-knot torch and seated himself alongside the Rickaree Kid, a slim younker who tended the outfit's pack string. The Kid at the moment was holding a little black metal disk up for all to see, before dropping it into the pile of chips and 'dobe dollars and scribbled IOUs making up the pot in the middle of the blanket.

"I'll see you, Boney, and raise you four bits, genuwine *americano* dinero."

Jace Blackwine, the cinnamon-whiskered boss who wore the greasy fringed buckskins of a mountain man, bent curiously to pick up the tarnished coin the Kid had dropped and tested it between his yellow snags of teeth.

"A four-bit piece, for a fact," Blackwine grunted. "Where'd you come by any hard money our last night in the hills, Kid? And you claimin' you was broke the past couple months."

The Rickaree Kid winked at Redding. "Funny thing about that coin, boss. You remember this afternoon when that ornery crop-eared jenny bolted on me. I chased her down a gully directly under Thimble Rock. Run acrost a man's skeleton there—what was left of it after the buzzard and lobos had finished scatterin' it."

Redding's eyes carried a quick interest as he waited for the packer to go on. The others merely looked skeptically amused.

"I found this four-bit piece plastered into a round hole in the skull. Looked like somebody had bored it there a-purpose, Damndest thing I ever see. Brought the coin back for luck."

Bull McArdle flipped a card to the Rickaree Kid, face up. The other gamblers were guffawing at this latest evidence of the Kid's fertile imagination—with the exception of Doug Redding.

"The Kid ain't lyin'," Blackwine spoke up. "Them bones prob'ly belonged to some trooper who let the 'Paches count coup on him. That silver piece in his noggin was a patch put there by some Army surgeon after a skull injury. Trepannin', the medicos call it. Cut out a chunk of damaged bone with a circular-shaped saw, inlay a hunk o' silver, and stitch the scalp back over it. Saw it happen more'n once durin' my soldierin' days."

Doug Redding's eyes, metal-blue in the flicker of the pine torch, were fixed on the black coin the Kid had anted. He seemed oblivious to McArdle's testy snarl for him to match the Kid's bet or throw in his cards.

Leaning forward, Redding reached a rope-calloused hand into the kitty and picked up the tarnished disk of metal. "Minted in '46," he said in a voice which carried a strange quality no man there could interpret, He repeated his statement, as if it were important. "Minted, in '46—"

McArdle cut in angrily, "Are we playin' poker, or is this, an old ladies' sewin' circle? It's your bet, Redding."

Redding's mouth hardened behind the curly black beard which four months without a razor had put on his jaw. There was a festering rivalry between these two, Redding and McArdle, for Redding had bested McArdle's mustang gather to qualify for the fat bonus Blackwine had promised the man who caught the largest number of *oreanas* which would meet the Army's rigid specifications.

"I'll stay," Redding said harshly, shoving the last of his chips into the pile. "I got a flush to fill here."

McArdle's porcelain-hard eyes held a crafty glitter as his thick fingers deftly scaled a deuce of clubs across the blanket to nullify the diamond flush Redding had in sight. The dealer's glance switched to Blackwine, next in line for the deal.

"Hold on, McArdle." Redding's voice was low-pitched, but the threat of it carried into the roundabout shadows and brought men jerking up in their blankets, sensing trouble about to break. "I don't cotton to getting a card off the bottom of the pack, even if you'd filled my flush with it."

Bull McArdle stiffened. He laid the pack of cards down carefully and came to his feet, a towering giant of a man, his legs thick as oak boles in his apron chaps.

"By Gawd, Redding, are you sayin' I cold-decked you?"

Redding was up now, showing a side of his easy-going nature these mustangers had never guessed existed.

"If the boot fits, Bull, haul it on. I got the top hand, so far. I don't aim to have no tin horn euchre me out of it."

Jace Blackwine came ponderously to his feet to stand between the belligerents, speaking with the tolerant amusement of a boss who had anticipated trouble long before this as the nerves of his tough crew were rubbed raw by grueling weeks of the hunt behind them, making them edgy and spoiling for fight.

"Come off, now, boys! What the hell, the pot don't amount to a hill of frijoles. We'll deal over an'—"

"Damn the pot!" Redding chewed out. "I'd call

4

McArdle for a slick-fingered crook even if we were playing for toothpicks."

The camp comedian, Old Boney the cook, sang out jocularly, "Why droop a horn this time, Doug? We all know McArdle monkeys with the cards ever' time he deals. Hell—"

But the thing had gone beyond the limits of a mere flare-up of tempers between two men who hated each other's guts. Redding had made his challenge, and McArdle had seized it, chuckling deep in his throat as he unbuckled his double shell belts and dumped them onto the blanket.

Spitting on his fists, McArdle thundered gleefully, "Unlimber your hardware, Redding, and we'll see if you got what it takes to finish this play you've started."

Redding's cold gaze was oblivious to the scrambling withdrawal of his fellow hunters. Without haste he unbuckled his cartridge harness and tossed it on the blanket, matched Peacemaker .45s in basket-woven holsters.

Blackwine and his mustangers had automatically formed a ring to fence in this arena. There was little doubt in any of their minds how this fight would go. McArdle outweighed Redding by a margin of eighty pounds; the Bull had a long record of gouged-out eyeballs and stomped guts behind him, schooled as he was in the ruthless art of barroom brawling, abiding by no decent rules of combat, giving no quarter and expecting none.

No man knew much about Redding, on the other hand. He had been an unobtrusive member of the expedition all summer, friendly but never speaking of his past. With guns, Redding might have a chance with the slow-moving McArdle; in a bare-fisted brawl, he was foredoomed to being chopped into a bloody ruin, maybe killed, at the least crippled by McArdle's murderous boots and sledge-hammer fists.

Redding lifted his palms to wipe them on his calfhide vest. McArdle chose that instant to charge, head down like the bull he resembled. Men yelled in dismay, then in excitement, as they saw Redding side-step his Gargantuan opponent's rush and clip the bigger man hard to the left ear, a blow that made McArdle gasp and shake his head dazedly as he wheeled to follow his nimble-footed adversary.

Roaring like a hurt grizzly, McArdle lunged at Redding, not trying to slug him this time but bent on overpowering the lighter-built man in one of his bone-crushing hugs. Redding met the attack with a stinging uppercut that pulped McArdle's bulbous, nose and sent a spray of crimson juices flying. Retreating to let McArdle's charge exhaust itself, his fists cocked to hammer another punch at the big mustanger when he could get McArdle off balance, Redding's left spur caught a mesquite root underfoot, and he felt himself falling.

He hit the ground on his back, the hunter's roar of dismay in his ears. He knew this bad break could cost him his eyes, if not his life; before he could roll clear, McArdle's two hundred and fifty pounds of bone and gristle avalanched on him in a flying tackle.

Desperation was in Redding. Already McArdle's great thighs straddled his belly, and McArdle's traplike fingers, clawing at his eyes, locked around his right ear.

With the pure malevolent gusto of his kind, McArdle slapped his right hand to his belt, and his fist came up with the torchlight winking off the whetted steel of a ten-inch bowie.

Redding saw the blade come to the top of its arc

6

directly above his head, knew there was no escaping the downward stabbing thrust that would impale his throat to the ground.

The crack of a gunshot ripped through the pound of blood in Redding's ears. He saw McArdle's leonine head rock back to the shock of a point-blank bullet riving his temples. The knife dropped impotently from the mustanger's fingers to land on Redding's shirt.

Gun smoke drifted across the campground to put its acrid bite in Redding's nostrils as he rolled out from under McArdle's toppling bulk and came to his feet, gasping air into his lungs.

He saw the horror in the frozen postures of Blackwine and his men, ringing this scene about; all were staring at the twitching corpse of the Bull, spilling his brain tissue into the boot-trampled dirt.

Redding glanced around in time to see the tail end of the Rickaree Kid's gesture of holstering his smoking gun. A stub of cigarette waggled on the mule packer's lower lip as he drawled, "McArdle had the thing won without goin' for a sticker. Any of you got any objections?"

Old Boney broke the following silence. "Reckon not, Kid. The Bull had it coming."

Redding stalked over to the rumpled blanket and picked up his shell belts and holstered guns.

Jace Blackwine remarked irrelevantly, "The pot's yourn, Redding. We'll bury Bull *mañana*."

Redding squatted down to pick up the 1846 half dollar from the litter of chips. Looking around, he saw the Rickaree Kid heading into the darkness to see after his pack mules for the night. Redding followed him, overtaking the Kid out of earshot of the others.

"Reckon I'm in your debt, son."

"Forget it, Doug. Never had any use for McArdle, nohow."

Redding said, "That skeleton you found. Any chance of you taking me to it?"

The Rickaree Kid's cigarette coal glowed to the suction of his draw, illumining the quizzical expression on his cheeks.

"Sure. I had a hunch you had your reasons for callin' the Bull. What was it?"

Redding hesitated imperceptibly. "I'm no mustanger, Kid. I signed on with Blackwine to see if I could cut the sign of a brother of mine who was lost in these Navajadas. A doctor over in Taos removed some bone from his skull, after a drunk Indian bashed him with the flat of a tomahawk. The medico plugged up the hole with a lucky piece my brother carried—a half dollar minted in 'forty-six, the year he was born."

The Rickaree Kid made a soundless whistle with his lips. "We can make it over to the Mesa and back," he said, "before Jace breaks camp in the mornin'."

Doug Redding's voice carried a husky note as he said, "Be with you as soon as I can roust up a shovel, Kid, The least I can do is give my brother a decent burial."

CHAPTER 2

RANGE DETECTIVE

SUNDOWN OF THE FOLLOWING DAY TEMPERED THE punishing heat which rolled off the eastern desert to pool against the Navajada's foot slopes. Day's end brought welcome promise of relief to Fort Paloverde's garrison and the squalid cow town which lay between the railroad and the Rio Coyotero.

That promise of twilight peace was rudely breached by a sudden break of hoofbeats topping the ridge above the river. A dozen shaggy riders, hazing fifty head of wild mustangs hitched two abreast of a long rope, showed briefly against the flaming sky line and then dipped down the purple slope at a dead run.

Above the snare-drum roll of pounding hoofs came a banging of guns and rowdy yelling, shrill as Apache war whoops. Paloverde knew by these violent signs that Jace Blackwine and his tough crew of mustangers were back from a summer of scouring the lofty mesas and canyons for wild horses; and the townspeople braced themselves for the shock of their arrival with dismay or apprehension, depending on individual memories of Blackwine's hell-raising visits.

Doug Redding brought up the drags with the Rickaree Kid's string of pack mules not sharing the exuberance of the Kid and the other horse hunters, the hungers they had built up over this period of weeks away from their last taste of whisky or the softness of a woman.

Topping the rise with the slow-plodding mules, Redding saw Blackwine swerve off the Rio Coyotero Bridge at a gallop on his grulla, leading his whooping cavalcade through the yawning gates of a holding corral. He would be glad to see the last of this rowdy bunch.

The riders were crowding around Blackwine's buckskin-clad figure by the corral gates, waiting to draw the pay slips which they could cash at any deadfall or brothel in town, when the squat shape of Dorf Chessman; Marshal of Paloverde, came across the street from the near-by jailhouse, his star catching the sundown glint like a bloody eye.

9

Chessman wore a truculent look as he elbowed through the press of bearded roughnecks to confront Jace Blackwine. He was a lawman soured by past experiences with these mustangers, and he aimed to move in fast tonight and nip a riot in the bud.

"I'm toleratin' no trouble in town tonight, Jace," the marshal warned the dusty crew collectively. "Ever' summer you come in out of the hills loaded to the neck with bad intentions and itchin' to see how much hell you can raise. By God, I won't have you turn my town into another shambles like last time."

The Rickaree Kid gave Chessman a boisterous shove which staggered the frog-built marshal. Chessman slapped his low-slung gun and eyed the rambunctious mule skinner with an oldster's hard effort to curb his temper against the horseplay he had suffered. But to arrest the Kid would be risky, at these odds.

"Don't git on the peck, Marshal," the Kid jeered. "We've worked like hell for the doubtful privilege of leavin' our pay in your flea-bit town. Don't douse our happy spirits this way!"

Chessman ignored the Kid. "You all been warned," he ground out doggedly. "I'll jail the first mustanger who shoots out a window light tonight. And I'll hold Blackwine personally responsible for any fights you men pick with a soldier. The commandant over at the fort has got a belly full of you hellions jumpin' ever' uniformed trooper you ketch with a girl on his arm. One wrong move tonight and I'll declare this town closed to you from here till who laid the chunk, savvy that?"

The marshal had beat a retreat, and Blackwine had paid off his men before Doug Redding hazed the Kid's mules across the Rio Coyotero Bridge and into the corral.

10

"I'll send a man over to unpack them jacks," Blackwine said, as Redding closed the gates and led his roan over. "Here's your pay check, includin' bonus."

Redding muttered his thanks and pocketed the voucher.

"Rest of the bunch have signed up for my next hunt, except you," Blackwine said, pocketing his pay book and running splayed fingers through the whiskers which hung like a red flag from his blocky jaw. "We're heading north Sunday a week. Gives you plenty of time to hell around and buck the tiger."

Redding started leading his horse toward the street entering town, Blackwine falling in step beside him.

"You'll ride out without me next hunt, boss."

"Pay don't suit you?"

Redding shrugged. "I signed on with you to get a stake. I got it. I'll be drifting."

No more was said as Redding reached the odorous archway of Colburn's livery barn and led his horse inside, turning the roan over to a game-legged hostler for grooming and graining. Coming back outside, Redding was faintly annoyed to find big Jace Blackwine still waiting for him.

"You're my ace hunter, Redding. Hate to see you bust away to nurse a fiddlefoot. Tell you what. I'll pay—"

"No dice, Jace, but thanks." He started walking toward the bright lights in mid-town.

Blackwine followed him, arguing persistently. "Doug, you're a hard man to figger. Never talk much. But I had you spotted as havin' joined up with me for some other reason besides ketchin' the wild ones for pay. You got something up your sleeve. That brawl with Bull McArdle—there was more to it than met the eye. Plus you and the Kid bein' away from camp all night."

11

A frown cut its quick crease between Redding's brows. "I told you I was after quick money, Jace. Let it ride."

Blackwine said, "If you're on the dodge, it's no skin offen my nose. Is Redding your real brand? Seems like you remind me of somebody I've ran across sometime—"

Redding thought, *Shave off my beard and you'd spot me for some kin of Matt's?* It irritated him that this nosy buckskinner was skirting the edges of his secret, closer than Blackwine could know.

"Quit tagging me like a hungry mongrel, Blackwine. You want to see the baptism certificate of every hand you hire?"

Blackwine dropped back, watching Redding strike up the canyon of false-fronted buildings through the latticing bars of lamplight which spilled from honky-tonk windows to stain the silver street's thick dust.

At the corner of Main and Agave, Redding put his back to a porch post of the Crossed Sabers Saloon and built himself a smoke. He waited there until he saw Jace Blackwine shoulder into the saloon to start his evening's spree.

Unfired cigarette sloping from his underlip, Redding moved out into the flow of foot traffic, rubbing shoulders with chap-clad punchers with the desert's white soda dusting their clothes. A blue-coated corporal from the military post up on the bluff side-stepped Redding with an underbreath curse, catching this man's horse smell; it pointed up what Redding already knew of the deep-rooted hostility the Army felt toward any Blackwiner.

A heady whiff of cheap perfume from a promenading harlot touched his nose, reminding Redding of how long he had lived in a world without women. That thought was brooding in him when he turned into the inky gut of an alley, between a wagonwright's shop and Alfred Keaton's store and post office, and knocked at a door of the latter building where lamplight leaked over the threshold.

As if this was a rendezvous long planned for and awaited, Alf Keaton himself opened the door: hand outstretched in welcome. The old postmaster's face held its question as Redding stepped into the redolent warmth of the room and slumped into a barrel chair, at once letting the fatigue of this long day's trek out of the hills seep from his muscles.

"Find any trace of him, Doug?" Keaton spoke with the apologetic tone of a man who knew he should wait for news.

Redding nodded. "I buried his bones last night, Alf. Above timber line, a place they call Mustang Mesa. Shot from behind. The skull had Matt's 1846 half dollar in it, so I know there's no mistake."

Keaton's long-jawed face showed its shock, the anti-climax that meant the end of long hoping for these two. He gestured toward an oilcloth-covered table where steaming food was set out.

"Knew you'd be in tonight," Keaton said. "Tomorrow is Blackwine's deadline with the fort's purchasing agent."

Watching Doug Redding attack his food, Keaton read the heavy toll this summer had taken. Redding's hickory shirt, plastered stiff with stale sweat and trail grime, hung loose over his leaned-down frame, and his big-boned wrists and bearded face were a shade more brown than they had been the last time these two had met in this room.

13

Redding's bullhide chaps bore a new webwork of scuffings from cactus and jagged rock. His Coffeyville boots were due for repair, their spike heels filed to nubs by the abrasion of a hundred nameless canyons and creek beds in the high country.

"I'm sorry, son," Keaton said. "No sign of Blaze Tondro's hide-out anywhere near this Mustang Mesa where you found Matt?"

Redding paused to pour a third cup of coffee. "There ain't a canyon or a bench in a fifty-mile radius of that grave that I haven't fine-toothed, Alf. Ridin' solo most of the time. If Tondro holes up in that locality, I muffed my chance of finding it. But I will."

The old postmaster stepped out of this room which served as his living-quarters and went to the front of the store to rummage inside his safe. He brought back a cardboard box which Doug Redding had left with him four months ago.

"I got a letter from Colonel Regis here," Keaton said, handing Redding a brown envelope gobbed with scaling wax. "Come last week, registered."

Redding, his appetite satisfied, pushed back his chair and reached for the cardboard box Keaton had put beside his plate. From it he drew a dog-eared envelope and a ball-pointed silver star, etched with the words, *Detective Stockmen's Protective Association.*

A sardonic grin touched the corners of Redding's mouth as he flipped the law badge back into the box. "Regis is either assigning me to a new case," he drawled, "or telling me to turn in my star. That's what I'm doing. As of now, Alf, I cease to be a range detective."

Keaton blinked. "Meaning you've writ off Matt's murder as a closed case?"

"I'll locate his bushwhacker if it takes me the rest of my life, Alf. But on my own. Colonel Regis wouldn't let me waste any more of the SPA's time on this job. But Tondro's den is up in those mountains somewhere. I'll find it."

Keaton tongued his cheek thoughtfully, wanting to this hard-bitten man some advice but not knowing how to go about it. Redding was twenty-nine; he had worn a star since he was twenty, like his brother Matt and his father before him.

"Doug," the postmaster coughed, "there wasn't a saltier range dick alive than your brother Matt. He disappeared into them hills eighteen months ago, trying to track down Tondro's rustler hide-out. He failed. I hate to see you buck a hopeless th—"

The sound of the store's front door rattling under someone's urgent pounding cut Keaton off. The desperate urgency of that knocking put a sudden suspicion in Keaton's eyes.

"Anybody know you're in town?" he asked. "Anybody that knows you're a star toter, that is?"

Redding said, "Go see who it is. It won't concern me."

When Keaton left the room, all show of ease left Doug Redding. He had been playing a chancy game these past months, where death was the price of a misstep, for Blackwine's crew numbered more than one man who, like Bull McArdle, would consider a John Law fair target for a shot in the back.

All the instincts of a man who lives on borrowed time surfaced in Redding as he blew out the lamp on Keaton's table and stepped to the connecting door, watching through the crack of it as old Keaton, carrying a lighted candle, groped his way through the littered

15

counters of his store to unbolt the street door.

The candle's shine revealed a girl waiting on the porch there, a girl dressed in a gray traveling-suit and an aigrette on her hat. A girl whose eyes, even at this distance, held their plain signs of a deep unrest, set in a face that was strikingly attractive.

"Howdy, ma'am," Keaton said. "What—"

The girl's voice, low-pitched, carried down the room to reach the ears of the man in Keaton's living-room. "Did a man named Douglas Redding get in with those mustang hunters tonight, Mr. Keaton? I was to meet him here at the post office—it's terribly urgent—a matter of life or death to me."

CHAPTER 3

LAVARIM BASIN RIDERS

KEATON KNEW THIS GIRL, KNEW HER NEED FOR reassurance; yet it was not his right to betray Redding's trust. He chose, therefore, the middle road of evasion.

"Why, Miss Joyce, them mustangers only got in thirty forty minutes ago. If this Redding hombre shows up, you want me to send him to meet you anywheres?"

The girl glanced anxiously up and down the street, shrinking from the candlelight as if there was some urgent reason why she should not be seen at Keaton's door.

"Tell him—tell him I'll be stopping overnight at the Foothill House, Room Seven in the new annex." She reached out to touch his hand with gloved finger tips. "Please, Mr. Keaton, don't mention to anyone that I'm in town. I had the stage driver drop me off across the bridge, so I could walk in after dark."

Keaton's head bobbed. "Why, now, I'll sure do that, ma'am." He coughed. "I'm sorry about the Major, Miss Joyce. A real loss to the Basin."

In the back office, Redding heard the words of thanks, which this girl choked out, then her departing footsteps as Keaton closed and barred the door. Redding was relighting the table lamp when the old man returned.

"You heard, Doug?"

"Yeah."

"Thought I'd play it safe. How come she knew you were here? Does she know you pack a star?"

"Never laid eyes on her before. Who is she?"

"Joyce Melrose. Her dad owned the Crowfoot Ranch over in Lavarim Basin, other side of Cloudcap Pass. He was gulched five-six weeks back. Talk over in the Basin is that Tondro did it."

Redding harrowed his memory for some clue as to where he might have crossed Joyce Melrose's trail.

"Seems she had a date to meet you here tonight, anyways," Keaton said. "One thing, I took close notice to see if she might be wearin' Matt's lizard ring. She wasn't. Gloves fit skintight. Thought she might have knowed your brother."

Redding reached into his pocket, a hunch striking him. He took out Colonel Regis's letter and ripped open the envelope.

"Five gets you fifty," he said, "Regis is back of her visit tonight."

He read his superior's letter aloud to the old postmaster.

" 'Friend Doug: I hope your scout of the Navajadas

17

brings you some trace of your brother. If not, I have a case lined up for you in that part of the country which should fit in with your continued search for Matt's whereabouts.

" 'Briefly: on the 24th of June last, Major Sam Melrose, a director of our Association and a Territorial Legislator, was murdered from ambush. Ownership of his ranch, the Crowfoot, over in Lavarim Basin, passed to his sole living kin, a daughter, Joyce.

" 'Major Melrose had left the ranch apparently to pay a visit to the Pedregosa Indian Reservation, northwest of Lavarim Basin, to consult the Agent there regarding the government's annual contract to supply his Indian wards with beef. When he failed to show up at the Reservation, Joyce instituted a search. Her foreman discovered the Major's corpse in the lower Navajadas, directly opposite the direction he would have taken to reach the Agency. It is the accepted opinion of the Trailfork sheriff, Val Lennon, as well as others in the Basin, that Major Melrose was ambushed by Blaze Tondro's rustlers.

" 'Miss Melrose has reason to think differently. I have taken the liberty of informing her that you will reach Fort Paloverde not later than the 13th of this month and that she can contact you at Alfred Keaton's store there. She will supply you with the details of the case which lead her to suspect that Tondro did not kill her father.

" 'Inasmuch as your brother was assigned to track down Tondro's base of operations 18 months ago and has not been seen since, this assignment should interest you. You can contact me through Sheriff Val Lennon at Trailfork.

" 'Best of luck to you, and keep me posted. Clayton

18

Regis, President, Territorial SPA.' "

When Redding finished reading, the Paloverde postmaster waggled his head somberly. "A pity," he remarked dryly, "that you are resigning. It ain't often a case involves a woman as perty as Joyce Melrose. And both of you bereaved by a border ambush."

Redding picked up his cardboard box and crossed the room to take his Stetson from the antler rack. Humor showed through the fatigue ruts on his face as he fitted the chin cord in place.

"Drop the chief a line by the next mail," he said, "telling him the Melrose girl and I had our powwow as arranged. She's in Room Seven, didn't she say?"

"In the new annex, yeah. Luck, kid."

Stepping into the alley's black void, Redding turned left and groped his way to the vacant wagon yard behind the main street buildings and thus made his approach unobserved to the rear of the sprawling two-story Foothill House. It being the only hotel this desert town afforded, booking a room there had already been a part of Redding's plans. In view of Joyce Melrose's desire for secrecy, he would drop a note in her letter box to arrange a meeting tomorrow in Keaton's store.

He entered the Foothill lobby through a side door, pausing in the shadows of that shabby room until he was certain that the girl was not in sight. With the exception of this lobby, the Foothill's entire lower floor was given over to a gambling-hall and barroom, from which came the racket of reveling men through portiered double doors beyond the clerk's desk.

There was no one on duty at the moment, but there was a crudely lettered sign beside the dog-eared register which said, *Take a key and settle up when you leave.*

19

Keep key until you check out. Manager.

Jabbing the rusty nib of a pen into the gummy ink bottle, Redding glanced at the latest entries on the ledger. *Jason P. Blackwine, Uvalde, Texas,* headed the patrons who had registered under today's date, the ink still wet from his signing. Blackwine, Redding took pains to note, had booked Room F, upstairs.

Directly below the mustanger's name was an entry in a feminine Spencerian: *Jeanne Miller, Santa Fe, Room 7, Annex.*

Redding thought, *Funny how often an alias has a person's real initials.* He scratched out *Douglas Redding, Sage City,* on the blue-ruled line directly below Joyce's and, scanning the available keys on the hook rack, decided against going to the annex wing and scribbled *Room B* opposite his name.

He tore a strip of paper from a page in the back of the register, and jotted down a brief note concerning a meeting tomorrow morning at Keaton's store, and thrust it in Joyce Melrose's letter box, Number 7. He had not signed the note, knowing that a nosy night clerk might read it. Joyce would know the meaning of it and keep the appointment.

Taking down the key to Room B, Redding climbed the uncarpeted staircase to a corridor above the gambling-hall, its gloomy length only partially lighted by soot-fouled lamps in wall brackets. Room B was the third door on his left; it gave off a fusty odor of resinous pine boards and moldy bedclothes as he entered, fumbled on a marble-slabbed washstand to find a brass-bowled kerosene lamp, and lighted it.

His reflection in the blistered mirror above the stand told its own story of the trail weariness which throbbed in every tissue of his being. There was a touch of gray at his temples which had not been there four months ago, when he had headed for the hills with Jace Blackwine's mustangers. Worry over Matt had done that, more than the grueling daily chase of the high-country mustang herds.

He opened a door giving way to an outer balcony, to ventilate the room, and walked over to sit down on the bed, depositing his cardboard box on the greasy blanket beside him.

Memories crowded him hard. In this same hotel, six months ago, Doug Redding had first seen the message which Matt had sent to Paloverde in care of Alf Keaton. This had been the first news the Association had had from its senior stock detective since Matt Redding had gone into the Navajadas more than a year previously, searching for the rustler roost where the Territory's most-wanted outlaw, Blaze Tondro, was believed to have his den.

Turning up the lamp, Redding took his brother's letter out of the cardboard box. In the envelope with it was a finger ring, fashioned by some goldsmith into the likeness of a whiptail lizard with a tiny seed pearl between its jaws. A loop of rawhide was threaded through the gold band.

That ring had belonged to Redding's father. Its exact duplicate had been worn by his mother, and upon their deaths the golden lizard rings had been bequeathed to their sons. In a family of sparse traditions and a Spartan sentimentality, those baubles held a place of high value. Redding had left his ring in Paloverde only because he knew his return was dubious.

Redding looped the rawhide thong around his neck and tucked the ring under his shirt next to the skin. Then, with a renewed depression of spirit riding him as he recalled the fruitless search of the past hundred or more days, he unfolded his brother's letter.

Although he had memorized its text through a score of previous readings, he held it under the feeble glare of the lamp and read again the last message Matthew Redding had sent to the outside world, this side of eternity.

Bro Doug:

I've located Tondro's hide-out. Tell Regis. Through the melodramatic but effective method of posing as a man on the dodge and joining his wild bunch.

It's on the west slope of the Navajadas, but I wouldn't have located it in a thousand years working from the outside.

Meet me at Keaton's store in Paloverde on the night of the 18th of February and we'll talk over a showdown with Tondro.

Am sending this out by way of a girl I want you to meet, as I aim to marry her soon as we have finished this business together. Thought I'd always be a hairy-eared bachelor, didn't you? But she's wearing Ma's lizard ring, so you can see I mean business.

I'm calling myself Blackie Fletcher on this job just in case Tondro may have heard of us.

Your bro, Matt.

Crushing the letter between his palms, Doug Redding drooped chin to chest, trying to crowd out the agony that had deviled him since the Rickaree Kid had led him to the human skeleton, polished by fang and claw and beak, up on Mustang Mesa last night. The skull had had a circular opening in it where a skilled surgeon had done a trepanning operation, insetting a silver coin dated

22

1846. The half dollar that had indirectly caused the death of Bull McArdle.

That skeleton gave him the answer to Matt's failure to meet him here, in Paloverde, the night of February 18th. For two months he had waited for Matt to show up, and then he had jumped at the chance to sign on with Jason Blackwine's horse hunters, knowing this would give him an opportunity to scour the Navajada wastelands in search of Blaze Tondro's hide-out without attracting undue attention. Except for Matt's bones, he had nothing to show for his hunt. If Matt had given the location of the robbers' roost in his letter—but that was something far too dangerous to put in writing. At the time he had sent the message out, Matt must have been supremely confident in the security of his position as a member of Tondro's rustler band.

Somehow, Matt's secret had been betrayed. Doug meant to find out, if it took a lifetime, how and why his brother had met his doom on Mustang Mesa. And the girl who wore his betrothal ring. Did she know? Perhaps at this very hour, perhaps in this very town, Matt's choice for a helpmeet was grieving for her missing lover.

Redding had promised himself a shave, as his first luxury upon reaching civilization tonight. He had purposely let his beard grow, to diminish his close physical resemblance to his missing older brother. But the barbershops of the town, even those up at the cavalry post on the bluff, would be closed at this hour. The only thing to do was go down to Colburn's stable and get his shaving-tools out of his saddlebags.

Leaving the hotel, Redding reached the livery barn on the edge of town in a matter of minutes. He borrowed a lantern from the game-legged night hostler and went back to the runway between the rows of stalls, searching the pegged saddles there until he located his own high-horned Brazos rig. From an alforja pouch he removed the india-rubber bag containing his shaving-kit and headed back toward the front of the stable.

He heard two riders hammer across the Rio Coyotero Bridge at a reaching gallop and rein to a halt in front of the barn. The hostler's face was dimly outlined by the red coal of his cigar as he walked out. to take over the reins.

"You unhitch the Trailfork stage tonight, Joe?" One of the riders put a sharp question to the stableman.

"Reckon I did, Teague. How's things in Lavarim Basin?"

Teague said, "Listen. Was Joyce Melrose on that stage?"

Doug Redding halted, instinct making him swing the lantern behind him so its beams would not reveal him to the riders out there.

After a pause, Joe said carefully, "She's in town, sure enough, but she must have got off the stage on t'other side of the bridge."

"Meaning what?"

"Well," Joe said, "I seen her walkin' in half an hour after I'd unhitched. After dark, it was. Struck me funny, Miss Melrose bein' afoot. Knew she couldn't have hoofed it over the Pass from Trailfork. So—she must have had the jehu let her off on the t'other side of the river."

Redding heard Teague and his companion holding a short council.

"You haven't seen us, Joe, understand?" Teague called softly through the dark, as the two riders walked

24

on upstreet.

Redding handed the lantern over to Joe as the hostler led two lather-drenched cow ponies into the ammoniac stench of the barn. A gelding wearing a Crowfoot brand and a big blanco mustang without any visible markings. Crowfoot. That was the Melrose iron.

"Teague's on the peck tonight, ain't he?" Redding chuckled, wiping a match into flame on his Levi's and touching it to a cigarette. "Any of his damn business if the Melrose girl comes over the Pass?"

The hostler rolled his cigar across his teeth, studying this stranger for a long moment. Finally he said cautiously, "Would you want the woman you aim to marry to traipse over to a Army town like this one, on her ownsome?"

Redding grinned, studying the tip of his cigarette, his Stetson brim shielding his eyes from Joe's inspection.

"See your point, Joe. Who was that with Teague— one of Crowfoot's riders?"

This time the hostler retreated behind his professional code which forbade aimless bandying of trail gossip about his paying customers.

"Didn't get a look at him, you having the lantern. Might be a good idea, stranger, if you don't josh Darkin about the girl if you run acrost hint at a bar tonight. He's a touchy one on that subjeck."

Moving outdoors, Redding said, "Obliged, Joe," and heard the hostler leading the horses toward the stalls.

He felt a moment's anger at himself for not having put the lantern on the two riders from Lavarim Basin; now their identities would remain a mystery to him if he rubbed shoulders with them in town tonight.

One thing for sure, he knew Joyce Melrose was engaged to marry this Darkin Teague or Teague Darkin, whichever his name was. He recalled how the girl had cautioned the postmaster to let no one know she had visited Paloverde tonight. She had taken elaborate pains to leave the Trailfork stage outside of town, and she had forged a false name—albeit a transparent one—to the Foothill House register.

Yet this Teague, forking a gelding from Joyce's own cavvy, knew the girl was in Paloverde tonight. If he knew much, he might know she had come here to meet a Protective Association detective on business connected with her father's murder. Why, if Teague was her fiancé, hadn't he accompanied Joyce over the mountains today?

That puzzle was nagging Redding's thoughts when he drew abreast of the Crossed Sabers Saloon and heard the break of gunshots from the deadfall's barroom put their voice of calamity into this uneasy night.

The saloon, doors burst open to disgorge a jam of men bent on getting away from trouble fast. One shaggy bull-whacker clad in the verminous buckskins of his calling dove bodily through a colored window, picked himself up, shook off the splintered glass shards, and sprinted down the steps in such blind panic that Doug Redding had to jump back to keep from being trampled down.

The pandemonium in the Crossed Sabers took the form of thudding feet, a percentage girl's choked-off scream, the recurring crash of splintering furniture.

A roulette croupier stuck his head out the broken window and bawled into the night, "Fetch the marshal before they tear this place apart! Some troopers have got a Blackwiner cornered in here—the Rickaree Kid."

CHAPTER 4

BUSHWACK BULLET

REDDING THOUGHT, *WHY DID IT HAVE TO BE THE KID? I'll have, to go in there and side him.* He moved over against the saloon porch, out of the path of the barroom exodus. The awning's shadow shielded him from the guttering flare of the torches.

This town had been a powder keg since sundown, tensed for the inevitable flare-up between off-duty soldiers from the near-by fort and their hated rivals, Blackwine's crew.

No longer a member of the mustang faction, Redding wanted no part of this feud. But if it involved the Rickaree Kid, there was no shunning the obligation to reciprocate for what the Kid had done for him in killing McArdle and leading him to Matt's bones.

There was no bucking the flow of men still draining through the batwings. Climbing over the porch rail, Redding saw the cook from Blackwine's camp spill through the jammed entry and stagger to one side, quitting the saloon before he got sucked into any riot. Old Boney was too wise a rooster to give the bluecoats any competition where women were concerned—the crux of the feud—and by the same token saw no sense in mixing in the Kid's trouble.

Old Boney spotted Redding moving toward the smashed-out window, and relief went through him as he saw Redding wheel to face him.

"What happened in there, Boney?

The old man grabbed Redding's arm. "Rickaree caught the keno roller palmin' phony cubes out of the

27

goose, Doug, and called him on it. Houseman drawed a pepperbox and cut down on the Kid, but missed. Rickaree drew in self-defense, but you can't tell them damn troopers that. They got him cornered."

Redding broke the cook's grip with a jerk of his arm. "Is the houseman dead?"

Old Boney's reply was hard to catch above the rumble of boots on the plank sidewalk as the town grapevine, keyed to this trouble in the Crossed Sabers, sucked men from the other deadfalls up and down the street.

"Kid's slug smashed the roller's kneecap. That ain't it; Doug. Couple of them stripe-laig' soldiers in the game, they got the Kid cornered. Know the marshal'll be on their side even if he shows up. Kid's number is up, Doug."

Redding knew he was a fool, mixing in here. But he found himself straddling the jagged glass of the broken window to step into the barroom.

He spotted the Rickaree Kid at once, a bayed figure with his back to a nickelodeon which boxed off a corner behind the roulette layout. The Kid had a smoking sixgun in his fist; the muzzle was weaving like a reptile's head between a pair of Army privates who wore military police brassards. The two soldiers stood shoulder to shoulder behind an overturned poker table, their Springfield carbines trained on the Kid.

It was a stalemate, the Rickaree Kid's short gun holding the two troopers' rifles at a stand-off, neither of them daring to squeeze trigger for fear of being cut down.

In the background, Redding saw the keno roller clutching his bullet-shattered knee and vomiting with the pain of it. The broken glass globe of the keno goose had showered its numbered buttons over the area of open floor where the Rickaree Kid faced the two uniformed troopers assigned to police duty in town.

The Kid could not move from where he stood without provoking a shot. Ostensibly, these soldiers from the Fort were holding the Kid here pending the arrival of Marshal Chessman. But Redding had listened to enough mustangers' gossip out in the hills this summer to know that Paloverde's marshal would like nothing better than to find a Blackwiner dead or wounded.

A change flashed over the Kid's pasty face as he sighted Redding's big shape moving in behind the troopers. This was help none of the other Blackwiners in the house had dared bring him.

Their target's shift of glance warned the troopers of possible trouble behind them. One of the privates half turned, shooting a glance over his shoulder at Redding, and in that instant Redding got both guns from leather and came in fast to ram their muzzles against the Sam Browne belts of the two MPs.

"Hold your fire, Kid!" Redding shouted his warning and in a lower tone addressed the two privates. "Drop the carbeens and turn around slow."

The flesh on Redding's neck nape crawled as he heard the shocked silence of the barroom crowd at his back give way to a stirring of booted feet on the sawdusted planks. He was a stranger in this town, but if any member of the barroom audience spotted him for a Blackwiner he would draw a bullet from behind.

The two soldiers dropped their Springfields and eased themselves around to face Redding, their mouths working. One of them chewed out, "You drunk or loco, stranger? You're buckin' the law here—"

Redding knew he was living on borrowed time, his

29

back to the crowd this way. A glance past the two soldiers showed the Kid inching away from the nickelodeon, covering that crowd with his gun; but the odds were too heavy for him to hold it in check long.

"The Kid ain't holden to Army jurisdiction," Redding retorted. "I can spot a jobbed deck when I see one—"

As he spoke, pulling the troopers off guard, Redding whipped up his left-hand gun in a swift arc, the front sight smashing one trooper in the nose. That man went down like an axed tree, giving Redding his chance to circle the other trooper and back swiftly to the wall.

Halting alongside the Rickaree Kid, Redding said without visible lip movement, "Take the lamp on your right, then head for the window behind the chuck-a-luck cage," and as he spoke he lifted his own guns toward the big ceiling lamp which hung directly over the paralyzed tableau of the barroom crowd.

In the pinched-off instant before he and the Kid triggered their guns in unison, Redding got a mental photograph of that crowd, naked gun metal beginning to show here and there along its front rank. As their bullets snuffed out the overhead lamps, Redding glimpsed the corpulent shape of Marshal Dorf Chessman squeezing through the press and realized that darkness had come too late to avoid being spotted by the town's lawman.

The darkness which followed the shattering of the two main barroom lamps was not complete. Other lamps above the back bar put the crowd into silhouette, but there was a momentary illusion of total darkness, and on this Redding was pinning their hopes of a successful getaway.

The Rickaree Kid was already breaking for the chuck-table, crouched low. Redding saw the wrangler make his headlong dive through the open window

30

facing an alley. The marshal, or somebody else in his general vicinity, started shooting in a rapid burst which indicated a gun hammer fanned by the heel of a palm. Lead chewed into both sides of the window frame as Redding slogged after the Kid.

He flung himself floorward, waiting for the gun fanner to empty his chambers. Then he holstered his Colts, reached up for the low sill of the window, and vaulted it like a frog, gambling against being hit by a random slug as the crowd broke its paralysis and stormed across the gambling-hall.

It was pitch-dark in this alley and a rising moil of dust bit Redding's nose as he landed heavily on the Rickaree Kid's back. They helped each other up, hearing the marshal's wheezy yell, "Cover the alley! We'll box 'em in the alley—"

The Kid gasped, "They can do it, too. We got to shoot it out."

Redding grabbed the wrangler's arm and headed toward the rear of the alley. Reaching the saloon corner, he cut sharp left in the direction of the Foothill House.

A back door of the saloon pounded open, and its outflung light caught both of them as they crossed it. A man yelled, "That's them!" and a spray of wild shots ripped the ground ahead and behind them.

Redding pulled the Kid to a halt and thrust a key into his hand. "Room B in the main building, Foothill House!" he panted. "My room. Hole up there while I fade back toward the river and draw the wolf pack off your tail, Kid."

"Doug," the Kid protested, "you can't—I won't—"

There was no time for arguement here. Redding turned, laid a shot in the general direction of the men spilling from the rear of the Crossed Sabers, and

31

sprinted toward the river, shooting twice as he ran to let gun flashes attract the eye of the man hunters.

The ruse worked, and the marshal's men raced that direction, the cacophony of their yells breaking harsh in the night.

Unseen, the Rickaree Kid made it to the outside fire escape of the Foothill House and scuttled up the steps, hearing the hue and cry of the chase leading toward, the west.

Out there, Redding heard the sound of pursuit dropping off, as men lost their nerve, bucking armed fugitives in this dark. He kept going until a rank odor of rotting mud and willow wood told him he was nearing the bank of the Coyotero. Mosquitoes formed a cloud about his cheeks as he squatted in the darkness, listening to the men arguing with each other.

Hunkering down on the bank where he could see the frosty glitter of the stars on the glassy surface of the river, Redding let the tension relax from his body. The Kid would be safe in his room at the hotel by now. He himself was a marked man in Paloverde, he realized; it would be difficult to keep his rendezvous with Joyce Melrose after daylight tomorrow. He would have to see Alf Keaton tonight and arrange another meeting-place.

It helped to know that he had squared accounts with the Rickaree Kid. The debt was paid. A life for a life. Later tonight, after the marshal's hunt had had time to cool off, the Kid could shag his tail out of town and wait for the mustangers out in the hills.

Whether the Kid was in the right or in the wrong had no bearing on the case. Redding had moved into the limelight he would otherwise have shunned, because a man couldn't duck his just debts. And he owed his life to the Kid.

Chessman's men were fanning out, searching the night. It would be a simple thing to join his own hunters now.

A vast weariness was in Doug Redding as he left his riverbank sanctuary and circled wide of the town to approach Foothill House from the south. The night hid the furtive sounds of scared men beating the brush of these back lots, pretending to search for the fugitives. A prowling cavalry officer challenged Redding and drew a grunted, "I ain't cut any sign yet, have you?" for reply.

Redding entered the hotel through the same door he had used after leaving Keaton's. As before, the lobby was deserted, the night clerk's desk empty. He went upstairs and tested the knob of Room B, vaguely surprised to find the Kid had not locked it.

Stepping inside Redding knew an instant's alarm, wondering if the Kid had gone into the wrong room; the cheap mortise locks of this hostelry could be opened with almost any key.

But a sour odor of whisky and a sound of stertorous breathing from the bed told him different. When he touched match to lampwick arid turned it low, he saw that the Rickaree Kid had flung himself on the blankets, face down. An empty pint bottle was on the pillow. One arm dangled over the edge of the bed, clutching a sixshooter.

The Kid, arriving here, had drained his pocket bottle. He was dead drunk. Redding thought, *Might as well give him a couple hours' sleep against the ride he's got before daylight.*

He took the precaution of locking the hall door and pocketed the key. The smell of whisky nauseated him, and he walked through the open doorway onto the balcony, feeling the cool breeze on his hot cheeks, spiced with the sage scent off the desert.

The balcony overlooked a patio formed by the main building and its ell, with a two-storied annex completing the square.

Studying the dark face of the annex wing, Redding found himself wondering which of those windows across the patio might be Joyce Melrose's room, and whether he should risk visiting her tonight.

Thought of the girl who now owned the Crowfoot Ranch at once swung Redding's reflections to what Keaton had told him of the murder of her father, over in Lavarim Basin. Blaze Tondro was being accused of that bushwhacking. Redding was reminded of how much Joyce Melrose and himself had in common, before they had even met.

According to the letter from SPA headquarters, Joyce Melrose would have more details to impart. Standing here in the darkness of the courtyard balcony, Redding found himself wondering about the unknown girl who tonight might be wetting Matt's golden lizard ring with her tears. The thought sent Redding's hand reaching to unbutton his shirt, to finger the duplicate ring which hung from its thong around his neck. He was like that when his revery was interrupted by the faint sound of a key grating in the door of Room B.

Redding whirled, at once alert, hand dropping to gunstock. From his position between the balcony door and window, he saw the outer corridor door was being shoved open; and its draft caused the low-burning lamp to leap for an instant's brightness and then snuff out.

Surprise was Redding's first reaction, remembering that he had been careful to lock that door and pocket the key. Yet from his shielded position on the outer balcony he had full view of a man's shadow blotting the threadbare carpet of Room B, a man standing at a crouch on the threshold with a corridor wall lamp at his back.

The fanwise spread of light from the hallway fell partially on the shabby bed where the Rickaree Kid lay snoring.

No more than a second had ticked off since the door had opened; Redding had not yet lifted his Colt from holster to challenge the intruder when he heard an abrasive voice call from the doorway.

"Redding?"

The Rickaree Kid stirred from his drunken sleep, heaving up on the blankets and twisting his head to stare at the silhouetted shape in the doorway. The voice of the Kid was a sleep-husky monosyllable. "Whut?"

Redding was moving toward the balcony door when the Kid spoke. Before he could reach that opening, a gun's ear-numbing blast filled the room, and instantly the man's shadow on the floor was replaced by dim gray clouds of smoke.

The gun's report still seemed to fill the room when Doug Redding charged in off the balcony. His raking glance showed him the settling form of the Rickaree Kid, only his legs in the light from the hallway.

Boots were slogging away down the corridor as Redding crossed the hotel room in two strides and raced out in pursuit of the ambusher. He had the briefest of glimpses of a heavy-built man rounding the far corner of the hall.

That glimpse was enough to note the broad splash of white which made a skunk streak down the middle of the man's heavy pelt of Indian-black hair. That and the distinctive pinto-spotted vest which covered the fugitive's massive chest were all were all the details

Redding was able to pick out of his memory later.

Wall lamps fluttered to the wind of Redding's swift passage down the corridor in pursuit. When he turned the corner where the man had vanished, gun ready, it was to find the hallway empty, ending not ten feet away in a wall broken by an open window, the night wind stirring the cheap gauze curtains there.

That open window was made to order for the escape of a man finding himself in a dead-end hallway. Redding approached the opening cautiously, to see that it was but a short drop to the shingled slope of the roof which overhung the porch below.

The Rickaree Kid's attacker had had more than enough time to slide over the eaves, gain the street below, and lose himself in the anonymity of the foot traffic there.

Redding turned, vaguely aware of excited voices in the rooms opening on this short pocket of corridor. He retraced his way to Room B, knowing that the sound of the gunshot would shortly bring tenants out of their rooms to investigate.

As he stepped into the room and closed the door he noticed a skeleton key protruding from the lock, indicating how the gunman had gained entry here. A metal tag hanging from the lock was marked with the letter C. Anyone could have picked it off the rack in the deserted lobby downstairs. Using this key, he locked the door.

In the gruesome darkness of this room, Redding could hear no sound of breath or movement on the bed. He struck a match. The Rickaree Kid was dead, half of his skull ripped off by the killer's close-range bullet. Somebody, somehow, had traced the Kid here from the Crossed Sabers Saloon. Some friend, perhaps, of the

36

keno roller the Kid had crippled for life; or maybe a cavalry rider, bent on spilling a mustanger's blood.

Then out of memory came the realization that the outlaw had called his own name, not the Kid's, an instant before the shot. The truth was a shocking, inescapable thing to Redding now.

He said aloud, "That skunk-striped hombre came to bushwhack me, not the Rickaree Kid!"

CHAPTER 5

Gun Trapped

COMMON SENSE TOLD HIM HE WAS A FOOL TO REMAIN another minute in this room with a dead man. If Marshal Chessman caught him here, his gun bore freshly fouled by the shots he had fired tonight after leaving the Crossed Sabers, he could be railroaded to the hang rope.

The fact that he was a stock detective would count for nothing in this Army-dominated town. By clubbing down a military policeman he had put himself open to arrest and confinement in the post guardhouse, where he might rot for months on end. And by helping the Rickaree Kid elude the town marshal, Redding knew he had incurred Chessman's unbending wrath.

But these risks held no part of Redding's thoughts now. Who had singled him out for murder, locating his room number, no doubt, by checking the hotel register down in the lobby? This error of targets had no connection with the affair at the Crossed Sabers tonight. It might very well be linked to his forthcoming conference with Joyce Melrose concerning her father's murder over in Lavarim Basin.

37

The pressure of events gave Redding no time to wrestle with his personal riddles now. Feet were slogging up and down the hall outside, making the thin walls tremble. In the adjoining room a woman was screaming, peal on peal, her cries seeming to vibrate the peeled wallpaper on the flimsy partition.

A film broke from his pores as he held the match closer to look at the Rickaree Kid. The young wrangler whom Redding had long since ticketed as a man on the dodge had died instantly. The gun still clutched in his hand might appear to investigators as proof that he had had a chance to defend himself.

The match burned out between his fingers. In the following exaggerated darkness he groped with a hand and found the cardboard box beside the chipped china pitcher on the washstand. He retrieved the two envelopes it contained and stuffed them into his shirt pocket. Then his fingers sought out the cold metal of his Stockmen's Protective Association badge.

There was a babble of voices directly outside his door. The hysterical woman next door was shrilling, "The shot come from inside this next room here, Marshal, for a fact. Room B. I know there's been murder committed—right acrost this wall where I was tryin' to sleep!"

A heavy hand tried the doorknob. Marshal Chessman's authoritative demand made the door tremble. "Who locked this door? Stand back, damn it—"

In that moment Doug Redding made his decision. His law badge was clutched in his taut fist; he stepped across the room now and thrust the silver star deep in the Rickaree Kid's hip pocket.

Chessman's gun bellowed out in the hallway, and a

shaft of lamplight penciled in through the shattered wreckage of the mortise lock. Doug Redding faded through the balcony door and got it closed behind him just as the marshal's beefy shoulder knocked the hall entry open.

Out on the balcony, Redding heard the sharp suction of breath which told him Chessman had spotted the dead man on the cot. It would be but a matter of seconds before the marshal deduced that the balcony was the only possible exit for whoever had locked the corridor door from the inside. The man who, evidence would irrevocably point, had shot the Rickaree Kid.

Redding took advantage of this interval to climb the outer balcony railing and shinny up the corner pillar to reach the edge of the shingled roof. A moment later he had hoisted himself onto the eaves and was crawling swiftly up the gentle slope of the roof.

Beneath him he heard pandemonium break as the town marshal and morbid onlookers gathered around the Rickaree Kid. Redding used that covering noise to gain the ridgepole.

An overcast drifting off the Navajadas toward the warm floor of the desert blotted out the stars, concealing Redding's flattened body from the view of anyone on the main street. But to remain on this roof peak for any period of time would be fatal. Sooner or later Dorf Chessman would have men out on the balcony investigating.

Redding scuttled along the ridgepole until he reached the valley formed by the right-angle ell of the annex. Saloon lights shed a faint glow on the far angle of the roof facing the side street. This was enough to force Redding to cling to the ridge with his fingers and hunch his hips along the dark inner pitch of the annex roof.

It was his intention to reach the far end of the ell and somehow make his way to the ground. The sudden appearance of men crowding the balcony outside Room B caused Redding to freeze, knowing he was in the full view of those hunters.

"Whoever 'twas had to make his getaway through here." The marshal was expounding his theories. "Dick, fetch a lantern and have a look at the roof. Harry Fox, you and Bob Hill check the yard below this balcony for sign. Hardly likely a man could have dropped from the railin' to the ground without bustin' a laig."

Panting like a lizard against the steep slant of the annex roof, Doug Redding had his bad moment. A few minutes would see men with lanterns exploring both roof and patio. In any event the marshal, if he were any kind of a strategist, would fling an armed cordon around this building.

Directly below him was the flatter jut of another balcony's roof. On the theory that Foothill House itself would be his safest sanctuary while this hunt was in full cry, Redding dug his spur shanks into the shingles to check his momentum and skidded jerkily down to the balcony roof.

Clinging to its edge, he peered over the side and was relieved to note that the room facing this balcony was dark. Those on either side had lamplight shining behind shaded windows.

Redding bellied over the lip of the eave and locked his legs around a weather-beaten pillar which supported the corner. Shadows were curd-thick under the projecting awning; he slid down the post and felt his boots make solid purchase on the balcony's rail without raising an alarm from any of the men who still formed a group on the Room B balcony not fifty feet across the courtyard.

Redding lowered himself to the floor of the balcony, crawled to the door, and found the knob. This door was locked. He told himself this was standard procedure for an untenanted room. If it were occupied, this door would be open for ventilation on a sweltering night such as this.

Removing his Stetson, Redding balled a fist inside the felt crown and, holding the hat against a windowpane, smashed out a section of glass without undue noise. He paused a moment, ears keening the room inside that window. Hearing nothing to indicate it was occupied, he reached an arm through the aperture and unfastened the sash latch.

He ran up the window inch by inch, lest the rattle of pig-iron weights or the squeak of sash-cord pulleys reach hostile ears. When the window was open he paused a moment, one leg over the sill, as his nostrils caught a scent of a woman's perfume coming from this room.

If this room had a tenant, she was either asleep or had gone out to investigate the excitement in the main building. The question of whether or not to enter the window was taken out of his hands a moment later when a man with a lantern came out on the balcony of Room B and put its glare over the courtyard below.

Forking the sill, Redding was straightening up to reach for the window to close it when he felt the hard thrust of a pistol barrel ream his ribs, and a whisper broke the unnatural stillness of the room.

"Don't move or I'll pull this trigger."

CHAPTER 6

JOYCE MELROSE'S STORY

THE COMMAND WAS BACKED BY THE DRY METALLIC click of a gun hammer thumbed to full cock. Panic stormed through Redding, believing this was finish. Then a match blazed in his face, and he saw that the gun was held by a girl wearing a plum-colored quilted robe.

He gasped out, "Hold it, ma'am. I'm Doug Redding."

His quick whisper checked the girl's impulse to scream for help. As the match sputtered out in her fingers, Redding felt a swift wash of admiration for her self-control. Her whisper reached him above the clatter of feet passing to and fro in the corridor outside. "You—you know who I am?"

"Joyce Melrose?"

"Yes."

"I saw you leaving Keaton's store tonight."

He felt the gun muzzle relax its pressure on his ribs as the girl from Crowfoot Ranch stepped back. He heard her fumbling in a matchbox on the chiffonier, and a moment later a second light bloomed in her left hand.

Her eyes were searching his vest, as if looking for a lawman's star, eyes of a blue which reminded Redding of a glacial pond he had come across once in the high Absarokas. Her hair, shoulder-long, cascaded in chestnut waves against the shirred collar of her robe.

"Can you prove you're an SPA man?"

Redding, keeping his arms well away from gunstocks, lifted the globe from a hobnail lamp on the dresser and waited until Joyce, using only her left hand, had lighted it. Then he drew the window blind.

"I don't carry a star," he said, "but I have a letter here."

The girl's right elbow was pressed against her hip to steady the cocked Bisley which still covered Redding. She remained wary as a doe with a stalker's scent in its nostrils, alert as a coiled spring, as Redding reached carefully under his vest and drew out Colonel Regis's envelope. He flipped open the letter and handed it to her.

He waited with hands again at hatbrim height while she scanned the message writtten on the official letterhead of the Territorial Stockmen's Protective Association. It appeared to satisfy her, for she uncocked her gun and lowered it.

"All right, Mr. Redding," she said. "Isn't this a rather irregular way of contacting me?"

Redding grinned for the first time in several hours. In the lamp's soft glow, it was hard to keep his eyes from following the lines her body made under the quilted fabric of the robe, the firm uplift of high breasts, the provocative curve of hip and waist.

Joyce was not far past twenty, he judged, and he knew an obscure sensation of regret when he noted the flash of the diamond on her left ring finger and remembered that this girl was engaged to marry the man named Darkin who had followed her across the mountain range tonight.

"I'm not accustomed to banging into young ladies' boudoirs, this way," he admitted dryly, "but I was sort of crowded out of my own stall, across the court yonder. I came over the roof."

He saw some of the high color leave her cheeks.

"That shooting which has aroused the house—are you in trouble already, Mr. Redding?"

43

His shoulders stirred. "A peck of it. I pulled one of Blackwine's mustangers out of a fight in a saloon tonight. Let him hide in my room. Somebody bushwhacked him—while I was out on my balcony getting a sniff of fresh air."

Joyce Melrose slumped down on a bed which, Redding noted, she had not as yet turned down.

"Whoever fired the shot thought he was shooting me," Redding continued. "He called my name just before he pulled trigger."

The girl regarded him with horrified intensity. "Because—you are a range detective."

"Probably. It's a hazard for men in my line."

"Then I'm indirectly responsible—"

"Not at all. To throw the marshal off the scent, though I planted my badge on the dead man. Which accounts for my not being able to show it to you now, Miss Melrose."

He saw a troubled intelligence deepen in her eyes.

"You don't think I betrayed the fact I was meeting you in Paloverde to anyone, do you, Mr. Redding?"

"Did you?"

"No. I can swear to that. I told no one, no one whatsoever, that I was coming here. There—there are things I want to talk to you about, about my father's murder, before you reach the Basin, before you even agree to accept the case."

Redding plumbed his vest pocket for tobacco and papers. "You wear a diamond," he said casually. "Surely your fiancé knew you were coming to Paloverde?"

She lowered her eyes at the directness of his question. "No, not even he. Anyway, Teague Darkin is on the other side of the mountains. He is Crowfoot's foreman.

44

I didn't tell him I'd decided to call on the SPA for help. He's just like the Trailfork sheriff—passing off Dad's killing as just another of Blaze Tondro's bushwhackings. I—I'm not so sure."

Hearing this girl mention the name of Blaze Tondro reminded Redding sharply of his own personal tragedy, his own gun-smoke crusade. Cementing his smoke with a swipe of his tongue and lighting up over the lamp chimney, he forced himself back to another line of thought.

"This Teague Darkin—he didn't come to Paloverde with you?"

"No. I told you that calling on the Protective was my idea alone. I have no way of knowing but what Tondro has spies planted in my own bunkhouse, the way riders come and go, go and come. It's hard to hire men to work for a hoodoo ranch like mine, Mr. Redding. So I didn't let Teague know about this deal of ours."

Redding thought, *But Darkin's in town tonight*— Aloud he said, "Does this man you aim to marry—does he have black hair with a white stripe down the center?"

A faint glint of humor touched the girl's mouth. "What a gruesome picture! No. Teague is a redhead, Why?"

"Does this man with the streak in his pelt fit any Basin rider you know of?"

She shook her head after a moment's reflection. "Why do you ask?"

He flicked cigarette ash into a saucer of fly poison on the chiffonier, taking his time about answering that one.

"It was Mr. Skunk Stripe who shot the man in Room B, ma'am."

She came to her feet with the surprise of it. "Are you hinting that my fiancé would want you killed, Mr.

45

Redding?"

He scowled thoughtfully. "No-o. But if the word got around that you were meeting a range detective secretly in Paloverde, someone might have followed your stage tonight, found out I was registered here at Foothill, House—and tried to make certain I wouldn't show up in the Basin to investigate your father's murder."

Outside the girl's room, the corridor was no longer noisy with the tramp and thud of feet. Stepping to the window, Redding tipped back the shade and had a long look at the activity going on in Room B, its window blazing across the court. Two men were up on the roof, exploring with lanterns. Another group swarmed in the yard below, looking for sign.

Redding took advantage of this diversion to debate whether he should tell this girl that Teague Darkin was in town tonight. But until he knew something more of the ramifications over on Crowfoot, he decided against it. As the stable hostler had theorized, perhaps the Crowfoot ramrod, getting wind of Joyce's visit here, had trailed her over the Pass for her own protection.

"You'll work on this case, won't you, Mr. Redding?" The girl's query pulled him back to reality.

He turned to face her. "I'm already working on it, Miss Melrose. I have reasons of my own for wanting to track down Tondro. If he murdered your father—"

She broke in. "I'm not sure—I can't be sure Dad *was* killed by the Tondro bunch, Mr. Redding. That's the main thing I wanted to talk over with you. It's common knowledge that Tondro hides out in the Navajadas, where the country is too rough for the law to penetrate."

Redding remained silent, remembering the letter from his brother now reposing in his shirt pocket; a letter confirming the fact that Tondro's den was in the

46

Navajada malpais east of Lavarim Basin.

"You see," the girl went on, "Dad wanted to sell our beef to the Pedregosa Indian Reservation this fall. That's on the northwest side of the Basin, across the mountains. Year after year, the Wagonwheel Ranch wins the bid on that government beef issue. Wagonwheel is owned by an English cattle syndicate with its home office overseas. Dad—and the other Basin ranchers—thought it was high time a Territorial outfit got the Reservation business."

Redding scowled, wondering what all this had to do with the murder of Crowfoot's owner. "A simple matter of underbidding Wagonwheel," he suggested.

"So Dad thought," Joyce agreed. "Dad left Crowfoot on his way to interview the purchasing agent over at the Reservation. That is northwest of the Basin—remember that carefully. When a week passed and Dad didn't return, I telegraphed the Agency."

"And your father hadn't arrived there?"

A storm of emotion kept the girl silent for a moment. When she had recovered, she continued in a taut whisper. "No. I was frantic. I called my crew off the range, had them start a search. Three days later Teague Darkin brought my father in. A bullet in his chest. Teague saw buzzards wheeling over a ridge—"

"Your foreman found your father?"

"Yes. Lying off the trail which crosses the east range toward Paloverde, Mr. Redding. Fifty miles from the Indian Reservation road, in the opposite direction. His horse had been shot, too."

Redding picked this information over in his head, as he would do many times in the days ahead. "In other words," he said, "it would seem your father didn't head for the Indian Reservation at all, but turned southeast

47

into Blaze Tondro's country instead."

She nodded, looking up at him with a little girl's soulful entreaty in her eyes. "So it would seem, Mr. Redding—but it doesn't make sense. It isn't a thing Dad would do, without telling me beforehand. I told Teague as much, but he laughed at me for imagining things. He said it was obviously a Tondro ambush. That—that's when I decided to call on the Association for an investigation."

Redding pinched out his cigarette, knowing it was time to terminate this discussion. Joyce Melrose, sensing his restlessness, went on quickly. "Teague thinks I went to Sage City to shop. He will meet my stage at Trailfork day after tomorrow to take me back to the ranch. You understand I'm not being intentionally disloyal to my future husband when I ask you not to—"

Redding reached for his Stetson. "Sure," he cut in. "Suppose I show up at Crowfoot in a few days. Is there any chance of hiring on as a cowhand?"

She answered eagerly, "Yes, there is. Our beef gather is coming up. Teague and I will be picking up extra riders in Trailfork, as we always do at this season of the year. If you're there, I'll make certain you're put on Crowfoot's payroll."

He gripped her hand. "I'll see you in Trailfork day after tomorrow, then," he said, and stepped to the door. "Right now, I'd best be on my way yonderward, ma'am, before the marshal takes a notion to make a room-to-room hunt of this hotel."

Looking out into the hallway, he found it deserted. A flight of stairs led down to the dining-room under the annex, and Redding headed that way, not once looking back at Joyce Melrose's room.

He crossed the darkened dining-room and let himself

out on the Agave Street side, fully expecting to be challenged by the guards Marshal Chessman should have posted around the hotel by now. He was surprised and relieved to find none on duty.

Cutting through the night toward Colburn's barn. Redding reached it to find the game-legged hostler nowhere about. Doubtlessly the man had been drawn uptown by tonight's excitement at the Crossed Sabers Saloon.

Ten minutes later Redding was fording the Rio Coyotero downstream from the bridge, on the off-chance that the marshal might have posted guards there to check outgoing riders.

Ahead of him loomed the dark, mysterious notch of Cloudcap Pass, where the stage road looped over the Navajadas on its way to Trailfork, the next county seat west.

Avoiding that road, Redding put his big roan along a game trail on the south flank of the Pass, in the direction of Lavarim Basin and Tondro's domain.

CHAPTER 7

TO IDENTIFY A CORPSE

MARSHALL DORF CHESSMAN DRAGGED A BLANKET over the dead man on the cot and chewed thoughtfully at his cigar. He had already formed his conclusions as to how this man had died, and he took a certain detached satisfaction in the memory that this was the salty kid who had insulted his dignity over at the stockyards at sundown; the same Blackwiner who had caused the ruckus at the Crossed Sabers a little later.

Chessman was alone in Room B at the moment. A burly Army sergeant had been pressed into duty to keep the morbid ones out of the way. The door opened now and Laury Church, the night clerk, entered with the Foothill House register under his arm.

"His name is Douglas Redding, Marshal," Church said, opening the book and running a finger down the list of today's guests. "Sage City man. Must have picked up his key when I was away from the desk, which is why I couldn't identify him before."

Chessman entered the name on the back of a grubby envelope for his official report to the coroner. In the act of closing the book, his eye caught Jace Blackwine's signature two lines above Redding's.

"Take the sergeant to Room F," the lawman instructed Church, "and fetch back the man who rents that stall. Tell him I want to see him."

Laury Church started for the door, then turned on his heel, a new excitement glittering in his eyes.

"Room F's Jace Blackwine, Marshal. Paid me his week's tariff in advance. You don't figger he killed this Redding?"

Chessman spat out a shred of tobacco and glared at the clerk. "I think this was a case of suicide, son, and I figger the coroner will concur. This hombre worked for Blackwine. I want Jace to confirm the identification before we move the body."

Church hesitated. "Jace has got a woman with him, Marshal. Fifi. Agin the rules of the house, you understand, but Jace slipped me a sawbuck to look the other way. If the boss—"

Chessman's pudgy face purpled. "Damn you, Laury, a man's been kilt under this roof. Rustle Blackwine down here and leave Fifi out of it."

Two minutes later the hotel clerk reentered Room B, accompanied by Jace Blackwine The big mustanger was shirtless and in his sock feet. His is ruddy face was mottled with drinking, and his eyes held a long-festering contempt for his old enemy, the marshal.

Chessman stood looking out the balcony door, thick fingers laced behind his back. Blackwine growled, "You want me, Dorf?" and stood waiting, his eyes fixed on the blanket-shrouded shape on the cot.

Chessman turned ponderously, his eyes bright with pleasure at the prospect of grilling his long-time feuding opponent. At a savage gesture from the marshal, Church and the blue-coated sergeant retired from the room, leaving Blackwine and the marshal facing each other across a fog of cigar smoke.

"Been in your room these past thirty-forty minutes, Jace?"

Blackwine ran a horny hand through his cinnamon whiskers. "Damn you, Dorf, I didn't shoot this hombre, so keep your hints to yoreself. I been chattin' with Fifi Latroux since eight o'clock, not budgin' a hoof outside o' Room F." After a long pause during which his glare challenged the marshal to dispute his statement, Blackwine added, "I was pourin' Fifi a drink when we heard the shot. She'll back my word as to that. You don't pin this gunplay on me, Chessman."

The marshal grunted. "Take more'n Fifi's word to convince me you weren't lyin', I thought so, Jace. So happens I ain't tryin' to pin this killin' onto you—not sayin' I wouldn't like to."

Chessman rolled his cigar across his lips for a moment, savoring his fun with Blackwine, and then stepped over to the cot and drew the blanket back to expose the Rickaree Kid's blood-laced head, the blue-green cavity of a bullet hole punched through his left eyebrow.

"You can identify this hombre?" Chessman asked.

Staring down at the dead face of his mule packer, Jace Blackwine experienced a genuine shock. When the hotel clerk had summoned him front Room F a moment ago with word that Doug Redding had been shot to death, Blackwine had accepted the news without question. Now, seeing the Rickaree Kid lying here, Blackwine felt the alcoholic fog lift abruptly, leaving him somberly alert.

"Sure, I can identify him," Blackwine grunted. "One of my mustangers, as you well know."

"What's his brand?"

Blackwine took a moment before answering. "Wouldn't know. I made out his pay check to cash. We called him the Kid."

"His name," Chessman supplied, "is Douglas Redding."

The Paloverde marshal stepped over to the washstand and reached in the bowl there to remove a ball-pointed silver star, the furbished metal shedding sparks of light from the high-wicked lamp. Chessman tossed the law badge over to Blackwine, who juggled it a moment as if it were a poisonous thing.

"Range detective's tin star," Jace Blackwine muttered. "What you showing me this for, Marshal?"

Chessman blew a smoke ring toward the ceiling. "Found it in the dead man's pocket, Jace. You didn't know you had an Association man on your wild-hoss hunt, eh?"

A shine covered Jace Blackwine's steamy temples as he met the marshal's glance. There was a slight tremor in his hand as he passed the star back to Chessman, saw the marshal replace it in the china wash bowl, which contained the other items removed from the dead man's pockets.

"News to me, Marshal. Come to think of it, the Kid—Redding, you say his name is—always played his cards close to his chest. I had him sized up for a man with a bounty on his topknot."

Chessman jotted something on the grimy envelope. "I got to telegraph SPA headquarters in Sage City about this matter," he said. " Redding being a range detective changes the whole aspect of this business. You knew Redding shot the keno man, Lew Graytrix, over at the Crossed Sabers tonight?"

Blackwine made a vague gesture. "Told you I spent the evenin' with Fifi, here in the hotel. I was in the saloon long enough for one drink, yeah. You expect me to play nursemaid to my boys?"

Chessman grinned. He had waited a long time to get Blackwine where he wanted him. He was savoring the sweet nectar of fulfilled revenge now.

"This will be your last spree in a Paloverde, Jace. I'll give you all day tomorrow to round up your mustangers, sober 'em up enough to fork a saddle, and clear 'em out. You're finished in this town. Like I warned you when your bunch breezed in tonight."

A rap sounded at the door, and one of Chessman's deputies poked his head in. "Nobody on the roof, Marshal, and no snake sign under the balcony. You know what we think? We think this hombre was drunk and used his own gun on hisself. Knew he'd be caught sooner or later for shootin' Graytrix over at the saloon, and—"

Jace Blackwine moved over to the washstand and turned to regard the marshal's broad back as Chessman interrupted his deputy's theorizing.

"We'll let the coroner do the thinkin', Bob."

"Well, he's waitin' out here with his pallet now, Dorf. Ready to have the body moved?"

Under cover of this talk, Blackwine poked a big hand into the washbowl and, from the odds and ends of loose change and matches and tobacco which comprised the gleanings of the dead man's pockets, grabbed the law badge the marshal had shown him. He dropped the star into his pocket just as Chessman was pulling the door wide to admit the contract surgeon from the fort, who also ran a civilian undertaking parlor and the coroner's office here in town.

"You finished with me, Marshal?" Blackwine demanded.

Chessman turned to lay the flat strike of his gaze on the red-bearded mustanger he had warred with for so long.

"Finished for keeps, Jace. 'Y Gawd, any mustanger I find inside the town limits by sundown tomorrow gets jailed."

Blackwine's grin held no malice. "Ultimatum accepted, Marshal. We'll take our trade elsewhere."

As Blackwine shouldered it into to the jam of people blocking the outer corridor he caught the tag end of what Chessman was telling the coroner. "—a case of suicide, Provart. No evidence to p'int to its being murder. But I'd give plenty to latch eyes on the big feller who helped him make his getaway at the saloon tonight."

Blackwine elbowed his way free of the crowd and went back up the hall, turned the corner, and paused a moment outside the door of his room, his big fist opening and closing on the law badge he had purloined from Room B.

"Way I see it," he mused, trying to arrive at the truth behind this tangled skein of events, "Redding pulled the

54

Kid out of a tight at the Crossed Sabers and stashed him in his room. Question is, where was Redding when Tondro shot the wrong man?"

After a moment's puzzling, Blackwine gave up. Of one thing he was positive. Doug Redding was still on the loose. And he was a Johnny Law, as Blackwine had suspected. This tin star might prove to be worth its weight in diamonds in future, if revealed to the right man at the right time. Obviously, Redding had visited the Rickaree Kid after the shooting, in order to plant the SPA badge in the dead man's pocket.

"One thing," the mustanger decided, "I got to make sure none of my boys attend the Kid's funeral and let the cat out o' the bag. The marshal wantin' us out o' town will take care of that."

Stepping into Room F, Blackwine put his beady gaze on the woman who was brushing her peroxide-bleached tresses in front of a blistered mirror. Fifi Latroux's washed-out eyes held the sharp fixity of the fear that was in her as she waited for the big mustanger to close and bolt the door.

"It appears one of my boys blew his brains out down the hall," Blackwine announced, in a too-loud voice. "Douglas Redding. Had his gun still in his hand."

"Fifi sure hopes nobody got wise to Blaze ducking in here," the jezebel said, showing a snag-toothed grin of relief.

Blackwine stepped over to a curtained corner of the room and whipped the soiled burlap aside to reveal the beefy shape of a man pressed against the wall there.

"Coast is clear, Tondro. The marshal just wanted me to identify the corpse. He'd already figgered it was Doug Redding from the hotel book."

Blaze Tondro emerged from hiding, his half-breed

face never looking more Indianlike as he relaxed from the strain of these past ten minutes. Raking brown fingers through his white-streaked shock of raven hair, the Navajada rustler stepped over to a bedside table and poured himself a stiff drink of whisky in a tumbler, downing it with a quick snap of his head.

"And you were right about Redding being a star-toter," Blackwine said, giving Tondro a glimpse of the silver badge. "Thought you'd like proof that you tallied the man you were after, Tondro."

A grin lifted the drooped corners of Tondro's wide mouth as he watched the law badge disappear into Blackwine's pocket. "You think it's *bueno* for me to leave now?"

Blackwine shrugged. "So far as Paloverde is concerned, you're just a stray saddle bum. And that thickheaded Chessman has already written off Redding for a suicide. Heard him tell the coroner as much. Provart won't argue the matter."

Relief showed on the sunken planes of the half-breed's cheeks. "I'll drift, then," the rustler said. "Sorry I broke into your party, Fifi."

Fifi went on with her hair brushing, ignoring Tondro.

"Chessman's give me and the boys the heave-ho, honey," Jace Blackwine remarked, dipping his cigar butt into a shot glass of whisky and sucking it. "Looks like we're finished in Paloverde."

Blaze Tondro donned a flat-crowned sombrero with greasy ball tassels girdling its brim. Blackwine and Fifi had already forgotten his presence; this room had served its purpose as a temporary refuge.

Stepping out into the hall, Tondro headed down the annex corridor and took the back stairs to the dining-room below. He left the hotel by the Agave Street door, an unnoticed shadow against the background of the night. He was in time to see the body of his ambush victim being lugged into Coroner Provart's lean-to morgue across the street.

Tondro lighted a black-paper Mexican cigarillo and made his unhurried way down Agave until he reached an adobe-walled, tarpaper-roofed shanty down by the river. The place was dark, but the door opened as Tondro mounted the steps.

The tense whisper of Teague Darkin met Tondro. "Job finished?"

"Sí."

"No hitches?"

"An hombre chased me down the corridor right after I shot, but I ducked into Blackwine's room and whoever it was figgered I had skun out the window."

The Crowfoot Ranch foreman joined Tondro outside, and the two started skirting the river bend toward Colburn's stable.

"You're positive Redding hadn't visited Joyce in her room?"

Tondro's cigarillo coal bobbed sideways to a negative shake of the head. "I saw her go into her room, señor. Redding was not in the annex at all." After a pause, Tondro added, "Blackwine was called in to identify Redding. He choused Redding's law badge."

Darkin bent a sharp stare at his partner. "Blackwine doesn't know I'm in town? I can't have that nosy mustanger suspecting I got cards in this deal."

Tondro laughed softly. "Blackwine knows I got reasons of my own to go after range detectives, *amigo*."

They approached Colburn's barn from the rear and waited while Joe, the game-legged hostler saddled their horses for the return trek up Cloudcap Pass. This Joe had once ridden with Tondro's wild bunch, until a line rider's slug had smashed a kneecap and ended his border-hopping career.

"Funny thing," the hostler commented as he turned the reins over to the waiting riders. "Feller name of Redding got himself shot at the hotel tonight. One of Blackwine's' hunters. Left his bronc here."

Swinging into stirrups, Teague Darkin laughed. "He won't be calling for his bronc, Joe."

The hostler grinned. "I know that. Somebody hears about the shooting, belts it down to the livery here, and steals the dead man's bronc. What do you make of that?"

Tondro, in saddle now, pondered this information briefly. "One of Blackwine's boys, most likely," the border hopper vouchsafed, and then he and the Crowfoot foreman spurred away toward the Rio Coyotero Bridge and melted into the night. The hollow rumble of their ponies' hoofs wafted back to where the stable hostler stood.

"Shouldn't have left the barn to find out what the brawl was about," Joe said aloud. "There'll be hell to pay if Colburn finds out a hoss was stole out of his place while I was playin' hooky."

CHAPTER 8

THE GOLDEN LIZARD

DUSK WAS POOLING THE VAST REACHES OF LAVARIM Basin when Redding arrived in Trailfork, after an all-day trek from Cloudcap Pass, where he had camped overnight.

The only event to break the monotony of his entry

58

into this range land which for the past decade had known the raids of Blaze Tondro's rustlers from south of the border was a minor one. At noon, encountering a horse-trader at Willow Springs on the stage road out of the Pass, he had swapped his roan for a white-stockinged sorrel which bore a brand from outside the Territory. There might be men who would link the roan with Doug Redding—and Doug Redding was supposed to have been killed in Paloverde last night.

He stabled the sorrel and engaged a room at the town's only hotel, the Emigrants' Tavern. According to Colonel Regis's letter, an ally to contact in Trailfork was Val Lennon, the local sheriff. That meeting, Redding decided, could wait until he had had a night's rest and a chance to get rid of his whiskers.

The day's ride had served to point up his knowledge of Lavarim Basin's geography. This was his first visit here, but he had seen the Basin almost daily from the high roof of the Navajadas, as a member of Blackwine's horse hunt.

The Basin was roughly two hundred miles long by sixty wide, bracketed on the east by the Navajadas and on the west by the granite-toothed lift of the Axblade Mountains. The two ranges met at the north, deep in the Territory, and at the south, below the Mexican border. Ever since the Spanish regime, Lavarim Basin had been plundered by rustler bands similar to the one now ramrodded by the elusive Tondro.

Redding had had plenty to occupy his thoughts during this day-long journey. Uppermost in his mind was his own personal crusade, knowing that the rugged western slopes of the Navajadas, flanking his left stirrup all day, held the secret of Tondro's hide-out, a secret which his brother Matt had learned at the cost of his own life.

As an SPA operative, he already faced a problem with many facets. Major Sam Melrose's murder at unknown hands; Joyce's doubts that Tondro had bushwhacked him. Teague Darkin, who had somehow learned of Joyce's visit to Paloverde and had followed her there with an unknown accomplice. The British-owned Wagonwheel Ranch, across the Axblades, and its annual beef contract with the Pedregosa Indian Reservation.

At a Chinese restaurant, Redding got on the outside of a square meal. Full darkness had come to the town when he stepped out on the main street, relishing a cigar.

Strolling the spur-scuffed sidewalk, taking in the night smells and sounds of this typical border town, Redding was aware of a brooding melancholy, wondering if Matt had left his footprints in the thick dust of these streets.

He located the Wells Fargo station, where on the morrow he would see Joyce Melrose alight from the stage from Paloverde, to be met by Teague Darkin. Opposite the stage stand was the big Fandango Saloon, obviously the center of Trailfork's night life, a deadfall built on the same lines as Paloverde's Crossed Sabers Saloon.

A vagrant impulse caused Redding to enter the Fandango. He found himself a spot at the bar and waggled his finger for a drink.

Waiting for the apron to serve him, he had his casual look at the inevitable poker games in progress along one end of the barroom. In an adjoining annex, percentage girls in gaudy crinoline were dancing with buckaroos in off the range for a week-end session of bucking the tiger and whooping it up.

Paying for his drink, he was toying with the shot glass of amber liquor when he observed one of the dance-hall girls approaching him, a striking Spanish-American type with ivory skin and a resplendent costume of rainbow colors, twinkling with sequins at and set off with gold pumps.

The girl had spotted him as a newcomer and prospective customer. Glancing in the back-bar mirror, Redding watched her pause to adjust the red rose in her combed-back hair of glossiest black. For a dance-hall hussy, she was uncommonly beautiful, young and yet to reap her harvest of disillusionment which was the inevitable prospect for a girl plying her profession in a town as rough as this one.

A half-drunk cowpoke at Redding's elbow swung around and swayed forward to touch the girl's bare shoulder as she approached. Redding heard the waddy's thick greeting. "You look perty as a li'l red waggin in that git-up, Zedra. You honin' to shake a hoof with ol' Monte, hey?" In the blistered mirror, Redding saw the girl's flash of teeth as she made some bantering remark to Monte and wheeled artfully from under his pawing hand. An instant later Redding caught the subtle fragrance of perfume and felt the lightest of touches on his sleeve.

"You wish to dance with me, good-looking?"

Redding had his moment of wry self-appraisal, eyeing the reflection of his grubby beard, the deep pockets of fatigue under his eyes, the trail dust still making its thick veneer in the fibers of his Stetson.

He turned to meet the girl's sparkling glance and professional smile. Instantly he saw her expression alter, her ripe ruby underlip sagging as she recoiled from him as if he had lifted a hand to strike her; and a single word

61

was torn involuntarily from her.

"*Matt!*"

The bantering remark which Redding had been about to make died on his lips. He felt the scrape of her bracelets, as she withdrew her hand from his sleeve, and caught the blurred streak of the gold ring she wore.

"I—I reckon I will dance with you," he said huskily, a voice somewhere in the recesses of his brain crying loudly, *She mistook me for Matt—Matt must have worn a beard down in this country.*

He forced a grin, meeting the girl's eyes. "I'll take a whole book of tickets, *paloma mía.*"

The girl started to turn back toward the dance-hall annex, and Redding stepped quickly to block her path. Pitching his voice low, he asked her, "You called me Matt. Why?"

This girl, whom the cowboy Monte had called Zedra, turned on a brassy smile intended to let a casual onlooker to this byplay know that this man was not molesting her with his attentions.

"It—it is nothing, señor. A mistake. You remind me—of a *caballero* I once knew. A man now dead. I must go now—"

He caught her wrist. "I've got to talk to you, señorita—"

A heavy fist grabbed Redding's shirt and hauled him bodily around , and he caught the whisky-fouled breath of the cowboy Monte in his face.

"If Zedra Stiles don't want to dance with yuh, stranger, 'at's her privilege. You want to make something of it, step into the alley with ol' Monte. Zedra's m' gal, savvy?"

Redding broke Monte's grip on his shirt and turned, in time to see Zedra Stiles's willowy back vanishing through the purple plush curtains of the dance hall.

He pushed his way through the ebb and flow of barroom traffic toward that door, his ears meeting a din of sound as the guitar orchestra struck up a lively fandango. He saw no trace of the girl he sought anywhere in this smoke-blued room. She was nowhere among the dancers.

A wench in a wine-red dress slithered up to Redding and linked an arm through his.

"Wanna dance, cowboy? Get your tickets from the cashier yonder. Dime a dance, twelve for a buck. I'm Flossie."

Redding jerked his gaze away from the swirling couples on the floor to meet the invitation of this woman's eyes.

"That girl Zedra, Zedra, Stiles."

"That mestiza?" Flossie pouted. "What's she got that I—"

Redding thrust a gold coin into the girl's palm. "I'll match that if you bring Zedra out here, Flossie. Look in the dressing-rooms—wherever she might have gone. I'll be waiting here."

Flossie shrugged, appeared to be considering his proposition for a moment, and then was lost in the eddying semi-darkness of the dance hall.

Ten interminable minutes dragged by before the woman in the red gown reappeared, extending a hand, rubbing thumb and forefinger together. Zedra Stiles was not with her.

"I said I'd pay you if you brought Zedra back with you."

Flossie smirked. "She's lit out. Mister, a-horseback. She's gone. Vamoosed."

"Where?"

63

Flossie shrugged again. "*Quién sabe*, as the spiks say. Her old man is a prospector out in the Navajadas somewhere. She spends a lot of time in the hills with him. This time she didn't even bother to change her dress."

Disappointment laid its impact on Redding's facial muscles.

Before he could speak, Flossie went on in a conspiratorial whisper. "She left a note for you, Mister, if your monicker happens to be—you tell me first."

He hesitated, then said, "Redding. Doug Redding."

Flossie reached under the low neckline of her dress and drew out a tiny scrap of paper. "How much is it worth to you, cowboy?"

With a groan of exasperation, Redding fished another gold piece out of his pocket and received Flossie's paper in exchange. Before he could unfold it the girl was gone, seeking a customer.

By the dim flare of a wall sconce Redding looked at the message scrawled hastily on a bit of paper torn from a calendar sheet.

You will be Matt's brother Doug. Matt told me about you. Do not try to find me. Matt is dead. I don't want that to happen to you.

Redding made his way out of the Fandango, feeling the hot pound of blood in his temples.

Zedra had called him Matt at her first full glimpse of his face. Now she had fled Trailfork like a frightened quail.

Were it not for this hasty note by her hand, Doug Redding might have doubted the memory of the ring he had seen so fleetingly on her hand—a ring shaped in the design of a golden lizard, with a tiny seed pearl caught between its jaws.

CHAPTER 9

CROWFOOT RIDER

VAL LENNON WAS A SHERIFF AGED AHEAD OF HIS TIME by the responsibility of wearing a star in a border county well-known as a sinkhole of outlawry.

As he sat at his battered desk in the Trailfork jail office this morning, the bright sun pouring through the window at his back pointed up the premature white in his thinning hair, accentuated the deep wrinkles which seamed a weather-browned face and hands, revealed the resignation to his lot that had made him old and tired and stolidly wise.

Doug Redding's golden lizard finger ring was in the cup of the sheriff's palm. Studying it, the sheriff shook his head and looked up to meet the anxious stare of his bearded visitor.

"Can't say as I've seen a duplicate of this ring, Redding. But you know how them fillies at the Fandango load themselves down with joolry, Zedra could have wore a sidewinder coiled around her neck without me paying any notice. I'm twenty years too old to notice a woman's charms."

Redding leaned back in his chair, taking back the ring and looping its rawhide thong once more around his neck.

"It's a valid clue, Sheriff, even if I didn't have the girl's note to back it up. You saw from my brother's letter that he aimed to marry some girl he'd given Ma's ring to. Zedra Stiles is that girl—unless she stole or bought the ring, from whoever Matt gave it to."

Val Lennon shook his head. "Not Zedra. You needn't

be ashamed if your brother picked her out for branding, son. She dances at the Fandango, yes. But she don't sleep with her customers like the others do."

Redding started to shape a cigarette. "Who is she? And why should she have run away?"

Lennon laced his gnarled fingers over an up-drawn knee. "Reckon she had her reasons, son. As to who she is—I know she has a father back in the hills someplace. A prospector with a game lung. A gringo. Ferd Stiles. Was a medical doctor before he come West for his health. Her mother was pure Spanish. Long dead. Zedra's got good blood in her, son."

"Have you any idea how long she'll be gone?"

"Hard to say. She takes off into the Navajadas ever so often with a wagonload of grub for her old man."

"A wagon, you say?"

"Rented from O'Connor's wagon yard here in town. Dancing is a side line with her. Gives her something to do. Attracts a better class of trade to the Fandango, her boss thinks."

"Where is her father's prospect?"

"*Quién sabe?* Somewhere in the Navajadas, a day's ride off, mebbe more. Hills are full of old mine workings, since the Spanish days."

Redding tried another tack. "Do I bear any resemblance to anyone you have seen around town in the last year or two, Sheriff?"

Lennon grinned. "If you mean your brother, I couldn't say. You admit yoreself you look like just another shaggy saddle bum."

Redding said, "I want you to see me without this beard, but I doubt if that will tell you anything. Matt was ten years older than me, but we were often mistook for twins. Zedra saw some close resemblance, else she

66

wouldn't have known who I was. I got a hunch Matt let his whiskers grow, too."

The sheriff reached for a fly swatter and flattened a blue-bottle that had been annoying him. Lennon stared out of the window a moment, watching a lone man tool a buckboard into town, drawn by a pair of matched Morgans.

The wagon driver swung in at the rack in front of the Wells Fargo stand opposite the jail and tied up.

"You were asking about Teague Darkin," the sheriff said. "That's him in front of the Express depot. Brought a buckboard down from Crowfoot to pick up Joyce Melrose, likely—"

Redding stepped quickly to the window for his first daylight look at the rider he had heard talking with the stable hand over in Paloverde two nights ago.

Joyce Melrose's intended husband made a commanding figure as he angled across the side street toward the bank. He was wearing a brown town coat, full-skirted in the ranch-boss tradition, and his sixty-dollar Stetson, coffee-colored, rode his head at a jaunty jack-deuce angle.

The bulge of gun holsters showed under Darkin's coat. He wore buckskin-foxed California pants tucked into shop-made Justin cow boots, giving him the over-all look of a prosperous ranch owner rather than a foreman.

As Joyce had told him the other night, Teague Darkin was a fiery redhead, with the ruddy complexion to match. He scaled around two hundred, without an ounce of excess fat, and Redding saw where a woman could find this swashbuckling man handsome.

"Darkin's past forty," Val Lennon volunteered, "and he's been Major Melrose's *segundo* since Joyce was a

67

tomboy in pigtails. She showed up wearing his engagement ring just before the Major was bushwhacked. Natural enough that Darkin should fit in as Crowfoot's new owner. The man knows cattle. He built up Crowfoot when the Major had it on the downhill grade. Professional soldiers got no business ranchin'."

Darkin vanished into the vestibule of the bank Redding turned slowly to face the sheriff.

"Joyce tells me you've written off the Major's death as a closed case."

Color stained the taut skin over the sheriff's cheekbones, although Redding had not intended his statement of fact to sound like an accusation.

"What else can I do? Darkin brought in the body, and he's a citizen who carries weight in Basin County. Claimed he found it at aspen level due east of here—in territory known to be swarmin' with Blaze Tondro's gun hawks. Major Melrose has been fightin' rustlers for thirty years. He should have known he would be bushwhack bait if he showed up alone in those hills."

Redding said gently, "If you know now where Tondro hangs out, if you know he hazes a good share of the Basin's beef south of the border year in and year out, how come you haven't smoked him out into the open?"

Lennon sighed patiently, in the manner of a man to whom this question was an of oft-heard heard challenge. He gestured out the window toward the vista of terraced, canyon-corrugated Navajadas, a maze of light and shadow under the morning sun.

"Take another look at that country, boy. None of it surveyed as yet. A man could get lost forever if he wandered fifty yards off a trail. Old time Apaches shunned it like the back yard of hell. You think I haven't tried to locate Tondro's den? You think I'd have been reelected to this job if I hadn't tried?"

Redding fired his cigarette and stared abstractly at the match in his fingers. "I grant it's rough country," he conceded. "Scouted the top side of it this summer with Blackwine's mustangers. But Tondro's hide-out isn't impossible to ferret out. Matt did it. I aim to do it."

The sheriff grinned skeptic skeptically. "And where is your brother now? No, Redding. I doubt if a regiment of U. S. cavalry could smoke Tondro out of cover, let alone a range dick workin' solo. You ask my advice, Redding, I'd tell you to drop this assignment like a hot spud and tell your Colonel Regis to go to hell. It ain't his skin he's riskin'."

This session with Trailfork's sheriff was getting nowhere. Redding consulted the battered clock on Lennon's desk, saw that he had less than an hour before Joyce Melrose's stage was due from east of the mountains, and made his departure.

Thirty minutes in the barber's chair and he emerged on the street looking like another man, the clean lines of a cleft chin and leathery checks exposed now, his flesh oddly bleached over the blue roots of his beard.

Leaving the barbershop, he met Sheriff Lennon coming down the street. The old lawman eyed him a moment, then shook his head. With a beard or without it, Lennon saw nothing to link Doug Redding up with any visit Matt might have made to this cow town.

At ten-thirty a feather of dust coming from the section-line road from Cloudcap Pass resolved itself into a red-and-yellow Concord drawn by four Morgans. Nearing town the jehu whipped his team into a run and hit the main street in a great boil of dust, the stage lurching dramatically on its bullhide thorough braces.

69

Redding was standing in the shade of the Fandango Saloon porch as the Wells Fargo rig pulled up in front of the Express station immediately behind Teague Darkin's wagon, the driver tossing his lines down to a stock tender and hauling mail sacks out of the boot to throw down to the waiting postmaster.

Teague Darkin emerged from the bank, as if he had been waiting there for the stage to arrive, and reached the coach in time to open the door for Joyce Melrose.

Alighting from the Concord, Joyce was wearing the gray bodice and traveling-skirt and the feathered hat Redding remembered from the girl's visit to Alf Keaton's store in Paloverde. She put her hands on Darkin's shoulders and kissed the Crowfoot foreman on the cheek before he lifted her off the iron footstep.

Redding gave this scene his strictest attention. He heard Darkin say, "How's Sage City?" and heard Joyce's answer.

"Frightfully crowded. How can folks live all penned up that way? It's good to be back, Teague."

Darkin led the girl into the shade of the stage stand's awning. This put the couple less than a dozen feet from the Fandango porch where Redding stood, idly rolling a cigarette; his eyes met her traveling glance and received no sign of recognition. He thought, *Without the whiskers she might not know me, at that. Or else she's a damned good actress.*

Joyce's next words told him it was the latter. "How about the roundup, Teague? Are we still shorthanded?"

Darkin appeared to remember something. He reached in his pocket and took out a square of pasteboard. "Forgot to post our notice," he said. "There are plenty of drifters in town, I notice. Unless Crowfoot's hoodoo rep has shied 'em off, we ought to round out the crew this

70

morning."

Darkin excused himself and headed past Doug Redding to mount the steps of the Fandango. A big bulletin board nailed to the side of this saloon evidently served as the cow town's public forum; as Darkin approached the board he had to wait while a pot-bellied man in a Mormon hat and high-polished Hussar boots searched for extra thumbtacks and fixed a large official-looking poster to the collection of stud-horse bills, auction notices and other bulletins there.

Redding heard Darkin and the Mormon-hatted man exchange greetings; then the latter went back into the barroom, and Darkin stuck his card to the board under a painted heading: *Men Wanted.*

A group of chap-clad cowhands got up from a bench farther along the porch and strolled up to read these latest signs. As Doug Redding joined them, turning his back as Darkin rejoined the girl at the stage stand, he heard a grizzled old range rider remark with a wry humor, "Injun Reservation Agent callin' for bids for fall beef again. Why tack up his notices here? That Limey outfit over to Wagonwheel will underbid the Basin outfits, nohow. Always does."

Another rider grunted, "No Yankee would work for the pay them Britishers offer on Wagonwheel, is why."

Peering over the shoulders of the gathering cowpunchers, Redding noted that the large poster which the Mormon-hatted man had just tacked up was an official government sign calling for bids for 1,000 head of prime steers to cover the fall beef issue at the Pedregosa Reservation, contract subject to delivery at the Agency holding pens on or before October 15th.

But Redding's attention was centered on the cardboard square which Joyce Melrose's ramrod had

71

just posted.

Cowhands Wanted

Apply Crowfoot Ranch, 15 miles north of Trailfork, on Pass road. $30 a month and found. Fall beef gather. Riders experienced in brush-popping work preferred. No objection to Mexicans.

Teague Darkin
Foreman

The garrulous oldster who had remarked on Wagonwheel's certainty to garner the Indian contract had had his look at the Crowfoot advertisement by now. He drawled acidly at no one in particular, "Damned if I'd sign on with Darkin for a hundred a month and whisky six times a day."

The oldster caught Redding's curious eye on him.

"This Crowfoot outfit a Jonah, old-timer? I was thinkin' of bracing this Darkin for a job."

The oldster grunted. "Crowfoot's range runs into the foothills where Blaze Tondro's border hoppers draw most of their beef ever' fall, stranger. Why pop a steer out of the brush and draw a slug where your suspenders cross before you've hazed the critter into the herd?"

Another waddy added, "It's happened before, my friend. Shy clear o' Crowfoot and grow up with the country."

Redding thanked his informers and turned around to see Darkin removing Joyce's carpetbag from the rear boot of the stage, the girl still standing under the Wells Fargo awning where her foreman had left her.

Descending the Fandango steps, Redding sauntered over to Teague Darkin with a confidence that came from knowing that this man, whatever secrets might lie back of his officious exterior, had never laid eyes on Redding before.

72

"Crowfoot?" Redding asked. "Saw you tack up the sign."

Darkin's yellow-flecked eyes ranged over the big puncher before him for a moment before he nodded. "I'm Darkin, foreman of the outfit. Lookin' for work?"

"Right the first time."

Darkin's penetrating glance came to rest on Redding's clean-shaven jaw, his nostrils catching the scent of fresh bay rum. Something was chewing the foreman; Redding thought he saw a hint of suspicion enter the big man's narrowed eyes.

"A man who shaves off a beard as old as yours must have been either fresh out of jail or trying not to look like a picture on a bounty dodger. Which boot fits you, stranger?"

Redding thought, *Could be he's trying to place me with somebody he's known on his back trail.*

Before he could answer, Joyce Melrose spoke from behind. "Teague, you mustn't talk like that. Since when are we choosing a man by his looks on Crowfoot? We're in no position to turn down a rider on what you imagine his past history to be."

Anger flared behind the metallic surfaces of Darkin's eyes. He snapped to Joyce without taking his gaze off Redding's newly shaven jaw, "I don't cotton to making our bunkhouse a hide-out for men on the dodge, Joyce. Something about this hombre—"

Redding grinned. "I know I look tough, sir. I landed in this town with a Mex dollar in my pants. Spent half of it for a meal and the rest of it for a shave."

Joyce, coming around to face him, said gently, "What's your name?"

Redding removed his Stetson. "Blagg, ma'am. George Blagg."

"Where from?" Teague Darkin cut in.

"Texas. Nueces country."

Darkin's scowl faded. "Good at popping the brush for ladino steers, I take it?"

"No thickets anywhere can touch a Nueces *brasada* patch, sir."

Darkin said in an altered tone, "No offense, Blagg. Miss Melrose here owns the outfit. If she says so, you're hired. You can throw your war sack and bedroll in the buckboard yonder."

Redding replaced his Stetson, thinking, *Darkin will bear watching. He's not clear in his mind about me yet.* Aloud he said, "Be with you soon as I throw a saddle on my crowbait, Mr. Darkin. How do I get to this Crowfoot Ranch?"

Joyce said quickly, "Mr. Darkin and I will be driving out in the wagon shortly. Meet us here. Will two o'clock be time enough, Teague?"

"Reckon." Teague turned on his heel, carrying Joyce's luggage to the buckboard and stowing it under a tarp. Then he lifted a pair of empty five-gallon kerosene cans from the box and headed downstreet toward a mercantile store.

Joyce was thus legitimately alone with her new cowhand. Pretending to be engrossed in drawing on a pair of elbow-length gloves, she spoke in the lowest of tones. "You're a Crowfoot man now, Doug. What next?"

There was something Redding urgently had to settle in his mind, and since privacy between them would be an uncertain thing in the days to come, he phrased his question bluntly, not sparing her feelings. "Do you trust Teague Darkin completely, ma'am?"

His question froze the girl, her eyes staring down at

her gloves without seeing them. Redding saw a nerve twitch at the corner of her mouth and got the distinct impression that she was wavering between outrage at the inference he had cast on her future husband and an instinct to cover her true feelings with a lie.

Her reply came as a surprise to him. "No."

"Nor has he got my trust." Redding spoke swiftly. "I'll tell you why. He has made you think he was on Crowfoot these past three days?"

"Yes. Yes, he has."

"Well, I saw Teague Darkin in Paloverde the night you arrived. He and another man rode over the Pass that night, before the shooting in the Foothill House. Which means he's either a jealous lover, checking on your whereabouts—or he may have got wind of the fact that you were in Paloverde to meet a cattle detective."

Joyce had not altered her posture during his speech. She forced herself to go on with the business of smoothing the gloves snug to her finger tips now.

"I've got to know why your faith in Darkin has wavered," Redding went on ruthlessly. "I know you want to be loyal to him, that you feel guilty about calling on the SPA without his knowledge. But if I am to work on this case—"

Joyce turned as if to head for the sidewalk. Her eyes were bright with moisture. "All I can tell you, now or ever," she whispered, pulling the traveling-veil down over her face to shield the movement of her lips from the possible notice of onlookers, "is that I think Teague lied when he said he found Dad's body over in Tondro's foothills. I think Dad was killed on his way to the Indian Reservation—and I think Teague knows it. I think he may have even learned the truth about Dad's death. Don't ask me why. Call it—intuition."

75

CHAPTER 10

GRUB-LINE VISITOR

FOUR NEW RIDERS, INCLUDING DOUG REDDING—OR George Blagg, as his name appeared in the pay book— had supper in the Crowfoot cookshack at sundown.

The ranch headquarters occupied the head of a narrow valley between two rocky spurs of the Navajada range, less than twenty miles north of the Mexican boundary. Crowfoot's range formed a belt across the entire Basin, from the summit of the Navajadas on the east to the summit of the Axblades on the west, its drift fences paralleling the Mexican boundary. It was thus one of the largest working outfits in the Lavarim country, and its barns and corrals and other outbuildings were lavish in proportion.

Joyce Melrose's home was a rambling tile-roofed adobe, boxing in a patio in the tradition of a Mexican hacienda; the site of Major Melrose's donation claim cabin of a generation ago, his bonus for distinguished service in the war with Mexico.

During supper, Redding noticed that Teague Darkin did not eat with his crew. As Joyce's foreman and fiancé he took his meals in the main house—a habit he had adopted, Redding learned, immediately following Major Melrose's bushwhacking.

A poker game got under way at the bunkhouse. Redding declined an invitation to join it, on the excuse that he wouldn't have the price of a stack of chips until after payday. Lying on his bunk, studying the faces around the blanket-covered deal table under the glare of a lantern hanging from a crossbeam, the range detective had his try at sizing up what breed of men Darkin had gathered on Crowfoot for this, the first beef roundup since the boss's death.

His first impression of the Crowfoot crew was that Joyce had had ample grounds for wondering if Blaze Tondro might have spies planted in Crowfoot's bunkhouse. Without exception, these tough-visaged waddies carried sixguns, even while engaged in a friendly poker session.

Long schooled in making snap judgments of character, Redding took this display of guns as the mark of men who had been, or were, riding the owlhoot trail. With a few exceptions—oldsters from the Major's original crew—Darkin's riders were of a tough stripe who might easily fit in with a midnight crossing of the border, hazing stolen stock ahead of them.

Joyce had done her part well this morning, giving him a spot on Crowfoot, a vantage point from which he could dig up evidence that Blaze Tondro's hide-out might well be located on Crowfoot soil. He had wondered, on the ride out from Trailfork, what had been behind Darkin's catechism regarding his past. On the face of it, it would seem that Darkin was striving hard to keep the outlaw element out of his crew. Judging from his riders, the foreman had done the opposite.

At midnight, Darkin came into the bunkhouse and ordered the poker game to break up.

"You new men," Darkin said, "will be assigned your personal strings by the wrangler tomorrow. Crowfoot runs cattle on two ranges, the home spread here on the Navajada side of the Basin, and leased graze abuttin' our holdings in the Axblades over west. Which means we got two roundups to handle."

Darkin dug a notebook out of his pocket and

consulted it.

"Blagg," he said, glancing at Doug Redding, "you and the other new riders I hired in town this morning, will work with the straw boss, Shorty Hadley, chousing anything that wears a Crowfoot brand out of the canyons on this side of the Basin. It's rough range, brush and rocks. Hadley will show you where to bunch the stuff you pop out of the thickets."

Darkin paused to make sure his roundup orders were clear to everyone concerned. Then he resumed.

"The bulk of our beef are on the west side. With luck, both our crews will finish about the same time, and we'll pool the stuff for the drive over the Pass to the railroad at Paloverde. Any questions?"

A stripling in his late teens whom Darkin had hired along with Redding at Trailfork this morning spoke up hesitantly. "Seems from where I sit you're givin' us new hands the dirty end of the stick, boss. What's this talk I hear about it bein' risky business chousin' beef critters out of the Navajadas?"

A scowl drew Darkin's brows together. Redding thought, *He'll be a tough man to buck.*

"Referring to the poppycock that Blaze Tondro's bunch is waitin' to pounce on any Crowfoot herd you gather out of the foothills on this side of the Basin, Seymour?"

Seymour clamped his, jaw doggedly. "Maybe it was whisky talk, maybe not, boss. I don't cotton to workin' the Navajadas."

The straw boss, Shorty Hadley, spoke up from a corner bunk. "Darkin needs experienced men to handle the main beef gather over on the west lease, kid. My crew won't have one cow to round up agin ten that Darkin's boys will be handling."

Young Seymour cleared his throat, not wanting to admit to a kid's misgivings in front of these men. "But Tondro's bunch don't bother beef on the west side. It was my understandin' when I signed on in town this mornin' that I'd work the Axblade lease."

Darkin snapped his book shut with a force that made the lantern jump. "You're free to drift in the mornin', Seymour. Other outfits in the Basin are hirin'. Tondro ain't choosy what ranches he raids, if that's what's gallin' you. Naturally Crowfoot gets hit the oftenest, our graze straddlin' the border."

Seymour's checks flashed, his temper crowding him hard. "It ain't that I'm yellow, you understand. It's just—"

"Shut up or get out!" roared Darkin. "I don't tolerate chuck-wagon lawyers stirrin' up trouble in my crew."

Seymour grinned. "Reckon I'll drift come daylight, boss."

Teague Darkin's glance raked the bunkhouse, singling out Redding and the other new riders. "If any of you other new ones feel like the kid, pull out after breakfast."

Redding grinned, drawling from his bunk, "Reckon we'll work where you tell us to work, boss."

Before daylight on the morrow, Teague Darkin left Crowfoot with better than half the crew, his pick including every one of the salty specimens Redding had ticketed for potential rustlers.

This puzzled him. If Darkin was working with Blaze Tondro here on the east side of the Basin, it would seem more likely that he would have remained in charge of the crew assigned to that part of Crowfoot's range which was exposed to Tondro's operations.

79

For himself, Redding had the assignment he wanted. He would even welcome an attack by Tondro's rustlers, for that would give him trail sign to follow back into the Navajadas to the lair Matt Redding had discovered before death struck him down from behind. Somewhere in these tangled uplands he might track down the riddle of Zedra Stiles, the girl to whom Matt had given his love and his golden lizard ring as pledge of that love.

Daylight was a gray stain in the east when Shorty Hadley's chuck wagon pulled out of the ranch grounds with a crew of nine, including Doug Redding, and a cavvy numbering six horses per man. Joyce Melrose had been nowhere in evidence at this early departure of her roundup crews.

By noon the straw boss had his roundup under way. They would work southward, canyon by canyon and ridge by ridge, gathering Crowfoot beef into a holding herd at a point near the Springs, where Redding had made his deal with the horse trader.

This roundup should be completed in two weeks, by which time they would be ready to pool their cattle with the main Crowfoot herd being rounded up under Darkin's personal direction on the leased Axblade graze across the Basin.

For Doug Redding, the next four days were filled with the man-breaking labor of popping the brushy Navajada draws for half-wild Crowfoot steers and she-stuff. The men worked in pairs, hazing jags of cattle down to the prairie flats whenever they had assembled herds which would be hard to handle without extra riders.

Redding found himself tormented with the thought that, for a range detective working on a case, he was up to now wasting his time. Joyce Melrose had called him to the Basin to investigate the mysterious murder of her father. This sharing the risks and grueling labor of a beef roundup seemed to fit no part of a manhunt pattern.

And yet, as Shorty Hadley's crew worked its dogged way southward, Redding knew that each time the chuck-wagon camp moved it was probably penetrating closer into the sprawl of foothills dominated by Tondro's renegades.

During his stint of nighthawk duty with the pool herd, every other night, Redding kept his senses keyed for the sudden break of gunshots and roar of hoofs which would signal a surprise raid from the outlaws hidden in the upper reaches of the Navajadas.

During the day, invading the chaparral with rope and peg pony to flush hidden cattle out of the brush, he carried the thought that this roundup might well be under the constant observation of some Tondro sentinel, posted on the lofty volcanic rimrock which gave the Basin its name.

If Tondro's band struck, Redding's part in this grim game would find him ready. His job would not be to defend the herd against attack, but to fade into the timber and keep an eye on wherever Tondro's rustlers headed with the cattle.

That trail might head into Mexico by some other route than the obvious one through the bottleneck at the south end of the Basin. Wherever it led, the answer to the mystery of Tondro's hide-out would surely be found at its end.

At noon on this fourth day of grinding range work, Doug Redding headed for the chuck-wagon camp to pick up a snack of bait and saddle a fresh horse from the cavvy. Riding down to the chuck wagon, camped five miles from the growing herd on the flats, Redding saw from a distance that a grub-line visitor had hit Slim-Jim, the cook, for a handout.

None of Hadley's other riders had appeared yet for their noon meal. During a roundup in country as rough as this, the cook of necessity had to keep his grub ready at all hours, for the job of combing the foothill canyons often took a rider miles away from the camp at mealtime.

Riding in, Redding thought he saw something vaguely familiar about the chunky-built grub-line rider and the grulla horse hitched out by the pile of wood Slim-Jim had had his visitor chop into kindling size as the price of a handout.

Redding was off-saddling out at the rope corral, where the cavvy was bunched, when he saw the grub-liner toss his dishes into the wreck pan and turn around to face Redding.

One glance at the shaggy red beard depending from the visitor's jaw identified the man. That and his greasy buckskins.

"Jace Blackwine!" Redding muttered, and felt the hair on his neck nape lift to the challenge of it. "What's that damn mustanger doing on this side of the range?"

Blackwine's presence in this Crowfoot roundup camp had all the makings of a calamity for Redding. Blackwine would know about the supposed shooting of Doug Redding in Paloverde last week. In any event, he would not greet Redding by the alias of George Blagg. Such a discrepancy would be sure to catch the cook's attention.

The beefy mustanger put a long look on the rider out by the cavvy corral and then turned to stroll over to his tethered pony. A wash of relief went through Redding. Blackwine had apparently failed to recognize him with his whiskers shaved off. The fact that Redding had gotten rid of his roan saddler had kept Blackwine from spotting the horse Redding had used this summer during the mustang hunt.

Redding tarried overlong at the business of unsaddling. The cook was out of earshot, tending his Dutch oven; as yet no other riders had shown up.

Hoofbeats made their abrasive crunch over the gravelly patch near the cavvy pen, and Redding glanced over his pony's withers to see that Blackwine was spurring straight toward him, a grin lurking behind his beard.

He's spotted me, Redding groaned inwardly. *Talking my way out of this will be rough.*

Five feet away, Blackwine reined up. "Mighty healthy-looking for a corpse, son. They got your name on a boothill headboard over in Paloverde."

Redding felt the fast race of blood in his temples. "What brings you to the Basin, Jace? Thought you were hunting *oreanas* up north of here."

Jace Blackwine shifted his ponderous weight in the stirrups to delve deep in a pocket of his buckskin pants. He glanced over his shoulder to make sure his next move would not be observed by the Crowfoot cook. Then he withdrew his hairy paw from his pocket, and Redding saw the flash of a silver star in the mustanger's hand.

"You played your cards wrong when you were workin' for me, Redding," Blackwine said softly. "If you signed up with my boys tryin' to get a line on where Blaze Tondro holes up, I could have told you. How was I to know you were an SPA bloodhound?"

Redding was silent a long moment, pondering how far he could trust Blackwine. He saw the mustanger thrust the badge back in his pocket and settle himself in saddle, waiting for Redding to speak. If Blackwine had his star, then Blackwine knew the Rickaree Kid had been the dead man on his bed at the Foothill House that night. Had Blackwine tipped off the Paloverde marshal that a law badge had been planted on the Kid?

"You say you know where Tondro holes up, Jace?"

Blackwine exhumed a briar pipe from his brush-popper jumper and jabbed the stem between his teeth. "You're closer to it than you realize right now, Redding."

After a long run of silence, Doug asked bluntly, "What's your play, Blackwine? Did Chessman put a bounty on my scalp and you aim to collect it?"

Blackwine grinned. "Do Chessman a favor? Hell, no. Lissen. I drifted over to Crowfoot huntin' you, all right, but not for the reason you think. What's it worth to you if I p'int out where Blaze Tondro is squattin' right this minute, bidin' his time to jump this herd you're workin'?"

Redding countered, "How'd you know where to look for me?"

Blackwine's eyes held a secretive triumph. "Played a hunch. Knew damn well the Rickaree Kid wasn't an SPA snooper. Knew Crowfoot's boss got bushwhacked this spring; plumb logical an Association dick might shift to that case. Visited Crowfoot's home ranch yestiddy; you weren't there. Knew you were either workin' this side of the range, or you'd be with Teague Darkin workin' the Axblade lease."

Redding glanced over at the chuck wagon, aware that Slim-Jim was watching them curiously.

"I'll grab a bite of chow," Redding said in a low voice, "and head back up this canyon I'm working. Meet me there inside of an hour. I'll make it worth your while on this Tondro deal."

Blackwine nodded, picking up his reins. "Thought you would, star man. You get your badge back when we close the deal. I'll give you the low-down on Tondro's den after we've come to terms."

Blackwine waved to the cook and spurred his grulla over the ridge in the opposite direction from the canyon Redding had indicated as their rendezvous point. But Redding knew the mustanger would be waiting for him. The man who led to the smashing of Tondro's border ring would be rich when the accumulated rewards were paid by the two governments seeking to break Tondro's grip on Lavarim Basin. If Blackwine had information that would enable Redding to crack Tondro's hide-out secret, the rewards would go to him.

Redding's appetite was gone, as he realized that he was nearer to cracking this case than he had hoped to be, this soon. But he forced himself to eat, fueling his body against a ride which probably would prevent his return to the chuck-wagon camp tonight.

Shorty Hadley and the other Crowfoot riders drifted in, singly or by pairs and threes, by the time Redding had finished eating. He cut his personal mount out of the *remuda* and saddled up, heading back to the short box canyon he was working.

An hour had elapsed since he had made his arrangement with Jace Blackwine, ample time for the mustanger to double back to this draw and wait it for him.

An ory-eyed ladino steer popped out of the chaparral as Redding put his horse into the draw. The dust of the animal's passage obscured his vision as the sorrel plunged through a spiny hedge into a further clearing.

Somewhere out of the roundabout mesquite and buckbrush he heard Blackwine's voice. "Over here, Doug."

As he hipped around in saddle, Redding had his quick

glimpse of the mustanger's hairy face at the edge of the clearing. Redding's arm was coming up with a rope, making his California underthrow at the steer. He was tensed like that in saddle when he saw Blackwine hurling a chunk of lava at him.

There was no time to dig his gut hooks into the sorrel, no time to dodge the oncoming missile. Instinct made Redding kick boots from stirrups as the rock struck his skull a glancing blow.

He was vaguely aware of the steer hitting the end of his *reata,* dallied to his saddle horn; the sorrel swung back, taking up the slack as he had been trained to do by a former owner; and Redding found himself toppling from saddle.

In mid-air he pawed at a gun butt, hoping his senses would clear enough for him to lay a shot at Blackwine's grinning face over there in the brush.

In landing, Redding's head struck a protruding boulder, and with that concussion all sensation faded in the man. It seemed he was plunging into a bottomless black funnel. Oblivion had smothered his senses before Jace Blackwine ran out to slash Redding's catch rope with a bowie blade and free the bawling ladino.

CHAPTER 11

TONDRO'S HIDE-OUT

FOR REDDING, THE RETURN TO SENSIBILITY WAS A slow ordeal, like a swimmer breasting a swift current through a black cavern, with daylight showing only dimly, an unattainable distance away.

His first conscious sensation was that of red-hot

spikes being pounded into his skull; it seemed an eternity before he was able to rationalize the peculiar pitching motion of his body enough to know that he was on horseback.

Hearing came next. The whisper of wind in tree crowns, the spongy rasping of hoofs in wet gravel. A bandanna had been knotted over his eyes. When he tried to claw it off, it was to find that his wrists were tied to a dish-shaped saddle horn which he recognized as that of his own Brazos hull.

His nostrils became aware of the spicy odors of dank moss and conifers. There was a chill moist wind beating his cheek one moment; and then at a turn in the trail he felt the radiated warmth of near-by rocks, holding the sun's stored-up heat.

Through the fabric of his blindfold he saw a blurred nimbus which he finally concluded was the moon. It was night, then. That fact gave him a concrete problem to conjecture about and brought back his last lucid memory—Blackwine knocking him out of saddle with a well-flung rock.

His tongue was blotter-dry in his mouth. He felt the stickiness of his own crusted blood on his left cheek, drawing the skin and lying still wet on the back of his neck.

All this must have happened six-seven hours back, maybe longer. A combination of coma and sleep, then, must have blotted out the intervening time. From the stiffness in his thighs and arms he reckoned that Blackwine must have had him on the trail most of that time.

When he tried to move his feet out of stirrups he found his ankles trussed together by a rope leading under his horse. This being made a prisoner was a question Redding could not immediately fathom. Was Blackwine a Tondro scout? If so, this kidnaping was out of character. Spotting him for a range detective, Blackwine would have thrust a knife into his back and buried him in a shallow grave or else left him for the coyotes.

Or was Blackwine taking him back to face the law in Paloverde? Perhaps Dorf Chessman had issued a warrant for his arrest as the Rickaree Kid's killer.

His horse was scrambling up a considerable grade. Off to the left, Redding could hear the brawl of shallow water cascading down a rocky bed, and from time to time his right shoulder brushed rock and foliage, proof that Blackwine was leading him along a narrow ledge trail.

This would not be Cloudcap Pass, then. And the direction of the moon, whenever he glimpsed it through his blindfold, was wrong if they were heading over the mountains toward Paloverde.

He knew from his mount's jerky gait that it was being led by a trail rope tied to the bridle. There was another horse immediately ahead. That would be Blackwine on his close-coupled grulla.

"What's the deal, Jace?" Redding's voice made a croaking, unsteady sound in his throat. It held the tremor of a man but lately out of the throes of the sickness of a mild brain concussion.

He heard saddle leather creak as his captor twisted to face him, up ahead. Then Blackwine's voice floated back. "Rallied out of it, hey? You had me worried. Thought I might have slung that rock a mite too hard for your noggin. And you're worth more to me on the hoof than if you were cold meat."

Redding was silent a moment, pondering this

implication that he was being hauled in for the bounty on his pelt.

"Where are we? Mexico?"

Blackwine laughed enigmatically. "The question you went into the Basin to find out was where Tondro forted up, wasn't it? Well, I'm takin' you there, like I promised."

The horses made a sharp bend in the trail, and the noise of spilling rapids somewhere far below was lost in a deeper organ roar of sound that indicated a sizable waterfall near at hand.

The night wind flung a stinging icy spray against Redding, shocking his senses back to nearer normal. "Why the blindfold, Jace?" he called above the cascade's roar.

"Tondro's finicky about keeping his hide-out under cover. Even for hombres makin' a one-way *pasear* to his place."

From somewhere out of this black void, Redding's keening ears caught the unmistakable metallic click of a Winchester lever cranking a shell into to a gun breech. It was not from the direction of Blackwine's horse. Higher up and to the left.

Blackwine caught that sound, too, for he reined up so abruptly that Redding's following sorrel collided with the grulla's rump.

"*Qué es?*" demanded a voice.

"Jace Blackwine," the mustanger answered the sentry's challenge. "That you, Panchito? I'm hauling in a gringo *jerife.*"

"Tondro will pay you well, señor."

They pushed on past the sentry's post. The thunder of the waterfall deepened as the horses came abreast, entering a belt of shadow which cut the thin diffusion of moon rays from Redding's vision through the bandanna.

Then he saw a smudge of illumination, which he took to be a lighted window, drawing nearer. A faint clamor of men's voices reached Redding as Blackwine halted the horses alongside the light and called out, "Señor Tondro *aquí?*"

Spurs chimed as several wen approached, gathering around Redding's horse. There was a confusion of voices speaking in Spanish gutturals and *pelado* jargon. Then Redding felt a knife sever his leg and wrist bonds, and he was hauled roughly out of stirrups.

It was difficult for him to stand. He sensed Blackwine's vast body close to his right elbow. Then a hush fell over the assembled men, and an odor of tequila struck his nostrils.

"Howdy, Blackwine," a voice spoke near at hand. "Who is this hombre you've brung in?"

Blackwine's shoulder brushed his prisoner's. "Douglas Redding. Your stock detective, Tondro."

Redding felt a sensation of pure shock go through him, knowing that within reach of his hand stood Blaze Tondro, goal of his manhunt in Lavarim Basin, the man known through the Territory as the kingpin of border rustlers for more than a decade. Perhaps the killer of his brother Matt.

He heard Tondro suck in a breath. Then the outlaw spoke incredulously. "What are you feeding me, Jace? I shot Redding in Paloverde. You showed me his star yourself, that night in your room at the Foothill House."

Something sharp stabbed through Redding's shirt— the pin of his law badge, which Blackwine was now returning to its owner.

"This hunk of tin?" Blackwine laughed cryptically. the genu-wine article, Tondro. But the man you killed that night in Paloverde wasn't Redding. It was a drifter on my crew who called himself the Rickaree Kid. He was using Redding's room that night."

Redding could feel the impact of Tondro's gaze upon him, hear the quickened tempo of his breathing.

"You told me it was Redding—you told the marshal it was Redding—"

Blackwine laughed. "A business proposition, Tondro. I knew if the marshal had found Redding's law badge on the Kid that it was a plant to throw the marshal off the scent. I knew Redding had made a getaway. I knew sooner or later I'd track him down and turn him over to you. For a price."

A hand reached up to jerk the blindfold off Redding's eyes. He found himself staring at the man with the skunk stripe running down the middle of his shock of black hair.

This was the killer of the Rickaree Kid. For mercenary reasons of his own, Jace Blackwine had kept Tondro in ignorance of his mistake in targets. But how had Blaze Tondro learned of a range detective's presence in Paloverde that night? It all led back to Joyce Melrose's visit there to meet him, and the mystery back of Teague Darkin's trailing the girl over the Pass.

Redding glanced around, seeing too much to absorb in one glance. Behind him, on all sides, stood a group of serape-clad Mexican *pelados*. Cartridge bandoliers formed crosses on their chests; the lighted window was set in a rough building of whipsawed lumber which the highwheeling moon revealed to be the shaft house of some abandoned mine.

On all sides lifted the sheer granite wall of a canyon. A hundred-foot waterfall was spilling through a notch in the box-end cliff brink a hundred yards beyond the shaft house, its flow a phosphorescent horsetail in the moonlight.

Tondro regarded Blackwine's prisoner for a long moment, the evil of the man showing in his close-slitted eyes. "You admit to being Doug Redding?" he asked.

Redding shifted his glance to Blackwine, who stood at his side, holding the reins of their two horses. "I don't," he shot back. "My monicker is George Blagg. Blackwine snatched me off the Crowfoot roundup. He's trying to wangle a ransom of some kind out of you, on the strength of a tin badge he picked up somewhere or other."

Tondro swung toward Blackwine. It was obvious that Redding's denial had planted the seeds of doubt in the outlaw. An angry chagrin was in the mustanger's eyes as he sensed how his prisoner had outmaneuvered him here.

"If you lied to me about Redding that night in Paloverde," Tondro said with a grim logic, "how do you expect me to pay a bounty on this stranger now?"

Blackwine grunted. "This man an worked for me all summer, Tondro. His pay check was made out to the name o' Doug Redding."

The object of this argument was the target of all eyes now. He fought to keep his expression inscrutable, knowing he had gained a hollow victory here. Tondro would never permit an outsider to leave his bastion alive.

It was obvious that Jace Blackwine had been affiliated with this owlhoot band at some time in the past, otherwise the sentry would not have let him pass. The fact that the mustanger knew the location of this hide-out pointed up some past association.

"Jace," Tondro said, "I will not pay off on such slim proof."

Blackwine curbed his mounting anger with an effort. "If you won't pay off on this man, Tondro, I know a couple of hombres who will."

"Not without better proof than you've given me, *amigo*."

Blackwine reached for Redding's arm. "Teague Darkin won't ask questions. Neither would the Englishman you work with over on Wagonwheel. Duke Harrington."

Blackwine pulled Redding's horse forward and gestured for his prisoner to remount.

"Wait!" Tondro's snarl was like a whipcrack. "No stranger leaves this place alive, Blackwine. But I'll do this—if Teague says this man is an SPA trouble shooter, I'll match his bounty."

Blackwine grinned his relief. "Fair enough," he said.

Tondro wheeled to single out one of his henchmen. "Rafael, I want you to ride down to the Basin and bring Señor Teague Darkin here. Tell him we are holding a man who may or may not be Douglas Redding of the SPA. You will find Señor Darkin working the Crowfoot lease in the Axblades. You *sabe?*"

One of the *vaqueros* nodded, flung his greasy serape over a shoulder, and stalked off into the darkness.

Addressing another of the group standing around, Tondro snapped, "Lock this man in the assay room, Doc. Jace, you are free to ride out or stick around until Darkin gets here."

A salt-bearded oldster, who seemed to be the only *americano* in the group, shuffled forward at Tondro's command and gripped Redding by the elbow. This man wore no guns. His fingers on Redding's arm were skeletal and trembling as if from the ague.

"Come with me," he said in a tired voice.

Redding heard Blackwine say, "I'll stick around, Tondro. That man is worth a couple thousand to me."

Redding stumbled forward as Doc escorted him through the ranks of garlic-smelling Mexicans, up a flight of steps to a doorway entering the shaft house.

Blinking his eyes against the battery of gas-mantled lanterns rimming the walls of this building, Redding saw that this shaft house had been converted into living quarters for Tondro's outlaws. A mine shaft had been planked over; a rusty donkey engine was still in place in one corner of this barnlike room, rusty cables leading to an overhead windlass drum that had once lifted ore from the bowels of the earth.

At a far wall, a long table sided by benches was set up. Two persons were seated at supper there; one of them, incredible in these surroundings, was a girl whose back was to Redding as Doc led him toward the black maw of a door in the back wall.

The girl's companion was a paunchy gringo with a porcine, jowled face which was instantly familiar to Redding. Sight of a black Mormon hat hanging from a peg behind the table gave Redding the reminder he needed, the fat man was the one he had seen posting the Indian Agency's beef bid notice on the bulletin board of the Fandango Saloon in Trailfork five days ago.

In the act of following Doc through the rear doorway, Redding glanced around to see the girl's profile as she shifted position to reach for a salt shaker.

Recognition put a sudden paralysis on Redding. He cried out involuntarily, "Zedra! Zedra Stiles!"

CHAPTER 12

LAST CARTRIDGE

REDDING FELT HIMSELF BEING JERKED BODILY through the doorway before Zedra Stiles had time to look his direction. He was not even sure that his voice had carried to her. But, brief as his glimpse of her had been, Redding knew he could not be mistaken.

The girl he had met in a Trailfork saloon, the girl who at first glimpse of him had mistaken him for his martyred brother, was for some unaccountable reason a resident of Tondro's hide-out, a lone woman surrounded by the off-scourings of border riffraff. Or was as it possible that she, like him, was a prisoner here? When she had fled Trailfork rather than talk with him, had this robbers' roost in the Navajadas been her destination?

It added up. Matt, working incognito, had become a member of Tondro's band; this box canyon had known his voice, his shadow. In the note which Matt had sent to the outside world he had added incidentally the glad news that he had given his love to some unnamed woman, that she was wearing his golden lizard ring as a betrothal pledge. Zedra Stiles was wearing that ring. And she was here. It all made sense.

"Doc," Redding whispered into the curdled blackness. "That girl—Zedra Stiles—what is she doing in this hellhole?"

Doc was tugging at his trussed arms, leading him across a pit-black void between the shaft house and the base of the canyon wall, a distance of less than a score of paces.

"My daughter warned you what would happen if you

95

sought to track down your brother," old Doc's voice came from the darkness. "This will be trail's end for you, Douglas Redding, just as it was for Matt. Just as it is for me."

There was an undertone of lost hope, of utter despair in this old man's voice. Redding said, "Your daughter? Zedra is your daughter?"

He got no answer. Doc halted to wipe a match alight on his pants leg, revealing the narrow maw of a prospect hole chiseled out of the face of the granite wall directly ahead of them.

While the match light held, Doc Stiles pushed Redding into the cavelike opening, past a rusty iron-latticework door built into the rocky fissure. Then darkness closed in, like a curtain.

As the match went out, the old man withdrew; Redding wheeled about as he heard the iron door closing, its hinges wailing their rusty protest. The roar of the waterfall made less of a thunder in this confined space.

A massive padlock clicked metallically. Then another match flared in the old man's scraggy paw, its lambent glow undisturbed by air currents, its light making Stiles's eyes glow in their deep sockets like marbles in a skull.

"Stick your hands out here, son," the old man ordered, drawing a clasp knife from his pocket with his free hand and snapping it open. "You understand this business is not to my liking."

The match guttered out as Redding thrust his trussed arms through the interstices of the iron-webbed door, felt Stiles's blade sever the bonds Jace Blackwine had knotted there.

"You knew my brother," Redding said, desperation in

96

his voice. "You've got to tell me what happened, Doc!"

Like a voice from an opened tomb, the old man spoke from beyond the iron grating. "Your brother did not die because Tondro found out he was a lawman, Doug, for that was a secret he shared only with Zedra and myself. Matt died because he won my daughter's love. You see, Tondro intends to make Zedra his wife."

Redding's knuckles squeezed tight against the heavy iron straps of the door, his ears aching to the strain of picking up the old man's quavering words.

"I am as much a prisoner here as you are, my son," Stiles went on in his panting, asthmatic whisper. "Alone of all Tondro's crew, I am not permitted to carry firearms or to leave this canyon of lost hope. Only for my daughter's sake have I not destroyed myself long before now."

Redding shook himself out of the dazed stupor which had enveloped him from the moment he had laid eyes on Zedra. There was too much of human tragedy back of Doc Stiles's words for a man to grasp. The fact that his brother had died because of his love for Zedra Stiles, rather than because Blaze Tondro had discovered his true identity as a lawman bent on stamping out Tondro and all he stood for, made Matt's sacrifice all the more outrageous.

"This is the old Thunder Rock mine, Doug," the old man went on. "It was a peaceful enough place eleven years ago when Zedra and I found it. I was panning the old tailings for color, letting this high mountain country restore my wrecked health. Then one winter morning Blaze Tondro rode up the canyon with his Mexican crew, dodging a sheriff's posse out of the Basin."

Redding found himself caught in the spell of the old man's narrative. The drama of it made him forget, for

97

the moment, that avenging his brother's murder was now an impossible dream.

"Tondro recognized the benefits of this place for an outlaw hide-out. An earthquake had blocked the outlet of this canyon, making it well-nigh unapproachable from the Basin. There is a mine tunnel which makes an exit for his gang if they should ever find themselves trapped here, which would put them onto Mexican soil in twenty minutes' riding. In eleven years no outsider has seen this place, Redding."

The range detective nodded, still wondering if this nightmare were a figment of his imagination, a result of the clip on the head he had suffered at Blackwine's hands. "How come you were spared?" he asked.

"Zedra and I would have died had it not been for the fact that I was a medical man of considerable skill. Zedra was only a child of seven. You see, Redding, an outlaw band is subject to frequent gunshot-wound cases. A competent doctor is an asset worth sparing."

Redding said, "But Zedra is not kept a prisoner here—I saw her myself, in Trailfork. Surely she has told Sheriff Lennon of your predicament, Doc."

Stiles grunted bitterly in the darkness. "She would not dare. Tondro allows her to visit Trailfork whenever it pleases her. He has her vow of secrecy. How could she talk, knowing my life would be forfeit the moment a sheriff's posse came anywhere near this accursed place? No. Tondro holds us powerless."

For the first time, Doug Redding grasped the reason why Zedra had not dared talk to him that night in Trailfork. Her father's life was the grip Blaze Tondro held over her, a factor which made her as much a prisoner of Thunder Rock Canyon as if Tondro kept her in chains.

"Tondro is holding me here until Teague Darkin can identify me as an Association man," Redding said. "Darkin doesn't know me. Blackwine tricked Darkin into thinking I was dead, the same as he did Tondro."

Stiles said, "There is another alternative. Harrington."

"So far as I know, I've never seen Harrington, either. Except that he is connected with Wagonwheel Ranch, this Duke hombre is a total stranger to me. What's the deal?"

Stiles did not answer Redding immediately. When he spoke again, his voice came from farther away, as if the old man was edging toward the mouth of the prospect hole, afraid of lingering here with his prisoner.

"Harrington? He is one of Tondro's confederates on the outside. I have never seen him. He has not visited Thunder Rock in my time. Rumor has it that he is an English remittance man who runs Wagonwheel Ranch."

"Where does Blackwine fit into the picture?"

"Blackwine was once a *compañero* of Tondro's. He became too ambitious for his own good. There was not room enough for both him and Tondro in this organization. A vote was held as to which should be captain. Tondro won. Jace Blackwine chose to withdraw—knowing well that if he ever betrayed this place to the law, he would not live to enjoy his reward."

Redding fingered the bloody welts on his skull. It galled him to think that for four months he had rubbed shoulders with Jace Blackwine, not knowing the mustang hunter was a former associate of Tondro's.

"Whether or not Darkin can identify you," Stiles said bleakly, "Tondro will kill you tomorrow. I—"

"Send Zedra here to talk to me, Doc," Redding pleaded. "I've got to know how my brother died. I found his bones—"

"Zedra does not know the details," Stiles answered. "One day Tondro caught Zedra kissing Matt. A week later, Blackie Fletcher—as we called him here—was sent out to bring back some mustangs for our *vaqueros* to break to saddle. He never came back. Tondro told Zedra that he had trailed him and ambushed him, over on Mustang Mesa. It broke my little girl's heart."

Redding ground his teeth impotently. This was the answer to the main riddle he had come to Lavarim Basin to solve. Matt had died at Tondro's hands, as he had guessed, not having proof. He heard Stile's voice continuing from outside the cavern.

"Tondro does not know Matt gave Zedra the golden lizard ring she wears. He, of course, has not guessed your relationship to Matt. Let us hope he does not. Tondro is half Yaqui. I have seen him burn a man at the stake, Indian-fashion—"

The old medico's voice broke off; Redding heard him hurry away. A moment later he knew the reason for Stiles's retreat. A door in the shaft house opened, and Blaze Tondro came out carrying a lantern.

The half-breed entered the cavern, ignoring the prisoner beyond the iron grating, and checked the padlock to make sure Doc Stiles had snapped it. Then he heeled around and disappeared inside the shaft house.

When the lights in the shaft house went out, indicating that Tondro's men had turned in for the night, Redding rummaged in his pockets for a match. He lighted it, sizing up his prison.

A generation ago, when this mine had operated, this cavity in the cliff wall had been utilized as an assay office. A dust-covered table built against the back wall of rock was still littered with cupels and fragments of

100

ore samples, flux bins and empty acid bottles now gray with dust. The brick furnace had fallen into ruin, its smokestack long since removed.

He found a stub of tallow candle on the assayer's bench and lighted it. A short examination of his prison convinced him there would be no digging under the iron doorway; its frame had been cemented into the living rock.

A dry nettle-sting of suspense touched his pores as he groped inside his shirt to check whether Blackwine had stolen his golden lizard ring, as he had done his guns. But the bauble still hung by its rawhide thong around his neck, and the feel of that talisman between his fingers buoyed Redding with a strange, irrational belief that perhaps his luck had not yet played out.

The thunder of the waterfall plunging into the canyon prevented Redding from hearing any sounds outside the shaft house. Recalling his brief passage through that building, he found himself puzzling about the presence of the fat man with the Mormon hat who had some connection with the Indian Agency's bid for beef.

There was some common demoninator linking all these puzzles together, if he could live to put them in order. The Indian Agency invariably let its beef contracts to the English-owned Wagonwheel spread. That ranch was managed by the mysterious Duke Harrington, who Jace Blackwine said would be glad to pay blood money for his, Redding's, capture. It could only mean that Duke Harrington was an outlaw Redding had known by another name sometime in his checkered past.

The candle flame guttered and died in its own drippings. Redding knew that by now Tondro and his men would be asleep. He thought of Matt, who had once

101

occupied one of those bunks as an accepted member of Tondro's legion, the man who had brought Zedra the only happiness she had ever known in this living hell. He found himself wondering if Matt had been on his way to keep his promised rendezvous in Fort Paloverde when Tondro had bushwhacked him, and left his corpse for the buzzards, out on Mustang Mesa where the Rickaree Kid, hunting a strayed mule, had found him.

By an association of ideas, Redding groped fingers in his watch pocket, feeling for the 1846 half dollar the Kid had removed from his brother's skull.

The touch of that tarnished silver disk gave Redding a strange rapport with his dead kin, the same tug of emotion that sight of Matt's ring on Zedra Stiles's finger had given him that night at the Fandango Saloon.

He took out his watch, struck a match, and saw that it was nearly midnight. Obviously Tondro meant to delay any interview with his prisoner until tomorrow. All the time Redding could count on would be tomorrow; by the following night Tondro's messinger would probably be back with Teague Darkin.

The instincts of a trapped animal set him to exploring his prison anew. The floor of the assay room was paved with adobe, dirt carried into the tunnel by the winds of yesteryear. The walls and ceiling of the short dead-end tunnel dripped with seepage, enabling a slimy moss to grow there.

Reaching through the door bars, Redding examined the huge padlock Doc Stiles had placed in the hasp, on the off-chance that it might be unlocked despite Tondro's check. But the padlock was snapped shut. Tondro probably carried the only key.

Searching his pockets for another match, Redding's fingers closed over an oblong metal object which he

102

identified as a stray .45-70 cartridge. Fingering that shell, the hazy form of an idea took shape in Redding's mind. That cartridge might be the instrument of his escape from this place.

There was enough energy in the seventy grains of powder contained in that cartridge case to drive a copper-jacketed .45 bullet a mile or more. If that latent power could be harnessed to his own needs

Groping his way back to the door of the assay room, Redding fumbled for the brass padlock, reamed a finger tip into the big keyhole. A surge of hope went through him, like opium firing the blood of an addict's veins.

Removing the .45-70 cartridge from his pocket, he reached through the strap-iron ribbons of the door and inserted the shell into the big keyhole of the padlock. The cartridge went clean through the giant lock until the flange of the casing fitted against the keyhole's aperture.

"It's a chance," Redding whispered into the darkness. "If I can explode that shell it might spring that padlock."

CHAPTER 13

BLIND JOURNEY

A DOOMED MAN, THE SAYING GOES, SNATCHES AT straws.

That feeling of futility nagged Redding now as he set about his preparations for a getaway attempt.

Thanks to the singularly large size of the padlock, the Winchester cartridge was accommodated inside the keyhole. The problem now was to devise a makeshift firing-pin to detonate the shell's center-fire cap.

103

A nail seemed the answer. Redding struck another of his scanty supply of matches and located a tenpenny nail in the litter of junk on the assay table. The point of this nail Redding placed vertically against the percussion cap of the .45-70 cartridge, where a rifle's firing-pin would ordinarily strike.

Holding the nail in position would be tricky. There was no anticipating what direction the released power of an exploding shell would take.

He thought of the adobe dirt underfoot, and had his answer. Scraping up a handful of soil, he clawed wet moss from the ceiling of the prospect hole and squeezed it into the adobe until he had a gummy, pliable mass.

He worked the adobe until it formed a sticky ball, enough to encase the big padlock completely and at the same time hold the tenpenny nail in striking position against the center of the cartridge he had inserted in the keyhole.

He waited a half hour for the mud to set, using that time to explore the debris of the assay furnace and locate a chunk of iron suitable for use as a gun hammer.

The sedative boom of the waterfall filled the outer canyon with its never-ending monotone. Redding was counting on that heavy undertone of sound, plus the muffling effect of the adobe shell he had built around the padlock, to deaden the explosion he hoped to bring about.

With his left hand, Redding held the mud-daubed padlock flush against the iron framework of the door. Gripping the chunk of rusty grate in his right, Redding pushed his arm through the largest opening in the door's latticework until his elbow joint was outside the door.

In that position, he made s few practice swings with his forearm, bringing the iron chunk lightly against the nail head protruding from the ball of hardening adobe.

The thing seemed as ready as it would ever be. A wet film of perspiration covered Redding's cheeks. In a moment he would know if this gamble would pay off. He was not even sure he could exert a hard enough blow to match a rifle's dropping gun hammer on firing-pin.

Every muscle taut for the supreme effort, Redding brought his right arm around with all his strength, smashing the iron hammer against the nailhead to drive its point against the percussion cap of the cartridge.

The explosion came with a numbing slap on Redding's eardrums. Bits of flying adobe peppered the latticework door, stung his averted cheek, brought blood in a dozen leaking punctures from his exposed hands.

A rancid boil of powder smoke clogged the air. He was vaguely aware of metal splinters striking the wet rock walls outside the cavern door.

The explosion had not carried the volume he expected; then he recalled that the main noise of a gunshot was the slap of air, refilling the vacuum of a bullet's passage from a rifle's muzzle, rather than the powder blast in the breech. It was the same reason why a high-calibered shell exploding inside a hot stove made a firecracker's pop instead of the ear-riving blast of the same shell leaving a rifle's muzzle.

Dropping the iron chunk, Redding groped feverishly for the padlock. His fingers encountered the U-shaped brass prong. Stripped of its mud casing, the padlock was now a chunk of broken metal shards, its inner mechanism ruptured by the confined explosion in the keyhole. The wreckage was scorching hot to the touch.

Redding jerked the broken padlock out of the hasp which held it and flung the door open. He staggered through the doorway to reach the outer mouth of the tunnel, coughing with the fumes of powder gases that burned the passages of his nostrils and lungs.

He was free. The impossible had come about. What mattered now was whether the muffled explosion had carried above the roar of the waterfall to rouse the sleeping outlaws inside the mine shaft house.

The moon had westered beyond the canyon rim during the night, so that Redding had only the dimmest view from this point The roar of plunging river water covered the grind of his cow boots over the mine debris as he rounded the shaft-house wall, his ears still numbed by the blast of sound so close to his head.

No lights flickered inside the shaft house as yet. There was too much noise echoing and re-echoing from the box canyon's surrounding scarps for Redding to tell whether men might be tumbling from their bunks inside the building.

Working his way along the up-canyon wall of the shaft house, Redding came to the front end of the building.

There he froze. A lantern was burning midway across the flat area of ground between the shaft house and the deeply eroded bed of the river below the waterfall.

The lantern's rays revealed a light, yellow democrat wagon, hitched to a pair of mules down there, and the dim line of the trail up which Jace Blackwine had led him blindfolded earlier tonight.

Zedra Stiles, wearing a Spanish sombrero and an Army overcoat over her dance-hall costume, was seated in the wagon, holding the lines. Doc was busy hitching the tugs to the whiffletrees.

Redding stifled the cry of new hope which sprang to his throat. Zedra, whatever her fears of him might have been down in Trailfork, must surely be his ally now.

106

The old medico had doubtless acquainted her with the identity of the prisoner Jace Blackwine had brought to this place.

Fifty feet of open ground lay between the shaft house and the waiting wagon. He remembered that Sheriff Val Lennon had mentioned how Zedra often left Trailfork in a wagon, ostensibly to carry supplies to her prospector father. Perhaps Zedra was getting ready to return to the Basin now.

Redding crouched low and raced out of the covering shadows of the shaft-house wall. The strike of his boots was the first inkling either Doc Stiles or the girl had of his approach.

Redding heard the girl's low cry of incredulity, saw the pink cavern of the old man's gaping mouth as Doc Stiles wheeled from his work to stare at the apparition sprinting toward them.

Redding skidded to a halt alongside the wagon. He saw Zedra make a quick movement toward the lantern on the seat beside her, jacking up the chimney and extinguishing the wick flame.

"Daddy left your door unlocked, Doug?"

Redding panted heavily from the exertion of his run.

"No—Tondro can't pin this on your father, Zedra. I smashed the lock—tell you how later. Can you help me get out of here?"

Old Doc Stiles caught Redding by the sleeve. "Tondro is taking my daughter back to Trailfork tonight," the old doctor whispered. "Your only chance is to head for the river—maybe you could swim past the canyon guards—"

Zedra whispered hoarsely from it her elevated position in the wagon seat, "He can't do that, Dad. The grub box—the grub box—Tondro won't think to check that—"

Doc Stiles tugged at Redding's arm like a dog worrying a marrowbone. Redding stumbled around to the end gate of the wagon and saw the old man's scrawny paw tugging at the lid of an oblong wooden box built into the rear of the wagon.

With frantic haste Redding set foot to the bull bar and straddled the edge of the grub box. He flung himself in a cramped kneeling position in the box as Doc Stiles closed the lid and snapped the catch.

Redding felt a rush of fear akin to claustrophobia assail him at being encased in this coffin. But he realized how slim had been his margin of concealment when spurred boots made their approach from the direction of the shaft house, and the democrat wagon lurched on its leaf springs as a man climbed over the front wheel to take his seat alongside Zedra.

"*Vaya con Dios,* daughter," he heard Doc Stiles's farewell to his daughter, in the language of her dead mother. He heard the girl answer in a steady voice which gave no hint of the strain she was under. "I'll be back in a couple of weeks, *padre mío.*"

The heavy voice of Blaze Tondro reached Redding's ears as the wagon gave a lurch and the mules swung out onto the trail. "Not that soon she won't, Doc. I can't gamble on you two cookin' up a double cross any longer. The next time Zedra sees Thunder Rock will be as my wife."

The wagon jounced and lurched over rocky ruts. The boom of the waterfall standing guard over the outlaw hide-out faded in Redding's hearing.

A mile down the canyon, Redding shoved tentatively against the lid of the grub box with his shoulders, to confirm his dread that Doc Stiles had closed the hasp on the outside.

He was at the mercy of the fates that ruled his stormy years now. It was up to Zedra to find the time and the place to open the box which was smuggling Tondro's prisoner out of the canyon, with Tondro himself the unwitting instrument of Redding's escape.

Cramped there in the total blackness of this bouncing coffin, Redding thought, *That explosion didn't rouse the camp. But if a guard checks on that assay room at dawn, they'll send a rider to overtake this wagon sure.*

In the following hours, Redding lost all track of time, of mileage covered, of direction. Now his body was thrust against the rear of the grub box as the wagon climbed a sharp uptilt of ground; now he was flung against the forward wall as they zigzagged down a dizzy series of looping switchbacks.

There was no keeping count of the thousand twistings and turnings of this road out of Tondro's lair. He only knew for certain that their route was dropping them steadily out of the Navajadas.

If he lived to see daylight again, he would carry with him one faint clue to the route which he and Blackwine had traveled during his period of unconsciousness: Thunder Rock could be reached by a road wide enough to accommodate a mule-drawn wagon and wagons left wheel tracks. An old mining road, no doubt.

What might have been an hour or a day later, Redding became aware that sunrise had broken over the foot slopes of the Navajadas. The shine of it was visible through a a nail hole in the end of the grub box, against which his injured skull was being thumped with every jounce of the spring wagon.

Looking through that nail hole gave him no clue as to passing landmarks; he saw only the revolving spokes of

109

a hind wheel, the meaningless blur of rocks and brush beyond them.

Bruised and aching, dissolving in his own body juices, the air fouled with his own breathing, and asphyxiation warded off only by the fortuitous nail hole in the end of the box, Redding endured his torture with the dogged patience of a man who did not question the maneuverings of a capricious destiny. The ceaseless bouncing and twisting made his stomach churn, made him close to vomiting on several occasions. This was a purgatory little short of hell, but he was alive, and each revolution of the wagon wheels was taking him farther away from the canyon end where Doc Stiles endured the tortured existence of a lost soul.

From time to time he heard the guttural voice of Tondro talking to Zedra. Her replies were pitched too low for him to catch through the thick wooden shroud which encased him.

His groping hands found a moldy husk of bread, somewhere along the tortured journey and he chewed it ravenously. At the time it seemed to spell the difference between keeping his sanity or losing it.

The wagon emerged from the canyon, a fact which the sudden lack of confined echoes told him. Long afterward he heard the wheels churning through shallow water, as if Tondro's route was taking him off the road into a creek bed.

The spicy odor of wild mint filtered through the nail hole in Redding's coffin and served to identify, however vaguely, the place where the wagon finally turned out of the watercourse and climbed a gentle bank slope through whippy brush. Eventually the wagon leveled itself and hit a dusty, relatively straight patch of ground which could only be a traveled road.

He stored these scanty clues to his route away in a corner of his brain, against the time when he might be able to use them to retrace this hellish journey.

Tondro whipped the jaded mules into a trot. They were traveling an arrow-straight road now, level as a floor. The prairie. Lavarim Basin. The mountains were behind them at last.

Without warning the journey came to an end, as Redding had despaired of its ever doing. For Redding, this was the crucial moment. If for any reason Tondro should open the grub box—

He heard Tondro climb out of the democrat, Zedra following. Tondro spoke gruffly to someone. "Unhitch and curry 'em down, Clark. I'll call for the wagon and a fresh team in an hour. You might grease that off hind axle."

Redding could not be sure if the wagon had reached town or an outlying ranch. He heard the strike of boot heels on the wind-scoured hardpan as Tondro and the girl walked away. The wagon box jolted slightly as someone let the tongue drop between it the blowing mules. Trace chains jingled, and then Redding heard the mule span being led away.

The sudden following quiet seemed unreal. It was broken by the creak of a door being opened somewhere, and a splashing noise as the mules plunged their muzzles into a trough.

After an interminable interval Redding was startled to hear Zedra speak through a crack in the box lid as she unfastened the hasp. "Doug?"

"Yes."

"Listen close, *amigo*. This wagon is in O'Connor's stable yard at the edge of Trailfork. You will have one hour before Tondro comes for it. Wait ten minutes. Will you make me a promise, Señor Doug?"

Redding resisted an urge to shove his back against the lid. It suddenly seemed that he had to feel the sun's warmth upon his flesh or go berserk.

"Promise what?"

"That you will not stay in this Basin, *amigo mío*. Tondro will hunt you down, kill you as he did your brother. You have already used up all the luck God can give a man, *amigo*."

He protested desperately, "Zedra, I've got to talk with you—"

"Hush! This is *adiós*. Go with God."

She was gone. There was nothing he could do but remain in this cramped coffin until Zedra had her chance to get well away from O'Connor's wagon yard.

And she was right. He had used up all the luck a man could rightfully expect in a lifetime.

But she had not waited to get his promise. He would see her again, just as he would see the hide-out at Thunder Rock Canyon again.

CHAPTER 14

FLIGHT FROM TRAILFORK

BLAZE TONDRO, AFTER LEAVING O'CONNOR'S STABLE on the outskirts of Trailfork, walked along the town's main street with the easy assurance of a man who had no fear of being seen or recognized for what he was.

Throughout the Territory, this half-breed's name was a malediction on the lips of the frontier populace. His name was emblazoned on reward dodgers throughout Lavarim Basin; the Spanish version of those posters were common throughout Mexico's northern provinces.

But no accurate description, no photograph accompanied those bounty notices. No gringo sheriff or Sonoran *rurale* policeman had any means of connecting the name and the man. So far as Trailfork was concerned, this swart-browed visitor was one of the prospectors who still combed the Navajada wastes in search of his lucky strike.

Zedra had walked with him only the length of a block before returning to O'Connor's to pick up—so she had explained—a pair of boots for repairing. But so unchallenged was Tondro's status in this cow town that he had no fear of being seen in Zedra Stiles's company. The girl's frequent trips into the hills to visit her prospector father were well known to the patrons of the Fandango.

It was believed in a vague sort of way that this man with the strange polecat streak on his scalp was a partner of old man Stiles, and that the supplies he carried into the wastelands in his rickety yellow wagon every few months were intended for Zedra's father and himself.

Except for certain trusted individuals—such as Clark O'Connor, the stable boss—Tondro's alter ego was an inviolate secret. In Trailfork he went under the name of John Montalvo.

His purpose in coming to the Basin today had been to pick up mail, which would include cunningly disguised messages from various vendors of stolen goods in El Paso and Phoenix and Santa Fe who carried on a flourishing commerce in contraband with Tondro's couriers.

At this early hour, Trailfork's street was deserted except for a hostler making up the Paloverde stage in

113

front of Wells Fargo, a drunk or two sick or asleep in the dusty gutters under the high wooden curb fronting the Fandango Saloon, and a swamper polishing cuspidors on the sunny porch of Emigrants' Tavern.

Reaching the Trailfork post office, Tondro heard someone call, "Hey, Montalvo!" and turned to see Clark O'Connor running up the dusty street toward him.

Sensing the urgency of the stableman's pace, Tondro waited on the outer edge of the plank walk. O'Connor's ruddy Irish face held a pallor of excitement now. Glancing up and down the empty street, he spoke to Tondro in a hoarse whisper.

"Blaze who was that jasper who made the trip with you?"

"What hombre?"

"The one I seen crawlin' out of the grub box on your wagon."

Tondro's granite eyes showed their sharp surprise as he reached a hand up slowly to remove a black cigarette from his lips.

"How's that?"

O'Connor knew by Tondro's reaction that his news was important. He said swiftly, "I was curryin' your mules inside the barn. I went out front to get some screwworm dope to rub on a cut in the crop-ear's gaskin when I saw this jasper crawl out of your grub box and high-tail it out of my yard like the devil was after him with a hot pitchfork. I says to myself, this is something Tondro ought to know about."

The rustler boss flung his cigarette into the street and said, "Must have been old Doc. Hooked a ride in the box as we were pulling out of Thunder Rock. I been careless with him."

The Irishman shook his head. "Wasn't Doc Stiles.

114

Big husky feller, stranger to me. Gringo. Wore a calfhide vest. Don't fit any of your *mejicanos*."

Tondro's cheek muscles stiffened. He mused half to himself, "Fits that Redding hombre, but—" He shook his head, rejecting that possibility. He had personally checked Redding's prison lock. And yet, O'Connor had identified the mysterious passenger as a gringo. Someone had smuggled himself out of Thunder Rock, and that was dangerous.

"Where's this *cabrón* now?"

O'Connor flushed. "Wouldn't know. He ducked acrost the road and vanished behind them cottonwoods."

Tondro dragged a knuckle across his jaw. The man couldn't have been Redding. Or could he? Was it possible that Stiles could have hacksawed the padlock to release Redding? There had been time enough for that. Ample opportunity for Stiles to have concealed Redding in the wagon.

"O'Connor," Tondro said, "saddle a pair of fast horses and bring them around behind the Fandango, *pronto prontito*."

"Two hosses?"

"I'm clearing out and taking Zedra back with me. Looks like one of the bunch got a cold gut and high-tailed it. I won't know who until I get back to the Rock."

When O'Connor had left on his way back to the stable, Tondro crossed the street to the Fandango Saloon, turning down an alley cluttered with tin cans and broken bottles which skirted the dance-hall annex.

"If Redding ain't there when I get back I'll get the truth out of Doc if I have to torture Zedra in front of him."

But it was impossible that old Doc Stiles could have

115

released Redding from the assay room. Tondro had checked the padlock himself. He possessed the only key. But who else could have been hidden in that grub box? No one at Thunder Rock owned a calfhide vest. And O'Connor had identified the interloper as being a gringo.

Tondro opened the rear door of the dance hall and stepped inside. A swamper was sweeping litter off the maple floor at the far end of the hall. The consumptive pianist they called the Professor was sprawled drunk or asleep on the bandstand.

Tondro headed for the row of doors in the back which opened on dressing-rooms used by the percentage girls. He headed or one of these, found it unlocked, and stepped inside.

Zedra Stiles was seated at a mirror, hiding the ravages of her sleepless night's journey with mascara and rouge. At Tondro s entrance she started violently, her eyes round with alarm as she saw the taut fixture of the half-breed's mouth reflected in the blemished glass.

"Who was the hombre in the grub box, Zedra?"

His, slurring whisper curdled the blood in her veins. Long schooled in masking her emotions toward this man who had held her and her father in bondage for so long, she gave no outward sign of the raw horror which Tondro's words put in her.

She turned slowly to face him as he strode toward her.

"What grub box?"

He halted alongside her, grabbing her wrist with a pressure that whitened her cheeks with the pain.

"The grub box in our wagon."

"I don't know what you're talking about, Blaze. Let go my arm. You're hurting me."

116

He released her, curbing a restless urge to smash his fist in her face. His own vanity made him draw back, refraining from ruining this girl's beauty. Some day she would be his, and he wanted the border underworld to look up to the beauty of his wife.

"Clark O'Connor saw a gringo crawl out of the grub box and high-tail it after we left the wagon at the stable yard."

Zedra shook her head slowly. In her heart she was more happy than terrified, now. At least O'Connor hadn't captured Doug Redding. She had worried about that.

"It wasn't my father, if that's what you're hinting, Blaze."

He laughed harshly. "We're heading back to Thunder Rock, anyhow. Now. Both of us."

Despair touched her then, showing in the black pools of her eyes. She had made up her mind to contact Doug Redding and tell him how to reach Tondro's lair, thinking that by so doing she could prevent him from attempting such a suicidal mission.

" '*Stá bueno*," she said heavily. "I would rather be at the Canyon with Dad than working in this dime-a-dance hovel."

CHAPTER 15

WATER-HOLE MAN-TRAP

AFTER LEAVING TONDRO'S WAGON, REDDING HAD gone directly to Sheriff Val Lennon's quarters behind the jailhouse. The two of them were now bellied down in the cottonwood *bosque* across the road from Clark O'Connor's wagon yard.

"Tondro was to pick up the wagon in an hour," Redding whispered, hands gripping the .30-30 carbine the sheriff had provided him. "It shows the gall of the man, showing up in your town this way."

Suspense laid its cutting edge on the old sheriff's spirit as he squinted along his rifle sights at the yellow spring wagon parked in front of O'Connor's barn.

"From your description of the man," Lennon muttered, "I'd say that Tondro is a breed prospector we call Montalvo around town. Supposed to be some kind of a pardner of Zedra's father. If Doc Stiles is Tondro's prisoner, it fits."

Redding stiffened imperceptibly, nudging Lennon's bony shoulder as he saw O'Connor leave the barn with two saddled horses. The Irish stableman was heading into town.

"Means nothing," the sheriff grunted. "He delivers horses to customers who stop overnight at the Tavern."

Fifteen interminable minutes later O'Connor returned. The two lawmen waiting in the cottonwoods saw him go into the barn. When O'Connor appeared again he would probably be bringing a harnessed team to hitch to Tondro's wagon. The hour was about up.

They had chosen to wait here, spying on the wagon, rather than risk an open hunt along the main street business houses or any of the various honky-tonks and deadfalls on side streets where Tondro might be trading. That method would have invited an ambush shot, if Tondro caught sight of his erstwhile prisoner in the sheriff's company, or might have tipped the rustler boss off to go into hiding or take flight.

As they watched O'Connor's barn, they glimpsed two horsemen heading across the Basin in flats toward the eastern foothills, too far away to be recognized. These were probably the customers who owned the saddle horses O'Connor had taken into town.

Minutes dragged into another quarter hour, a half hour. O'Connor finally reappeared, leading an a apaloosa mare over to his blacksmith shed. There the Irishman started cranking the bellows of his forge preparatory to shoeing the animal.

"Sheriff," Redding said, consulting his watch, "Tondro's half an hour overdue back to his wagon. I think our birds flew the coop. I think those horses O'Connor led off were for Tondro and Zedra."

"The hell you say!"

"I think O'Connor must have spotted me leaving the wagon and lit a shuck to tip Tondro off. Tondro figured he couldn't risk taking the wagon back for fear he'd be followed."

After another futile quarter hour of waiting, Sheriff Lennon reached the end of his patience. "I'm goin' over there and brace the Irishman," he said. "Cover me in case O'Connor spooks."

Redding, cursing himself for a fool, remained in the concealment of the cottonwoods as the sheriff got to his feet and crossed the road, toting his carbine. O'Connor was shaping a horseshoe at his anvil when the sheriff's shadow fell across the shed opening. The blacksmith glanced up and gave the sheriff an easy smile of greeting.

"Who belongs to that yeller wagon yonder?" Lennon asked.

O'Connor laid down his hammer and tongs. "To John Montalvo, Sheriff. The breed prospector."

"When's he headin' for the hills?"

O'Connor reached under his leather apron, the gesture causing Redding, across the road, to lift his rifle

119

to the ready. But the Irishman merely carried a plug of tobacco to his mouth and worried off a quid.

"Why, he's already left, Sheriff. Had me saddle him a couple hosses. Said him and the Stiles gal were ridin' back to their minin' claim in the hills."

"He come into town on that wagon, didn't he?"

"Yeah. Wanted me to re-tire a wheel and set some loose felloes. Said he'd call for the wagon in a couple weeks."

The sheriff's shoulders slumped. Without explanations he turned and shuffled off up the street toward the jailhouse.

Redding, having listened in on Lennon's conversation with the stable tender, rejoined Lennon in the sheriff's office ten minutes later.

"Tondro outfoxed us?" Redding asked.

"Looks that way. I ast Madame Carlotta over at the Fandango where Zedra was. She said her and Montalvo headed for the hills a-hossback. Reckon that was them we seen, Redding."

Redding sat down on Lennon's cot and buried his face in his hands, anticlimax tugging at his keyed-up nerves. Tondro had been in his grasp, here in town this morning. Something had warned the outlaw to leave Trailfork in a hurry. The fact that he took Zedra back with him might be ominous or otherwise.

Finally Redding looked up, his red-shot eyes holding their bleak look of frustration and defeat. "I told you what this Thunder Rock Canyon looked like," he said. "Does it fit any of the country you know?"

The sheriff walked over to peruse a big survey map of his county. Most of the Navajada mountain area was frankly labeled: *Unsurveyed, Unexplored Territory.*

"Well, the waterfall don't mean anything. Every crick

120

that drains the Navajada watershed has a few waterfalls. As for the abandoned mine, them mountains are speckled with old mine workings. Thing that buffaloes me is you sayin' Tondro's hide-out can be reached by a hoss and wagon. That stumps me."

Redding said, "We followed a creek for the last couple of miles in. We hit the stage road maybe five-six miles east of town. Lots of wild mint growing close to where the wagon left the creek. That give you any notion which creek it might have been, Sheriff?"

Lennon shook his head. He tapped a half-dozen spots on the map where squiggly lines indicated the approximate course of creeks which flowed out of the Navajadas to link with Whetstone River, the watercourse which drained the Basin.

"Could have been any of a dozen cricks. Like lookin' for a grain of sand on a beach, to find which one."

Redding stretched himself out on the sheriff's office cot, his brain sluggish with fatigue. Suddenly he knew he had reached the limit of his physical endurance. Two nights without sleep, coupled with the head injury he had suffered at the hands of Jace Blackwine, had drained utterly dry his capacity to think anything out.

"Your string is frayed out," the sheriff said gently. "After a few hours' rest, we'll tackle this thing again. I'd haul O'Connor in and make him talk if I thought—"

"No," Redding said bleakly. "It's very possible O'Connor is innocent. We couldn't prove he knows that Montalvo and Tondro are one and the same."

Redding spent the rest of the day sleeping like a drugged man inside Lennon's personal quarters at the rear of the jail. Late afternoon's westering sunrays brought him awake; he sat up groggily to find Val

121

Lennon busy cooking a meal at his rusty stove in the corner.

Something that had nagged his troubled dreams during this refreshing slumber came to him now. He shot a question at the grizzled sheriff. "Who's the fat hombre who wears a black Mormon hat, the one I saw tacking up a notice of the Pedregosa Indian Agency's beef bid at the Fandango the other day?"

Lennon thrust a chunk of 'squite wood into the stove and went on slicing onions into a fry pan.

"Sounds like Joe Curtwright. The Agent over at Pedregosa. He drops over to town this time every fall tackin' up his beef-contract notices around the county."

Redding walked over to the zinc-lined sink, pumped himself a basin of water, and started working up a lather with a cake of lye soap.

"Curtwright's crooked, then. He was visiting Tondro's camp yesterday. I saw him."

The sheriff showed no sign of surprise. He pulled a pan of steaming potatoes out of the oven and carried them over to his deal table. "This range has thought all along that Curtwright had some kind of a shady deal worked out with Wagonwheel. Leastwise that British combine always nabs the beef-issue contract. As for Curtwright workin' with Blaze Tondro, that don't surprise me none whatsoever."

During the meal which followed, Redding amplified the morning's brief recital of his experiences at Tondro's hide-out, on the slim hope that his detailed description of the place might rouse some clue as to its whereabouts in Lennon's mind.

But the sheriff had no theories to offer. Redding's sense of distance covered and time consumed, both on his ingoing ride with Jace Blackwine and his outcoming trip in the grub box of Tondro's wagon, was too meager to be of any value.

Concerning the mysterious Duke Harrington who ramrodded the Wagonwheel Ranch for its British owners, the sheriff could supply little more information than that which Doc Stiles had given Redding.

"Duke Harrington is supposed to be a filthy-rich remittance man who spends most of his time in California," Lennon said. "He's never been to Trailfork to my knowledge. Fact is, I don't know of anyone who has actually laid eyes on him."

"Heard anything about his background? Apparently he knows me by sight—knows I'm an Association star-toter."

"Well," the sheriff drawled, "the gossip is that Harrington was chased out of England, Wales to be exact, for some crime against the Crown. His blue-blooded family keeps him across the ocean to save the family honor, or something. So far as runnin' Wagonwheel's affairs, I reckon the Duke is just a figgerhead."

Redding ferried a slab of apple pie over to his plate to wind up his meal. "Our friend Darkin's probably up at Tondro's hide-out by now," he said. He grinned, visualizing the excitement at Thunder Rock this morning when the empty assay room and its smashed padlock had been discovered. "I'll bet Jace Blackwine is a sorry critter about now. That's one mustanger who'll do no more hunting in this Territory. As long as he knows I'm on the prowl Blackwine will keep his distance."

At sundown, Doug Redding rode out of Trailfork astride a pinto gelding he had borrowed from the sheriff's *remuda*. He carried a repeating Winchester in the boot under his saddle fender and a pair of matched, ivory-butted Peacemaker .45s strapped at his flanks, having selected the weapons from the arsenal of guns Lennon had confiscated from sundry evil-doers during his many terms in office.

He was heading for Crowfoot; he wanted a council of war with Joyce Melrose, during this roundup period when Teague Darkin would be on the Axblades side of the Basin gathering the fall beef herd.

He had covered half the distance to Joyce's ranch headquarters when a dollar-round moon wheeled over the jagged peaks of the Navajadas and flooded the Basin flats with its argentine glow.

Riding at a steady lope, steering for a landmark butte he knew to be above Crowfoot Ranch, Redding occupied his thoughts with the sticky problem of trying to retrace mentally the route of Tondro's wagon back into the hills, drawing on the scanty clues that he had gained from his blind ride out of Thunder Rock Canyon in the grub box.

It was paradoxical that he had actually visited Tondro's den but was still ignorant of even its approximate whereabouts.

Off to the south of this short cut he was taking across the bunch-grassed prairie, he saw a motte of dwarf willow and salt cedars marking the water hole where he had made his deal with the horse trader, the morning of his arrival in the Basin.

He swung the pinto that direction, with the intention of letting the horse have a needed drink. His mind, refreshed and keen after this day's sleep, was dwelling with a warm anticipation on his imminent visit with Joyce Melrose.

The girl had never been far from the edge of his thoughts, since the whispered intimacy of their conversation concerning Teague Darkin's loyalties, that morning on Trailfork's street.

He found himself thinking now, *Strikes me she's fallen out of love with that walloper,* and that thought set off a train of speculation as to why he so urgently wanted to believe that was true. There was no room for romance in the life of a man who wore an SPA star. A woman's love had been responsible for Matt's finish.

With that distraction taking the edge off his usual alertness, Redding jogged up to the prairie water hole and dismounted, letting the pinto plunge its muzzle into the muddy pool.

He was easing the cinch when a pony's whicker broke the utter stillness of the night from a near-by willow growth. In that same instant, two horsemen spurred into view, the moon's rays flashing on naked gun metal as they separated and bracketed him between double gun drops.

"Reach, bucko!" came the harsh order from the big rider who covered him from the right. "No booger moves, Redding."

Being called thus by name told Doug that he had ridden into a trap here; that his approach had been spotted as he crossed the Basin flats, by these riders who had been at the water hole ahead of him.

Redding stepped away from his horse, hands upraised knowing that to buck this crossfire setup would be suicidal. Then his shuttling glance saw the moon's full radiance strike the faces of these converging riders, and shock welded its paralyzing chains on his reflexes.

The man on his right, who had barked the showdown order, was Jace Blackwine.

125

His companion was Joe Curtwright, the Mormon-hatted Indian Agent from the Pedregosa Reservation whom he glimpsed last night at Blaze Tondro's hide-out.

CHAPTER 16

BLOOD ON THE SAGE

"STAND HITCHED, REDDING."

Blackwine held his grulla broadside to the scene as he kept his gun trained on the range detective.

"Joe"—the mustanger lifted his voice—"hustle your fat carcass over behind this bucko. Dehorn those holsters and use his shell belt to dally his arms behind him."

Curtwright was wheezing stertorously as he swung his porky bulk out of stirrups, ground-tied his buckskin pony, and sidled in between the pinto, drinking at the pool, and Redding's back. The Indian Agent was not cut out for physical violence; his forte was behind-the-scenes political string pulling, and he showed his distaste for what Blackwine had ordered him to do.

"Why play it so risky?" Curtwright demanded sourly, gingerly stripping the ivory-handled guns from Redding's holsters and tossing them to one side as if he were drawing a rattler's fangs with his bare fingers. "Once you seen it was Redding, you shoulda dropped him from the brush."

Jace Blackwine's taut hand on the reins kept his grulla confined to a back-and-forward dancing. Contempt was an acid in his voice as he rebuked the Indian Agent. "We'll not cash in his chips till we know

126

how much he's uncovered about this setup of Tondro's. We don't even know but what he's got deputies from the Association helping him."

Curtwright drew a .38 pistol from an armpit rig, cocking the gun as he reached a timid arm around Redding's body and started fumbling at the buckle of the lawman's outer gun belt. So far, Redding had not uttered a word.

"You're a slippery customer," Jace Blackwine commented with grudging admiration for his former employee. "When Tondro's boys found that busted padlock on your jail and saw you'd flew the coop, that place was buzzin' like a smashed beehive."

Redding made no reply. Curtwright had unbuckled one of his cartridge belts and had thrown it to one side. Now he was working on the others, which he would use to pinion Redding's arms.

"Don't mind admitting I was headin' back to my crew's camp at the north end of the Navajadas," Blackwine went on conversationally, "to pick up my possibles, and then light out for Mexico. Figgered the Territory wouldn't be too healthy with you knowin' I wore Tondro's collar."

Redding gave no sign that he had heard. Curtwright was reaming the muzzle of his Bisley against Redding's spine as his his fishbelly-white hand struggled with the buckle tongue of his prisoner's remaining shell belt. In his shaky condition Redding had a real fear that the Indian Agent might inadvertently put too much pressure on the .38 trigger.

"Teague Darkin expects to find you at Tondro's," Blackwine went on, "and by God he's going to. Joe, hurry that up. Redding won't bite yuh."

The Indian Agent's breath was warm against

Redding's neck as he shot back, "Suppose you give me a hand, damn you, instead of settin' on your rump and givin' me orders."

Redding took his gamble then. He brought his right foot up behind him in a lightning movement which drove his spur rowel into the Indian Agent's crotch. In the same instant Redding flung himself to the ground with a sidewise rolling movement which carried him out from under the blazing muzzle of Curtwright's .38.

The slug bored off into the night sky, fired by pure reflex as Curtwright doubled up with the agony of his spur-gashed groin. Close on the heels of the Bisley's report, Jace Blackwine's big Colt spat its nozzling stab of blue-orange fire.

But the mustanger had not followed his target's earthward dive; his wild bullet fanned Curtwright's grease-rimed cheek and struck Redding's pinto in the shoulder, dropping the horse into the shallow edge of the water hole.

The dying animal's threshing hoofs caught Curtwright's buckling knees from behind, and the beefy Indian Agent fell forward over Redding, shielding him from a follow-up shot from Jace Blackwine's swinging gun.

The crash of guns, crowded into the space between two ticks of a clock, spooked Blackwine's grulla saddler, and the mustanger lost his precious moment's advantage as he fought to retain his seat in the saddle.

Curtwright writhed free of Redding's legs, retching as paroxysms of agony laced through him. Redding's out-flailing hand brushed one of his grounded six-guns, and he snatched it up, swung his half-lifted arm, and drove a snap shot at Blackwine.

The big Colt recoiled violently against the crotch of

Redding's thumb, a snake tongue of fire slicing outward. His bullet drilled Blackwine's barrel belly at a glancing angle, just as the mustanger was about to curb his grulla's bucking.

Blackwine's gun clattered to the dirt. Hard hit, the redbearded giant made a gagging shriek and grabbed leather. Blood spurted through the moonlit dust which swirled around him. Then Blackwine lost his grip on his reins and the grulla bolted for the open prairie, out of control.

Behind Redding, the fat Indian Agent had regained his feet, but his Bisley was lost somewhere in the mud beside the jerking hoofs of the pinto, and he dared not retrieve it.

Knowing Curtwright was no immediate threat, Redding scooped his second gun from the dirt and came to his feet, laying an alternating pattern of slugs on Blackwine's bolting grulla.

He saw the big stallion swing sharply to the north, stung by a bullet. For an instant Redding thought Blackwine was guiding the horse in getaway; then he realized the horse had tripped on a dangling rein.

Redding was vaguely aware of the gargling screams of his pinto, head churning the edge of the water hole in its last agony. He saw Curtwright limping toward his own horse, reaching for the reins; but the buckskin shied off, and Redding kept his attention on Blackwine.

The mustang hunter's grulla was galloping in a circle now, sweeping momentarily out of sight behind the willows and reappearing due south, briefly silhouetted against the moon. Blackwine by some miracle was still in saddle.

Ignoring Curtwright, who at this moment was frantically dancing around his wheeling pony with one foot wedged in an oxbow stirrup as he tried to mount, Redding dropped his smoking six-guns and lurched over to the water hole where the pinto was still threshing the pond into a bloody spume.

He leaned over the downed horse and got his Winchester out of scabbard, realizing the part luck had played in the the pinto's not having fallen on top of the rifle.

Fifty yards yards out on the moon-gilded sage flats, Jace Blackwine was lying on the ground. He had either fallen from saddle or had been bucked off during the brief seconds when Redding's attention had been fixed on getting his rifle. The grulla had bolted into the distance with stirrups leathers flapping.

But before being unhorsed, the bearded mustanger had had the presence of mind to haul his Remington out of the boot. The moon made a silvery flashing on the blued barrel of the .45-70 as Jace Blackwine settled on one knee and leveled his piece toward the water hole.

Redding yelled, "Cut that, Curtwright!" as he saw the Indian Agent, in saddle at last, spur his buckskin gelding away at a tangent.

As Redding's .30-30 swung to follow the Indian Agent, Blackwine's Remington cracked. Redding hit the dirt on his belly as he heard the banshee wail of the steel-jacketed slug close off his right shoulder.

Prone behind the shielding bulk of his pinto, the animal now still in death, Redding thrust Lennon's carbine across the horse's rump and lined his sights on the gargantuan bulk of Jace Blackwine, kneeling out there amid the tufts of silver sage.

Blackwine was levering a fresh shell into the breech of his Remington, cuddling the walnut stock against a hairy jowl.

Redding laid a shot inches from Blackwine, seeing the dust puff up to spray the mustanger's big shape. Blackwine triggered his return shot, his bullet slapping the dead pinto and jolting the carcass under Redding's gun barrel.

"Come on in Jace!" Redding sent his warning yell across the night. "I can fort up here the rest of the night if I have to. I want to take you alive."

He saw Blackwine shaking his head to clear it. The mustanger's lifeblood was leaking from the bullet hole in his side—a liver shot, a fatal hit. All Blackwine had left was a savage thirst to take Redding to hell with him. He concentrated now on nursing his strength enough to bring his Remington to a level pointing, waiting for Redding to show his head above the carcass of the pinto at the far rim of the water hole.

Meanwhile Joe Curtwright had made a getaway. The Indian Agent, flogging his buckskin into a dead run, was pounding across the sage flats toward the opening of the valley where Crowfoot Ranch was hidden beyond the intervening ridge. The direction of his flight told a story of some kind, but at the moment the significance of it was lost on Redding.

Curtwright was already out of effective rifle range. Redding dismissed the Reservation Agent from his attention, knowing he could pick his own time for a showdown with Curtwright. At the moment he was pinned to the uncertain cover of his dead horse, facing a bear-shaped foe who, like a wounded grizzly, could be dangerous despite the slug lodged in his guts.

"Show, damn you!" came Blackwine's frenzied bellow across the prairie. It was as if the mustanger sensed death's quickening approach and wanted only one more shot at his antagonist.

131

Clawing at the chin strap which had held his Stetson against his shoulders, Redding flung the headgear aside. The blur of movement baited a shot from Blackwine which made the hat jump in mid-air its crown perforated by the snap shot.

That feat of marksmanship was no lucky accident. This summer, more than once, Redding had seen Blackwine crease a fleeing fuzztail's mane at extreme range—a mode of capturing an *oreana* which most professional horse hunters shunned as too risky.

Redding came to his knees, judging the interval it would take Blackwine to jerk the load loading-lever of his Remington. The mustanger was a big target, crouched there on one knee, the wind tugging his cinnamon beard.

Redding notched his gun sights on Blackwine's chest, dead center, deciding to finish this business.

Before he could squeeze off the payoff shot, he saw Blackwine suddenly topple sideways, a shudder wracking his limp form. In falling, the mustanger had flung his Remington to one side, out of reach.

An old Injun trick, Redding thought, *to draw me in closer.*

After a short wait, Redding left the shelter of the dead pinto, crawling on all fours toward the willow thicket, pushing his .30-30 ahead of him. Blackwine had a belt gun, but if he was playing possum, the mustanger did not elect to make a draw, now that his target was out in the open.

Then, from a different angle, Redding saw that Blackwine lay with his face ground into the dirt, facing away from the water hole. He believed then that his first slug had killed Blackwine.

Warily, Redding came to his feet, Winchester at hip

level. He made a wide circle, so as to approach Blackwine from the rear. A dozen feet from the man, he sighted the sprawling pool of blood crawling into the thirsty sand alongside Blackwine.

He called Blackwine. Then, emboldened by the surety that the man was dead, he walked up and rolled Blackwine's mushy, inert weight over on his back with a boot toe.

Blackwine's eyes were crusted over with dirt. This bounty hunter was cold meat now.

A hard-pent breath leaked through Redding's teeth, sounding like escaping steam. Grounding the butt of his rifle, Redding cocked an ear to the breeze, listening to the subsiding rataplan of hoofbeats marking Curtwright's continuing flight across the ridge a above Crowfoot.

He said aloud, "Jace and that Injun Agent were heading for Joyce's place, looks like," and knowing today, that these men had come from Tondro's hide-out he had his moment's puzzlement over their choice of destination. He concluded that Blackwine—on his way to pay a last visit to his hunting-camp before seeking the refuge of Mexico—had decided to visit Crowfoot on the off-chance that Redding might have gone there.

He wondered if Blackwine and Curtwright had met Tondro and Zedra on their way out of the Navajadas. There was no telling.

Turning his back on Blackwine's elephantine corpse, Redding returned to the water hole and buckled on his gun belt and retrieved his bullet-punched Stetson.

Now, thinking things over, Redding gave his first attention to Curtwright's escape and the direction his flight had taken. If they had been en route to Crowfoot, that accounted for their having stopped at this water hole.

Curtwright headed for Crowfoot when he had his chance, Redding recalled; and the thought that the Indian Agent would find the home ranch deserted except for Joyce Melrose and her Mexican *cociñera* and roustabout filled him with an urgent haste to get on his way.

Blackwine's grulla had halted to graze a hundred yards out from the water hole. Redding unbuckled the lariat from his pinto's saddle pommel and, shaking out a loop, made his way toward the dead mustanger's mount.

The grulla headed up at Redding's approach, and spooked, but ran head-on into his loop. Gouging his spike heels into the gumbo, Redding made his hand-over-hand approach of the lass rope and caught the grulla's bit ring.

He repaired the broken rein and mounted, finding Blackwine's horse docile enough, perhaps because it was gaunted out from its trek from Thunder Rock today.

He spurred back to the water hole, picked up his Winchester, and thrust it into the rawhide boot under Blackwine's saddle. Then, reining around, he put the grulla into a lope, heading toward the entrance of Crowfoot's valley.

Rounding the shoulder of the outthrust ridge, Redding saw the twinkle of lights, marking Joyce's ranch house at the head of the short valley. A clamor of ranch dogs came downwind as he hit the wagon road and made his approach. When he was within a quarter of a mile of the house he reined up, becoming aware that the dogs were not barking at him.

Through the moonlight, Redding saw three black dots emerging from the timber north of the ranch. Riders, approaching Crowfoot. One of them could be Joe

Curtwright. That left two unaccounted for.

Pulling the grulla off the road to where a clump of smoke trees would conceal him from the view of the trio quartering down the ridge slope, Redding saw two of the riders pass out of sight beyond the shade trees which rimmed the Melrose house.

The third rider spurred down to the road and turned into the poplar-bordered lane. His voice floated back to reach Redding's ears as he spoke to the dogs which swarmed clamoring around his horse. The collies at once became silent, by which sign Redding knew this third rider was a Crowfoot man, familiar to the dog pack.

Redding saw this rider's shape cut across the house lights and dismount before the whitewashed gate. Spurring out of the smoke-tree *bosque,* Redding skirted the fence bordering the road until he came to the outer end of the poplars.

There he saw the front door of the ranch house open and close, leaving its bright rectangle as a fading image on his retina.

That rider might be Joyce herself, coming in from a moonlit ride of the ridge. No, the voice that had silenced the dogs had been a man's.

Keeping outside the south now of poplars, Redding glimpsed the other two horsemen coming in beyond the Crowfoot barns, their horses limned distinctly against the whitewashed corral fences. Why this splitting up, this approaching Joyce's house from different angles?

A hundred feet from the ranch house, the dogs caught Redding's scent and came trooping out. Before they reached him the wind shifted, and the collies turned their attention to the other two riders, who by now had reached the Crowfoot bunkhouse and stopped.

135

Redding hastily dismounted and tied Blackwine's grulla to a poplar. He paused a moment, watching the dogs rush toward the bunkhouse, barking inanely. Redding decided that the bunkhouse would be his first objective.

A man's angry yell sent the dogs yipping toward their kennels behind the main house. Redding saw a match flare as one of the men at the bunkhouse fired a cigarette.

Keeping the blacksmith shed between him and the, bunk shack, Redding worked his way closer to the latter building. He heard the bunkhouse door open and close, and shortly thereafter a light glowed behind the gunny sacking which curtained the windows.

Redding left the black maw of the shop and, gun palmed, walked straight to the rear end of the bunkhouse, which had no windows. He found a spot near the rock fireplace, where a chunk of adobe chinking had fallen out, and squatted down for a look inside.

Joe Curtwright, his pouchy face bleached to the color of unbaked dough, was pouring himself a drink at the poker table in the center of the room. Over by the rusty Franklin stove stood a Mexican wearing a steeple-peaked sombrero and a rainbow-hued serape.

The Mexican was Rafael, the courier Blaze Tondro had dispatched to Lavarim Basin to bring Teague Darkin back to Thunder Rock hide-out to identify Blackwine's prisoner.

Redding felt a cold chill of alarm wash through him. That third rider, then, the one who had gone into Joyce's home, would be Teague Darkin. If Curtwright had told Darkin enough to let Darkin know who Blackwine's killer had been, then Joyce might be in danger of her life at this moment.

CHAPTER 17

THE WAY OF A WOMAN

LEAVING THE BUNKHOUSE, REDDING HEADED TOWARD the main house at a run. The collies came trooping from their kennel as Redding was climbing the picket fence, their barking nullifying any hope he might have had to approach the house undetected.

With the dogs nipping at his spurs, Redding mounted the porch steps and headed to the nearest window.

Relief went through him as he saw Joyce Melrose standing before a blazing fireplace, directly below a gold-framed oil portrait of a man in bemedaled Army regimentals—presumably the martyred Major Melrose.

She was wearing an apricot-colored rodeo shirt and split doeskin skirt, as if she had spent some time in the saddle today. Her complete attention was on her visitor, who was seated in a high-backed chair which screened him from Redding's view.

As the dogs continued their yammering Redding heard the voice of Teague Darkin addressing Joyce.

"—that's about how she stacks up, with our beef gather better than half finished. I hate to be always bringing you bad news, dear."

Joyce's glance shifted to the front door. Redding saw by the white set of her face that her foreman-fiancé had brought some manner of bad tidings to Crowfoot tonight.

"Go see what's the matter with those fool collies," she said. "If you have had supper, I won't—" Darkin stood up, with a bone-wearied slackness showing in him, and headed toward the door.

Redding was standing directly outside, thumbs hooked in shell belts, when Darkin opened the door.

It took the Crowfoot foreman a full ten seconds to recognize this stubbly-chinned apparition in the trail-dusty range garb.

"Surprised to see me, boss?"

Redding spoke the words as he stepped forward, not waiting for Darkin's invitation. His eyes were fixed on Darkin's guns, knowing that if this man had learned the truth of his identity from Curtwright and Rafael tonight, he might try to shoot his way out of this situation.

But Darkin only scowled. "Blagg!" he bit out, as it genuinely surprised. "How come you ain't on the job with Shorty Hadley?"

Redding laid his unblinking gaze on Darkin, thinking, *You're a damned good actor, or else you don't want to show your hand in front of Joyce.*

"Well," Darkin snarled, "speak up, Blagg!"

Redding answered Darkin softly. "I'm here to draw my time and vamoose, Darkin. A man's a fool to work cattle in the Navajadas. I was told that in town before I signed up with you. I've had enough."

Darkin slammed the door shut with unnecessary violence. "Meaning what?"

"Meaning I'm drawing my pay while my hide's still in one piece."

Joyce crossed over from the fireplace, her gaze on the livid gash visible on the range detective's scalp, a wound that hinted of unknown violence out in the Navajada foothills where Shorty Hadley's roundup crew was working.

"George, what on earth happened to your head?" the girl asked sharply, halting alongside Darkin.

The ramrod s big hands hung tensely at his sides now,

138

splayed fingers brushing his thonged-down holsters. Redding had his moment of amused suspense, wondering how badly this Crowfoot foreman had been caught off balance by his sudden appearance.

How much, if anything, had Curtwright told Darkin about the events at Tondro's hide-out? If Darkin and the Indian Agent were together in the mysterious Basin intrigues which even Redding could only guess at, then Darkin must know that this man facing him was a Stockmen's Protective Association detective.

Darkin must have learned from Curtwright the news of Jace Blackwine's shoot-out, as well.

"Run into trouble, Blagg?"

Darkin's voice gave no hint of what lay in his mind. If Darkin had received a complete report from the Indian Agent during their recent meeting on the ridge— accidental or planned—then Darkin must surely know now that Joyce Melrose was aware that this man's name was not George Blagg. Darkin must know that Joyce was responsible for his being here on Crowfoot at all.

It was a preposterously complex situation, and the next few seconds would reveal whether Teague Darkin was involved in the tie-up between Wagonwheel Ranch and the Indian Agent and Tondro's rustler organization.

"Trouble?" Redding echoed. "Well, I wouldn't exactly say it was in my contract when one of Tondro's bunch kidnapped me a couple of days ago, within gunshot range of Hadley's chuck wagon."

Darkin licked his lips, thinking this over. His slitted gaze flicked over Redding's shirt front, as if he might be wondering where Redding had put his law badge.

"I'm sorry, to hear that, Blagg," Darkin said carefully. "What happened?"

Darkin had side-stepped a showdown in front of

139

Joyce. Redding turned to the girl as he said, "I was working the brush for Crowfoot beef day before yesterday. One of Tondro's men caught me flat-footed in a box draw. I was taken all the way to Tondro's hideout somewhere back in the high country. I made a getaway. That was yesterday. I rested up in Trailfork today. Now I've come to draw what wages I got coming and head back over the Pass, Miss Melrose."

The girl's face took on a flush. She was plainly mystified by Redding's incoherent story, hinting of so much yet telling so little. She appeared uncertain of what he wanted her to say.

"Of—of course, Mr. Blagg," she said hesitantly. She glanced at Darkin. "It seems that bad luck isn't confined to the Axblade lease. Teague just rode in to tell me that at least fifty percent of Crowfoot's cattle have disappeared from the west range."

Teague Darkin's eyes were bright with the man's rapid-fire scheming. He dragged a hand across his chin and turned to Joyce, saying gruffly "Tally up Blagg's time and write him a check, Joyce. I'll go out and saddle a fresh horse."

"Aren't you stopping over here tonight, Teague?"

"No. After what Blagg tells me, I figger I'd better ride over to Hadley's camp and tell him to drop the roundup where it stands. I'll have him move his beef to safer range."

Teague Darkin brushed past Redding and ducked out of the house as if in a great hurry to quit this scene. Redding heard the foreman's boots crunching down the gravel walk outside as he hurried away from the house.

"Doug," Joyce asked in a sharp whisper, "what really happened to you? Have you uncovered anything that would incriminate Teague, or what?"

Redding put on his hat and carefully adjusted the lanyard under his jaw. He decided not to tell Joyce all he knew as yet. "Can't say as I have," he admitted. "This I do know—your foreman is in a hurry to get out to the bunkhouse right now and get a couple of his friends off the ranch before you get wise that they're here."

"Two friends? Who?"

"One of them is a Mexican from Tondro's hide-out. The other is Joe Curtwright."

Joyce's eyes showed a round-sprung dismay. "Curtwright—you mean the Indian Agent? Why should he be hiding in my bunkhouse?"

Redding shrugged. "I intend to find out. If we give him enough rope, Darkin will hang himself. Did your father ever have any dealings with Curtwright, Joyce?"

She shook her head. "Not directly. But you remember Dad was on his way to visit Curtwright's Reservation when he was murdered."

She was close to tears. Almost without conscious volition, Redding found himself reaching for her, pulling her against him. He bent his head, and in the next instant his lips met hers. He felt the yielding pressure of her against him, her softness and her aloneness in this rustler-infested range which had been the Major's doubtful legacy to her. Then her arms slipped over his shoulders, and her fingers laced through his hair as she responded unrestrainedly to his kiss.

Redding was the first to break the hot urgency of this moment. There was a shy guilt on his face as he felt her arms loosen their passionate embrace.

"There's no saying what gets into a man to shove him into a play like this, Joyce," he said hoarsely. "You hired me to restore your faith in Teague Darkin, not cut

141

his props out from under him. I'm sorry."

A tear made its glistening streak down her check as she stepped back to face him. "Don't be, Doug. I only know that whatever happens—that after this moment's closeness I can never let Teague touch me again. It—it was more to please an aging father that I consented to wear his ring, Doug, to be honest. That is something I want you to carry away with you tonight."

Her words snapped Redding back to the cold reality of the hour, reminding him of chores undone.

At this very moment Darkin must be closeted with Tondro's man and the Indian Agent, out in the bunkhouse. Redding's instincts warned him that events were fast racing to a climax on Crowfoot tonight, and that Joyce's arms were not for him. Not now. Perhaps not ever. As Matt had so often said, a man who wore a star could not afford the luxury of romance.

"Look," he said roughly. "When Teague comes back, tell him you paid me off and that I'm heading for Cloudcap Pass, on my way out of the Basin. Tell him that—nothing else."

"All right, Doug. But—"

"I believe you are safe enough here," Redding hurried on, "or I wouldn't leave you. Whatever kind of a man Darkin turns out to be, marrying you is the key to all his plans. He won't let any harm come your way."

As he stepped to the door Joyce intercepted him, something akin to panic showing in her eyes. "I've got to know what happened to you, Doug. I've got to know how things stand, where you are going—"

He gently removed her hand from his arm. "I want to see where Darkin goes, what he does when he thinks I'm heading for Cloudcap Pass, that's all," he reassured her. "I don't want you to worry about seeing me again. I think you and I were meant to be together, Joyce."

With that he was gone, stepping quickly out into the night. Joyce was glad that he was not here to see the quick tears which came to her eyes; it seemed wrong, somehow, to feel that she could come to love a man whom she had known so briefly, and yet she knew that love was the thing that was tormenting her now, making Doug Redding's safety the uppermost thing in her life.

CHAPTER 18

MESSAGE FROM TONDRO

AVOIDING THE FLARING SPREAD OF LIGHT FROM THE ranchhouse windows, Redding crossed the yard, noting that Darkin had taken his horse from the front rack by the gate.

As he faded into the shadows of the poplar lane, Redding saw the light in the bunk house wink out, followed at once by a sharp rattle of hoofs as someone headed away from the bunkhouse at a gallop.

He thought, *I wasted too much time in there with Joyce,* and indecision went through him.

If that rider should be the Mexican, Rafael, he would almost certainly be returning to Thunder Rock, and to trail him would be the easiest way to solving the enigma of the whereabouts of Tondro's lair.

But if Teague Darkin was allied with Tondro as closely as Redding believed, it was imperative that he be on hand to check on what Darkin's move would be upon on learning from Joyce that his new cowhand, so recently a prisoner of Tondro's, had left Crowfoot for Paloverde.

He headed toward the tree where he had left his horse. Coming clear of the poplars, he had a view of the horseman who had spurred away from the bunkhouse and knew from the bulk of him that it was Joe Curtwright. The Indian Agent was heading for the open Basin as hard as he could flog the buckskin.

Mounting the grulla, Redding headed down the wagon road. By the time he reached the end of the poplar lane, he turned for a last look at Joyce's house and was in time to see Teague Darkin's big shape opening the door and going inside.

The wind brought to his ears the sound of Curtwright's horse.

Redding had his choice of waiting for Rafael to leave the ranch and intercepting him on his return to Tondro's hide-out; or running down Curtwright. He decided on the latter target; he might waste valuable time scouting the ranch for the Mexican courier to leave.

With the wind at his back, Redding believed he was out of earshot of the ranch. He put the jaded grulla into a gallop, and as the poplars dropped behind he saw the moonlight touching the long feather of alkali dust out on the flats, marking Joe Curtwright's line of travel.

Looks to be heading for Trailfork, Redding thought, and came to the sudden decision that perhaps the Indian Agent was carrying some kind of message to a henchman in town.

The night breeze off the Navajada uplands carried a sudden drumming of hoofs to Redding's ears. Two horsemen were hammering up the poplar lane behind him, leaving Crowfoot.

Pulling off the road, Redding gigged the grulla into a jungle of chaparral and dismounted, holding a palm over the stallion's muzzle to throttle any betraying whicker when the two riders passed.

He lifted a gun out of leather, on the off-chance that he might have been seen getting off the road, although he believed the poplars had concealed him from the view of the following riders in this tricky moonlight.

Less than a minute later, Teague Darkin and the Mexican, Rafael, stormed past his covert, lashing their mounts at top speed along the wagon road.

Joyce told him where I was going and he aims to head me off before I reach the Pass, Redding concluded. He had his hunch confirmed when he saw Darkin and Tondro's courier leave the road and head up the north ridge, on a short cut which would head off any rider traveling north toward the Paloverde road over the mountains.

He waited until the two had vanished over the pine-hung ridge. Then he mounted and put Blackwine's horse out into the Basin again, heading for the remote twinkle of lights on the sky line which marked Trailfork town.

The grulla was nearly spent, but unless Joe Curtwright had saddled a fresh mount—which was doubtful, in view of the short lapse of time prior to the Indian Agent's departure from Crowfoot—Redding believed he had a fair chance of overtaking the heavier rider short of the cow town.

He picked up the prints of Curtwright's horse on the road, and a half hour's riding brought him once more in sight of the Indian Agent, as Curtwright topped a rise less than a mile ahead, sharp-limned against the moon's disk.

The grulla protested the spurs but maintained a steady canter. What reserve stamina the horse had left, Redding knew he must save for the final sprint when he had cut down Curtwright's lead.

Cresting one of the series of low, sage-dotted ridges which corrugated the floor of Lavarim Basin, Redding was startled to see an empty-saddled horse standing with drooped head among the tumbleweeds piled against the north fence.

This was Curtwright's buckskin. Its hipshot posture favored a lame foot, and Redding read the complete story of Curtwright's misfortune in an instant.

The buckskin had thrown a shoe somewhere back along the road and had gone lame to such an extent that Curtwright had decided he could make faster time on foot.

The westering moonlight made a bas-relief of the river of silver dust which was this road. In that soft sand Redding had little difficulty picking up the dragging footprints of the Indian Agent. Curtwright was heading toward Trailfork.

Redding followed these tracks to the crest of the next slope. At the crown of the bunchgrass-tufted hill, he saw where Curtwright had turned off the road, climbing the barbed-wire fence to strike off in a short cut directly toward the town lights.

Scanning the farther slope of this hill, Redding spotted his man less than two hundred yards away. Curtwright at the moment was skirting the rim of a dry wash which had put an unexpected barrier across his short cut.

Jumping the fence with a winded horse was out of the question. Redding moved along the barbed-wire strands for a hundred feet until he found a fallen post where his horse could cross.

He was fifty yards from the wash when he saw Curtwright stumble and fall, then pick himself up. A

146

shift in the breeze had carried the sound of the grulla's approach to the Indian Agent, and for the first time Curtwright realized he was being overtaken by a mounted pursuer.

Redding was close enough to hear the Indian Agent's involuntary cry of alarm. Remembering that Curtwright had dropped his Bisley out at the water hole, miles from this spot, Redding knew there was a chance that Darkin had supplied him with a gun back at Crowfoot.

To check on that possibility, Redding triggered a shot over Curtwright's head as he put the grulla into a trot, heading straight for the bayed Indian Agent.

Curtwright yelled something unintelligible and turned like a panicked calf to leap headlong into the shadowy gulf of the arroyo. As Redding reached the cut-bank and reined up, expecting to hear sounds indicating that the Indian Agent was trying to take cover or else claw his way up the far bank, he saw that once more Curtwright's luck had gone sour.

In his blind leap to get out of range of Redding's gun, the Agent had landed in a bed of lava boulders. His sprawled form now lay motionless less in those bubble-pitted rocks.

Redding dismounted and slid down the cut-bank, knowing the winded grulla would stay put. He worked his way over to where Curtwright lay, keeping his gun ready for treachery, and made a quick check of the man.

Curtwright was alive but unconscious. His left ankle was twisted at a grotesque angle in his Hussar boot, and blood was oozing from a tear on his onion-bald scalp. His Mormon hat lay several feet to one side.

Hauling Curtwright's two hundred pounds of dead weight out onto the sandy floor of the draw, Redding made a quick exploration of the fugitive's pockets. He found what he wanted in Curtwright's alligator-leather wallet, a scrap of paper he recognized as a page torn from a wall calendar of the Crowfoot bunkhouse.

Striking a match to augment the fading brilliance of the moon, Redding scanned the scrawled message which he believed Teague Darkin had given the Indian Agent to take to Blaze Tondro up in the hills.

I've nabbed Redding here at Crowfoot. Don't know as yet how much he's learned. How come he gave you the slip?

My reason for this message is that I need your help, Tondro. It's worth $500 to me to hire a dozen or so of your vaqueros *for a trail-drive job.*

Important I get the Reservation beef onto Wagonwheel at once. C. will be back at the Agency by the time you get this, but we can't be sure if he can finish deal as matters now stand. Depends on whether Redding has sent a report out or not. Will bring him up.

Redding pocketed the message, lips pursed thoughtfully. He was morally certain Darkin had written this in the Crowfoot bunkhouse tonight. At the time, Darkin had thought he would find Redding, waiting back at the ranch house with Joyce. How he had planned to nab Redding and return him to Thunder Rock, without the girl's knowledge, he did not waste time trying to figure out now.

He scrambled back up the bank to get Jace Blackwine's canteen off the grulla's pommel. Returning to the unconscious Indian Agent, he sloshed the water over Curtwright's face.

One thing was certain from the context of the message. Darkin hadn't intended Curtwright to carry this message as far as Thunder Rock. The agent was to have passed it on to a relay man, probably in Trailfork.

When he learned the identity of that courier, Redding knew his Lavarim Basin manhunt would be entering its final phase.

CHAPTER 19

To the Navajadas

CURTWRIGHT RALLIED WITH A SERIES OF ANIMAL gruntings and strangled moans. He strove to prop himself up on the blow sand, but the wrench on his fractured ankle made the man pass out.

Before using the rest of his water to revive the Indian Agent, Redding took time out to use Curtwright's pocket knife and cut the Hussar boot off the injured leg before swelling set in.

Returning to the grulla, Redding rummaged in Blackwine's alforja bags, remembering that the mustanger kept a bottle of whisky there. He found one with a few ounces of amber liquor left in it.

Leading the horse down into the arroyo, Redding squatted down beside Curtwright, forced the bottle between the man's lips, and tilted it.

The fiery stimulant roused Curtwright. The man's eyes were wholly rational behind their greasy hammocks of flesh as he saw the expiring moon's last rays touch the rutted planes of the range detective's face.

Redding saw in his prisoner's slack mouth the realization of complete and devastating defeat. This petty poliltician was at his rope's end. How black the record of this man was, Redding could not guess; nor was he especially interested. Curtwright was a pawn in a far bigger game being enacted on this renegade range. His chief value now would be as a bearer of evidence against his cohorts.

"You were carrying a message to Trailfork for somebody to relay to Tondro," Redding said.

Curtwright was in too great pain to bluster. He remained silent, watching his captor with the blinkless intensity of a wolf caught in a trap.

"This message," Redding went on, "involved a herd intended for the Wagonwheel Ranch. I take it that Teague Darkin has a finger in this government beef-issue deal at your Reservation."

Curtwright snatched for the whisky bottle in Redding's hand and sucked down the last swig it contained. Revivified by the bite of alcohol in his belly, Curtwright became abusive.

"A damned lie, Redding. You got nothing on me. I'm a government man. I—"

This was no time for bickering. Redding pawed Darkin's note out of his pocket and waved it in front of Curtwright's face.

"Who were you to deliver this message to?"

Curtwright overcame the agony of his broken ankle enough to rasp out, "I never saw that paper before."

Anger drew Redding's lips thin over his teeth. "You damned fat slob, it's in Darkin's writing and on a page torn from the calendar in the Crowfoot bunkhouse—where you and Rafael were waiting for Darkin tonight."

Curtwright's pain-bright eyes went crafty. "Then it was planted on me unbeknownst. You can't frame me, Redding."

Redding sighed. He got to his feet, slipped a Colt

150

from scabbard, and twirled the cylinder with his thumb tip.

"You'll make prime coyote bait down in this draw, Curtwright. Unless the buzzards spot you first. You forget I saw you at Thunder Rock, eating supper with the Stiles girl the other night."

Curtwright's slabby jowls quivered. Sheer panic was growing in this man as he saw Redding turn the black bore of the Peacemaker at his paunch.

"You wouldn't shoot a man in cold blood—"

"I'll give you five ticks to tell me who you were going to turn this message over to when you got to Trailfork."

"You wouldn't shoot me."

"Why the hell not? I've got no time for picayunes like you, Joe."

Curtwright made his try at bluffing it out, but the ominous double click of the gun hammer coming to full cock wilted him.

"I believe you would kill me, you damned savage— Well, it was Clark O'Connor. Friend of Darkin's who runs a stable over in town. I—I didn't know who it was intended for."

Redding tipped the .45 muzzle skyward, picking this information to pieces in his mind, testing it for truth. He already knew the Irish stableman had some affiliation with Blaze Tondro. A spy, most likely, acting as a listening-post at the county seat. Quite probably a man with knowledge of how to find Tondro's hide-out in the labyrinthian wastes of the Navajadas.

"*Bueno,*" Redding said, pouching his gun. "You can't walk, so we'll ride double on your friend Blackwine's nag."

Curtwright made a scared, whimpering sound. "What

151

are you going to do, Redding?"

"Turn you over to Sheriff Lennon. You've lapped up your last gravy at the Pedregosa Reservation, Curtwright."

Curtwright shook his head numbly. He had sold his accomplices down the river tonight, to save his yellow guts from a bullet. Right now, getting a doctor to set his shattered ankle was his only consideration.

It was hard work, boosting the fat Agent aboard the grulla. The pain of it wilted Curtwright in another faint, and he was only half-conscious when, an hour and a half later, Doug Redding hauled him from saddle in the alley alongside Val Lennon's jailhouse.

The old sheriff, roused from bed, answered Redding's knock clad in his drawers and carrying a gun in one hand and a stub of candle in the other. He only stared as the SPA operative stumbled into his living-quarters, lowering the beefy shape of Joe Curtwright to the rumpled cot Lennon had just vacated.

"The Injun Agent, eh?" Lennon commented, igniting a lampwick from his candle. "Had a hunch that hyena would overplay his hand one of these days. What's the setup, Doug? You look like you've done a good day's work since you left town ten-twelve hours ago."

Redding gave the Trailfork sheriff the high lights of this wild night's crowded events.

"Curtwright needs medical attention, Sheriff, and then I want you to lock him in your calaboose. I want him held incommunicado. His testimony should help wrap up the loose ends at the payoff. I have a hunch the Basin's rustling scare is about over."

Lennon bent over Curtwright, who was either unconscious or playing possum, and decided to play it safe while he was going for a doctor by shackling the

Indian Agent's good ankle to the cot with a pair of handcuffs.

Redding stepped to the door, drawing Lennon's sharp, "Where you think you're going son?"

"To leave Darkin's note where O'Connor will spot it. And I'll need a fresh horse; that pinto you loaned me is dead, Sheriff. And you might also rustle me up a pack of grub; say, enough to last me two-three days."

The sheriff thumbed his overall straps over his shoulders and tugged on his warped boots. There was a grin lurking under his waterfall mustache as he asked, "What joy ride are you cookin' up this time? Don't you ever sleep, man?"

Redding grinned as he opened the door. "I aim to follow O'Connor to Tondro's hide-out, Sheriff—without bein' blindfolded or inside a black box for a change."

Dawn was a scant two hours off, Redding estimated, as he stepped out of Lennon's door. He was glad he had fortified himself with a long sleep the day before, against the unknown rigors of the trek he had ahead of him.

Leaving the jail vicinity, he avoided the main street of Trailfork, although this cow town's deadfalls and honkies were locked up at this hour, most of its cowboy patronage, busy with roundup work at this season of the year.

With the moon below the Axblade peaks, Redding had only the starlight to guide him to Connor's barn and blacksmith shop on the southwest edge of town.

He had no way of knowing whether Tondro's liaison man slept on the premises and regretted not having obtained that information from Lennon. Entering the stable yard, he saw Blaze Tondro's yellow democrat wagon still standing where the rustler boss and Zedra Stiles had left it an aeon ago—was it less than twenty-four hours?

There was a lean-to connected with the blacksmith shed which had the look of a dwelling about it. Pausing alongside the front window, he heard a man's measured snoring inside. Peering through the open window, he saw a man sleeping in a cot, his face faintly illuminated by the cherry-red glow of a heating stove on which a pot of coffee simmered.

The sleeper was Clark O'Connor.

Taking Teague Darkin's note from his pocket, Redding creased it and wedged it under the door, knowing the bright red figures on the calendar page would catch O'Connor's eye immediately upon awakening.

That done, Redding made his leisurely way back to the sheriff's office. Lennon was waiting for him in the alley with a saddled steeldust gelding, his own personal mount.

Lashed behind the cantle was a grub sack, and a plump canvas water bag was hooked over the horn. Lennon was thorough. He had transferred his Winchester from Blackwine's saddle to this one, and had supplied a pair of Army field glasses in a scuffed leather case securely tied to the swell-fork pommel.

"Doc Ullman's in there working on Curtwright," the sheriff reported. "Ullman can be trusted not to let the word leak out that I got a federal politician locked up. What next, son?"

Redding checked the stirrups and let them out another notch to accommodate the length of his saddle-warped legs.

"I'm going to head east along the foothill road. Going

154

to post myself on a ridge where I can spot whichever crick O'Connor heads up on his way to Tondro's. The crick Tondro and Zedra traveled in the buckboard."

The sheriff chewed at the ends of his mustache. "What's your idea of what Darkin is up to?"

Redding shook tobacco into brown-paper trough between his fingers. The stillness of the alley was broken by a stifled groan from Curtwright, inside the lean-to, as the doctor worked on the Agent's broken leg.

"You'll probably dig that out of Curtwright before I get back from the Navajadas," Redding said. "Offhand, I'd guess that Darkin has been stealing Crowfoot stock from the west lease, venting the Melrose iron into Wagonwheel. He wants Tondro's crew to lend him a hand in getting that stock over to Duke Harrington's range, where it won't attract as much attention as it would on Joyce's Axblade graze."

The sheriff shivered, not entirely from the night's chill. "Wish to hell I was twenty year younger and spryer, son, "I'd give my eyeteeth, if I had any, to be ridin' with you."

Redding stepped into saddle the unlighted cigarette sloping from his underlip.

"You'll get your chance to flash that star at the payoff," he assured the Trailfork lawman "I'm no one-man Army. I don't intend to corral Tondro's border hoppers by myself. My job is to locate his hide-out well enough to lead a posse to it when the time is ripe And maybe get a line on this Wagonwheel deal of Darkin's while I'm at it."

He heard Curtwright bellow in oath inside Lennon's shanty, heard the cow-town medico's professionally brusque, "That does it, I guess. You'll wear this cast a few weeks, Mr. Curtwright."

Redding reached down to grip Lennon's hand in the darkness. "So long, *amigo*. I got to be linin' out, in case O'Connor gets up early. One thing sure, he'll light a fast shuck out of town soon as he spots Darkin's note."

Lennon said, "Luck, fella," and watched Redding spur past the jail and rein east when he hit the main street.

CHAPTER 20

THE LOST TRAIL

DAWN'S RUDDY PROMISE WAS STAINING THE SAW-toothed sky line when Doug Redding reached the first of the series of creeks which the stage road panned as it flanked the Navajada foot slopes.

This, if memory of Val Lennon's county map served him right, was the Sangre de Santos, emptying into the Whetstone River out in mid-Basin. He failed to locate any growth of wild mint which would indicate that this was the stream Tondro's wagon had followed out of the hills.

Redding followed the creek into the embracing foothills and put the steeldust gelding up a rocky splintered ridge which gave him a view of the entire sweep of road leading to Trailfork, ten miles west—the road Clark O'Connor would soon be riding.

He had a smoke and plundered his grub sack for a breakfast of jerked venison and a can of tomatoes, knowing events might crowd too hard to permit another meal during the day.

By the time he had finished eating, the sun had risen in fiery splendor, filling the vast length of Lavarim

156

Basin with its unearthly beautiful glow, tipping the remote Axblade peaks with pure gold.

Assuming that Clark O'Connor awoke at daylight, Redding figured the Irishman might be starting on his errand about now. An hour and a half should see him at the Sangre de Santos. From then on it would be a matter of trailing O'Connor without being seen. With luck, Tondro's lost trail would be revealed to Redding before a nooning sun made a bake oven of these uplands.

After slightly more than an hour's wait Redding saw a rider flogging his horse down the Trailfork road, eastbound. The hard drum-roll of iron-shod hoofs wafted to his ears as the horse forded the Sangre de Santos below him.

Using Lennon's binoculars, Redding saw without surprise that the rider was Clark O'Connor. A mile farther along the road, Redding saw the Irish blacksmith leave the road where it forded the next creek—marked Twelve Mile Creek on the map—and put his horse into its fetlock-deep wash until he disappeared behind a ridge.

Redding cased the glasses, went back to his horse, and put the steeldust down the ridge into the cactus-mottled valley which formed a saddle between the bracketing hills.

He picked up a game trail linking the ridges and followed it at a gallop, knowing the wind would keep the sound of hoofbeats from crossing the ridge into the canyon where O'Connor was riding. He could not risk losing sight of O'Connor. It was almost too much to hope that the canyon O'Connor had entered would form an unbroken route to Tondro's hide-out at Thunder Rock.

At the crest of the ridge overlooking Twelve Mile

Creek, Redding pulled up, searching the vista below with the sheriff's Army glasses. The sun's full light had not yet penetrated this pocket in the Navajadas, but a silver flashing caught Redding's eye, and he picked out O'Connor's horse still following the stream.

The creek bed was wide and level, with no visible rapids. A mule-drawn wagon could negotiate it to reach the Basin road without leaving any sign of its passage on the pebbly bottom. It was that lack of a visible trail which was the main lock on the door of Tondro's lair.

Redding moved along the ridge, keeping O'Connor abreast of him before he finally moved west of the crest to keep O'Connor from hearing or seeing him. If Tondro's messenger thought he was being followed, the whole plan would be ruined.

The ridge climbed steadily as it roughly paralleled Twelve Mile Creek. From time to time Redding dismounted to walk to the crest, but O'Connor was now out of sight, below vertical rock walls which the brawling stream had furrowed out of the country rock through millenniums of time.

Redding knew he was sky-lined now, but that fact did not worry him. So long as O'Connor was hemmed in by cliffs without visible ravines entering from the sides, he could not discover that he was being flanked.

A thousand feet of elevation were behind Redding when, unexpectedly, his horse broke out of the scrub brush above timber line onto a clearly defined trace of an old wagon road.

Tondro's spring wagon had not traveled these sand-filled weed-grown ruts, however, nor had any other vehicle passed in this way a decade. This was probably an old logging-camp road.

Because the road dipped down toward the canyon

O'Connor was traveling, Redding decided to follow it, giving the steeldust head and keeping his full attention on watching for O'Connor to show up in the canyon below. The road bent around a shoulder of naked rock which lifted hundreds of feet to form a lava sugar loaf which Redding recalled having seen from the sheriff's office in town. Glancing behind him, Redding had an unobstructed view of the Basin, with the roofs of Trailfork forming their indistinct blot in the middle distance.

The steeldust blew its lips and came to a halt. Looking ahead, Redding saw where this old-time road he was following had been obliterated by a rock slide which had stripped the mountain to the naked bedrock to form a scar hundreds of acres in extent.

An earthquake or some other cataclysmic upheaval had blocked Twelve Mile Creek's course with incalculable tons of granite debris. Beyond the avalanche pile, Redding could see the ancient cuts and fills of this road leading on up the canyon; below it, the natural dam had backed up the waters of Twelve Mile Creek to form a small lake which meandered out of sight around a far bend of the hills.

The creek's waters, or part of them, drained through the rock-slide boulders. O'Connor could never hope to pass that barrier on horseback. Therefore, this must be the first turnoff in his route to Tondro's lair.

Even as that thought touched Redding, he saw Clark O'Connor, reduced to specklike proportions at this altitude, putting his horse up a ledge which crossed over the opposite canyon wall.

Focusing the field glasses on the ledge O'Connor was following, Redding made out the unmistakable tracks of a wagon recently driven down that tilt of rock and brush.

"This is where Tondro drove the other night to reach the creek bed," Redding muttered, a vast satisfaction filling him. It was like seeing invisible hands put together the pieces of a mammoth jigsaw puzzle.

That creek had swallowed up the last five miles of Tondro's secret exit into the Basin. It was easy to see why no sheriff's posse had ever penetrated this deep into the Navajadas; there was no trail to lead them here, no reason for exploring.

Redding waited until O'Connor had scaled the farther slope and vanished over the ridge. Then he put his gelding down to the avalanche-blocked creek, picked his way across, and began trailing the fresh hoofprints of O'Connor's horse.

He was not prepared for the sight awaiting him at the high point of land above the avalanche scar. This was a lookout point commanding an unbroken view of the entire northwest extent of the Navajada range. Hundreds of feet below and perhaps two miles farther inside the mountain barrier, the nooning sun was as refracted by the crest of a dazzling white mare's tail of water spilling over the crest of a cliff.

O'Connor was not in sight, but the wagon track led down into the farther canyon formed by that waterfall's runoff. Even before he put his military glasses on the curvature of the distant cataract, Redding knew he had broken the secret of Blaze Tondro's hide-out.

Just visible over the intervening rimrock he saw the weather-beaten roof of the old mine shaft house marking Tondro's headquarters. Up there at the dead end of this canyon was Doc Stiles's bastille of lost hopes.

Swinging his gaze over the formidable vastness of

this unsurveyed domain of rock pinnacles and unscalable cliffs and ridges and caverns, many too deep for the sun's light ever to penetrate them, Redding realized how cunningly Tondro had selected his den.

At no other point in the Navajada range, probably, was Thunder Rock's waterfall crest visible to earthbound creatures.

Redding had passed this spot, wearing Blackwine's blindfold; he had returned over this ridge, locked in the grub box of Tondro's wagon. Now the landmarks were his to study and memorize against the time when he would make his last trek into Tondro's forbidden domain—backed by the strength of a posse that would rid Lavarim Basin forever of Tondro's reign of lawlessness.

CHAPTER 21

UNDERGROUND TO MEXICO .

REDDING WITHDREW INTO A JUMBLE OF TIME-furbished glacial boulders to ponder his next move. Any attempt to trail Clark O'Connor farther would mean inviting a bushwhack bullet from the sentries Tondro kept on duty around the clock. For all he knew, this spot might be within gun range of a guard post.

His horse concealed, Redding sized up the rugged country between him and the rimrock which overlooked Tondro's hide-out. He saw no cross chasms breaking that brushy slope, no indication of a ledge or avalanche scar which would block a man on horseback.

To be spotted out on that sun-baked expanse of steep, naked slope would be risky business but was a chance

161

he had to take. Darkin's message called for Tondro to send a crew from Thunder Rock large enough to move a sizable cattle herd onto Wagonwheel range. He was tempted to remain where he was, on the supposition that within a short while O'Connor would be returning, perhaps with Tondro's rustler crew.

Then he remembered what Doc Stiles had told him of a mine tunnel which served as an escape outlet from the gorge in case of emergency. It was possible that Tondro might dispatch the men Darkin had asked for through that exit.

Checking the magazine of his Winchester and the cylinders of his Colts, Redding put his horse out of the rocks and along the mountain slope, heading in the general direction of the canyon-end waterfall.

He could make good time along here, for the slope carried a webwork of hard-beaten game trails. With luck, Redding believed he could reach the rim directly above Tondro's hide-out before O'Connor reached his destination.

Redding had estimated the waterfall to be two miles from the ridge where he had had his first glimpse of it. But, reversing the usual error in underjudging distances in this high arid country, he found himself nearly abreast of the plunging waters within a an hour's riding.

Redding off-saddled in a brushy rincon, staked out the steeldust gelding, and provided himself with a hunk of rye bread and a can of peaches from the sack Lennon had supplied him. Then, unencumbered by his Winchester, he picked his way down an eroded barranca, eating as he traveled, until he found himself at the edge of the cliff, facing the dizzy abyss of Thunder Rock gorge.

He bellied down on the hot granite shelf and worked

his way with infinite caution to the rimrock's verge.

He was directly above Tondro's shaft house; he could have thumbed a pebble into space and landed it in the outlaws' horse corral. A dozen Mexicans were lolling in siesta in the shade of a loblolly pine down by the boiling whirlpool at the foot of the falls, the showering white spray giving them welcome surcease from the sweltering heat of the day.

A maul made its metallic music on an anvil in one of the *aguista*-thatched outbuildings down there. The place had an almost pastoral atmosphere of undisturbed peace, which Redding took as evidence that Clark O'Connor had not yet arrived with his message.

At that very moment a horse's hoofs beat up echoes above the muted organ roar of the falls. Redding swung his gaze down-canyon and saw O'Connor rounding the last bend of the gorge wall, his shout to the camp lost for Redding in the constant thunder of plunging water.

But O'Connor's shout had reached the shaft house. Redding saw the loafing Mexicans jump to their feet like startled quail and head across the flat area of old mine tailings at a run.

Peering almost straight down, Redding caught sight of Blaze Tondro as the *contrabandista* chief emerged from the shaft house, walking out to greet O'Connor as the Trailfork blacksmith climbed wearily from his lathered stirrup and handed Tondro the slip of paper from Darkin.

Before Tondro had finished reading the note, he was surrounded by sombreroed henchmen, coming from all sides. Redding felt his pulses race as he caught a flash of vivid color down by the river and recognized Zedra Stiles, wearing a scarlet fandango dress, come into view with a basket of clothes she had been laundering in primitive fashion.

Old Doc plodded up out of the river's channel behind his daughter, his salt-gray beard fluttering in the constant wind currents down there. Redding thought fervently, *You two won't be prisoners here much longer.*

Tondro was barking orders which did not carry up the cliff to Redding's ears. His Mexican henchmen scattered; some ducked into the shaft house, others trooped over to a low log-walled shed and emerged carrying saddles and bridles, some of them sparkling with silver work.

Watching the Mexicans sadddle horses from the *remuda* corral, Redding realized that Tondro was wasting no time in carrying out Teague Darkin's orders. O'Connor had turned his horse over to Doc Stiles and had vanished inside the shaft house. Men were running to and fro between barn and shaft house now, most of them carrying bedrolls and saddle guns, as if in preparation for a trip which would take them away front this camp for several days.

Despite the anthill-like confusion which Redding was witnessing from his hundred foot elevation over their heads, Tondro's men were performing like well-disciplined soldiery. This camp was poised for action at a moment's notice. Within five minutes of O'Connor's arrival at the camp, Redding counted fifteen *vaqueros,* equipped for several days' absence, grouped in front of the shaft house to get Tondro's final instructions before hitting the trail.

Redding saw Zedra return to her washing down by the river, carrying a maguey-fiber *canasta* such as peon women used. Her aging father was out by the cavvy corral now, currying down O'Connor's exhausted pony.

A wave of indignation swept Redding as he realized

that the old medico was forced to do this gang's menial jobs, in addition to ministering to their gunshot wounds and their illnesses.

Tondro reappeared from the shaft house and mounted a snowy blanco stallion which a *mozo* had saddled for him. The outlaw chief had his riders' complete attention as he addressed them, apparently outlining the job they were about to embark upon.

Then Redding saw Tondro lift a hand like a field officer signaling a cavalry charge, and the riders fell into a quick column of twos as they followed the half-breed away from the shaft house.

Redding's eyes narrowed with puzzlement as he saw that Tondro was leading his cavalcade toward the base of the waterfall, instead of toward the down-canyon trail. Then, shifting his gaze to the base of the cliff, Redding discerned the black maw of a mine drift cut into the rock, a spill of rubble fanning out from its mouth like the upcast dirt of an earthworm.

Knowing what the penalty would be if an up-glancing eye happened to spot him on his lofty perch, Redding inched back a way, exposing only the top of his head as he watched Blaze Tondro spur his blanco into the mouth of the tunnel, his riders going into a single-file formation as they followed him, like ants crawling into a burrow.

Within a minute's time the riders had been swallowed up in that subterranean cavity. A lone Mexican came back out of the mine tunnel, swinging a metallic object on the end of a thong, which Redding surmised was a key to some sort of door.

"The escape tunnel Doc told me about," Redding muttered aloud. "The question is, where does the other end of that tunnel see daylight?" On Mexican soil, Doc

165

had told him. But how far away?

The solitary Mexican made his way to the shaft house. Out by the barn, Doc Stiles finished rubbing down O'Connor's horse and plodded back down to the river where Zedra was washing clothes, out of Redding's view.

A brooding somnolence returned to this outlaw citadel. With it came a feeling of frustration to Doug Redding. It would be impossible for him to circle around and travel the canyon as O'Connor had done; even if he could, the chances of breaching Tondro's exit tunnel were next to impossible.

The only thing left to do, then, was to guess Tondro's destination and try to reach it by another route. Darkin's message had mentioned Reservation beef and Wagonwheel Ranch. If Crowfoot cattle were involved, then Darkin must have them waiting on some bed ground on or near Joyce's leased graze in the Axblade country west of Trailfork.

In that event, Tondro's rustlers must be bound for the west side of Lavarim Basin, by some secret route which they would reach through the Thunder Rock mine tunnel.

Figuring the geography of this country, Redding believed it would take Tondro's crew a day and a half at the outside to reach the Axblade range where Darkin's fall roundup was in progress.

"Reckon I can't lead a posse back to Thunder Rock as long as the kingpin and half of his men are away," Redding mused, mapping his future course. "It wouldn't hurt to take a little *pasear* to the Axblades myself and see about this herd Darkin is so anxious to turn over to Duke Harrington's outfit."

Heading back across the rugged slope with his horse

166

showing its need for water, Redding felt in good spirits. This trek into the Navajadas, trailing Clark O'Connor, had paid off with priceless information.

Tondro was no longer safe behind the shield of secrecy concerning the location of his hide-out. Thunder Rock was incredibly close to Trailfork. All that remained now was to give Sheriff Lennon time to assemble a posse of riders with guts enough to clean out this rattler's nest.

CHAPTER 22

BLOTTED BRANDS

SHORTLY BEFORE SUNDOWN, A PALOVERDE FREIGHTER drove his tandem-hitched Conestoga caravan into Trailfork and sent a kid posthaste to the jailhouse to report that he had picked up a dead man at Willow Springs, midway from Cloudcap Pass.

Val Lennon knew whose corpse it was before he climbed the bull bar of the caboose wagon and peered through the puckered oval opening of the covered wagon's hood. It was Jace Blackwine. A day's exposure to the burning sun had bloated the mustanger's face beyond all recognition, but having had Doug Redding's report of the shoot-out at the water hole, Lennon had no difficulty identifying the buckskin-clad body.

The old lawman made a pretense of jotting down what facts the mule whacker could give him—"There was a pinto nag lyin' dead in the water hole, Sheriff, that carried your brand on its rump"—and stood by until the local coroner arrived to transfer Blackwine's remains to his morgue.

167

It was dark when Lennon returned to the jail, carrying a tray of food from a near-by Chinese restaurant for his lone prisoner, Indian Agent Joe Curtwright.

Pausing at the jailhouse door, Lennon cast an uneasy eye toward the Navajadas, glowing a rich gold rose in. the aftermath of sunset. Doug Redd Redding was not yet back from his trailing job on Clark O'Connor. Neither was O'Connor; Lennon had kept a sharp eye on the incoming roads all afternoon.

A vague worry stirred Lennon as he unlocked the bull pen and carried the supper tray over to Curtwright's cell.

"Brought your grub, Joe. How's the ankle?"

Curtwright did not answer. Struck by a sudden prescience of disaster, Lennon set his tray on the floor and struck a match.

Joe Curtwright had cheated justice. The Pedregosa Agent had fashioned a noose out of his gallus straps. His body hung from a crossbeam of the cell, porcine face congested black, tongue protruding, feet dangling below the edge of the cot from which he had jumped to eternity. The man's death hadn't been instantaneous, from a snapped spine. An autopsy would probably indicate that Joe Curtwright had died of slow strangulation.

The match burned out in Lennon's fingers. The old lawman waggled his head, clucked his tongue thoughtfully. Two of Tondro's henchmen, Blackwine and Curtwright, would occupy adjoining slabs in the county morgue tonight.

Even if Doug Redding failed to return from the Navajadas tonight, the man had left his mark on the ranks of Tondro's bunch.

Lennon picked up the tray of food, feeling a strange

168

revulsion as he did so. These victuals intended for a man now dead wouldn't sit right in his belly. Shame to waste good grub, but—

He heard a horse blow its lips alongside the jail. A rider was dismounting at the rack alongside Lennon's lean-to shanty. Hurrying over to a barred window, the sheriff looked out. A stray beam of light spilling through a knothole in the saddle shop across the the alley revealed who the rider was.

Doug Redding was back safe.

Lennon let himself into his living-quarters through an adjoining door from the bull pen and was putting the tray on his table when the SPA operative stepped inside.

"Grub waiting for me." Redding grinned. "Sheriff, you missed your calling. You ought to be a headwaiter in some high-toned feedbag in New York."

Lennon snapped waspishly, "This chow was for Curtwright. He won't be needing it."

"Confinement spoiled his appetite?"

"Curtwright hung hisself. Body ain't cold yet, but he's toasting in hell just the same."

The shock of this news kept Redding silent a long moment.

"He have anything to say during the day?"

"Nary a word, except that he was being framed."

Doug Redding went over to the corner basin, pumped himself some water, and started washing up. "No matter. Sheriff, I spotted Tondro's hide-out. Know every inch of the trail. How long will it take you to round up a posse for the showdown?"

Lennon chewed his mustache. "I'd need two-three days. Already got my boys picked, but some of 'em are busy with roundup."

Redding toweled his face and hands and, without

169

waiting to be invited, sat down at the deal table and launched into the food intended for Joe Curtwright. As he ate, he gave Lennon a succinct review of his day's doings.

"So, I aim to take a jaunt over to Joyce's Axblade range tomorrow," Redding wound up, "to be on hand to see where Tondro picks up the Wagonwheel beef Darkin aims to sell to the Reservation. With Curtwright a suicide, it's anybody's guess when those 'Paches will get their next beefsteaks."

Lennon grumbled, "Always on the go, ain't you?" and went on to report the news of Jace Blackwine's final visit to town.

"I'll be away several days," Redding said. "You have a fifty-man posse ready to ride when I get back, eh?"

Before turning in, Redding took the time to pen his first case report to Colonel Regis at Protective Association headquarters at Sage City. Lennon's alarm clock roused him in the bleak hour between the false and the true dawn; he had eaten breakfast at the sheriff's table and was heading westward toward the Axblades by the time the sun rose.

Noon found Redding in the timbered foothills of the western range overlooking Lavarim Basin, within sight of Teague Darkin's roundup camp. Most of the Crowfoot beef had been choused out of the mountain brush by now; a herd numbering close to a thousand head was being hazed across the Basin today, a slow-moving russet column against the shimmering sage flats. Melrose cattle on their way to Cloudcap Pass and the rail road yards at Fort Paloverde, east of the Navajadas.

That herd would be joined with the jag of cattle

170

Shorty Hadley's crew had flushed out of the east range. The combined herd would eventually wind up at the slaughterhouses in Omaha or Kansas City.

But Redding was not interested in this orthodox routine of Crowfoot's roundup. He was remembering what Joyce had told him at the ranch house only last night—how Darkin had reported a fifty percent loss here on the Axblade graze.

That missing half of Melrose's cattle, Darkin had initimated, must have been rustled during the past spring and summer. If Redding's hunch was right, he believed those Crowfoot steers were still north of the border, being held in one of the innumerable back canyons on the Axblade edge of the Basin. It was this herd that Blaze Tondro's rustler crew would be hazing by some secret route over the Axblades, to throw onto Wagonwheel.

Taking care to avoid being seen by any Crowfoot cowpunchers who might be combing the range for strays, Redding made his dry camp that night on the lofty lava rim which gave the Basin its name. From this elevation a man had a clear view of the Basin where it tapered across the Mexican boundary.

It was around midnight when Redding was roused from a catlike sleep by the noise of mounted men entering the Axblade foothills below the lava rim. He broke camp at once, took his steeldust off picket, and, saddling with haste, moved down off the rim by way of a side canyon, making in the direction of those night-riding horsemen.

The moon was on the wane, but its light was sufficient for him to pick up, a few minutes later, the long column of riders threading their way across the grassy, rolling valley which pointed into the heart of

Joyce Melrose's leased range.

Keeping to the thin edge of the timber, Redding flanked the route of the night riders until he saw them turn due west into the rock-ribbed fissure of a pass which opened on the Pedregosa Indian Reservation west of the Axblades.

He had little doubt but that he was scouting Blaze Tondro and his *vaqueros* front south of the border. They had planned to cross the line after dark, after their roundabout way from Thunder Rock.

From the top of a cactus-spined ridge, Redding saw the riders making camp. Soon the smudge of three campfires burned their orange holes against the blackness of the cliff walls.

Redding selected a high point of rocks a mile north of the camp, to await the coming of daylight.

The following sunrise confirmed his hunch. With the aid of Val Lennon's powerful glasses, Redding watched Tondro and his dusky-hued rustler crew break camp and continue their push up this nameless mountain gap.

Working his way along the north shoulder of the pass an hour later, Doug Redding's attention was diverted from the riders he was following by a sound of cattle bawling somewhere in the recesses of a side canyon on the south.

This was just beyond the Axblade summit, judging from the way the silvery thread of a creek ran down in the pit of the pass. It was, therefore, outside the legal limits of the Melrose government lease, probably on Curtwright's Apache Reserve.

Redding settled himself down to play a waiting and watching game. Tondro's riders disappeared into the throat of the side canyon where the cattle were being held; they would show up presently with a herd.

Redding took advantage of the delay to wolf down a cold breakfast. It was shortly after midmorning when a herd of shorthorns swung out of the holding canyon, with Tondro's point riders in the lead.

Yipping Mexican *vaqueros* shoved the bawling steers westward toward the outer desert and the Indian Reservation. Redding, waiting until the drags had left the canyon, estimated the herd at roughly a thousand head—equaling the herd which Darkin had on its way to rail for Crowfoot.

The air held a din of clacking horns and creaking joints, bawling of thirsty critters and the deafening clatter of cloven hoofs on the flinty trail. When the flank riders began moving down the west grade of the pass and the stragglers had been bunched with knotted rope ends and much shouting of Mexican riders, Redding saddled the steeldust and continued along the high north shoulder of the pass, keeping Tondro's herd in constant view. When the herd was out of the Axblades, there was nothing to prevent Tondro from shoving the steers south into Mexican territory. If he carried out the instructions in Teague Darkin's message, this herd must move north, toward Wagonwheel.

The field glasses told Redding that this herd carried Wagonwheel's brand. Furthermore, the ranks of Tondro's crew were augmented at noon by a half-dozen other riders, strangers to Redding. These punchers, all of them *yanquis*, were not Crowfoot riders; but in all probability Darkin had sent them here, perhaps from Wagonwheel itself.

This pass was difficult terrain for a cattle drive, and as a result the herd would show up with a short tally before Tondro could turn it onto Wagonwheel graze. Redding drew on his cow savvy now to pull up and wait until the slow-moving herd was out of sight beyond a twisting of the pass.

Cutting down to the herd's trail, Redding had little difficulty in locating a straggler, overlooked by the drag riders. He dared not risk a shot, this close to the herd; instead, Redding hazed the steer into a pocket of rocks and dabbed his rope on the animal, quickly snubbing it to a piñon.

The animal was a two year old. Dismounting, Redding took a stock knife from his saddle pouch and, moving in on the ory-eyed brute with a range-wise caution, drove his blade expertly in the steer's throat.

This wanton butchery was repugnant to Redding, but it was his only sure way of checking on the authenticity of a brand. The killing and skinning out of a beef was a legal prerogative of the star he wore, practiced by brand inspectors or stock detectives throughout the western cow country.

When the steer had bled itself out, Redding made no attempt to butcher it. This carcass would be a feast for the *zopilotes*, already beginning to spiral on motionless pinions high in the blue.

Redding's keen-whetted blade made four slices of the hide to box off the Wagonwheel brand on its ribs. The brand, even to his expert eye, looked original, untampered with.

This critter, he thought, could have a Wagonwheel run on its hide while it was sucking a Crowfoot cow, and a pressing curiosity made him hurry the job of peeling off the segment of hide to have a look at the flesh side of the brand.

It was a blotched job. The original brand stood out distinctly on the underside of the hide—Melrose's Crowfoot brand, a letter Y with the vertical bar

174

extended up through the fork of the Y to make a triple-pronged crow's foot design.

But some artist with a wet blanket and a running iron had extended downward the two original prongs of the fork of the Y, to make a six-pointed asterisk, which had then been enclosed in a circle to form a wagon wheel.

These alterations, not visible on the hair side, were indistinct even when studied from the fleshy underside. Whatever brand blotter had altered Crowfoot into the Wagonwheel had done this job eighteen months or so ago when this animal was a calf.

"No wonder Teague Darkin didn't cotton to having strangers help with the Axblade roundup," Redding muttered, carefully rolling the rectangle of hide and stowing it in his saddle pouches against the day when he would submit it to a federal court as evidence of brand blotting. "Wouldn't do for it to leak out that fifty percent of Major Melrose's cattle carried the brand registered to Duke Harrington's syndicate."

Many obscure things were clearing up in Redding's mind now as a result of this brand inspection. Small wonder that Wagonwheel had been able to underbid every rancher in Lavarim Basin and get the government's Indian contract year after year. The beef Wagonwheel delivered to Curtwright's corrals at the Pedregosa Agency hadn't cost Duke Harrington a bloody shilling.

Removing his rope from the dead animal, Redding, wondered aloud, "It'll be interesting to get Teague Darkin and Duke Harrington face to face in a court of law. I wonder what Blaze Tondro's cut on the deal was?"

In a general way, he had accomplished what he had set out from Trailfork to do. But Sheriff Lennon needed time to assemble his posse for the attack on Tondro's citadel in Thunder Rock Canyon; there was no pressing need for Redding to return to Lavarim Basin today.

Seeing the dust of Tondro's trail drive turning the sun to a copper rivet in the enamel-blue sky, Redding made his decision. He would continue trailing this herd until it was shoved onto Wagonwheel graze, per Teague Darkin's orders.

That would put him close to the headquarters of the man of mystery, Duke Harrington. Indirectly, part of the cleanup job he had been sent to the Basin to accomplish would entail picking up Harrington, on charges of defrauding the Fedral Government.

A better opportunity to visit Wagonwheel would not present itself. If he delayed too long, Harrington might skip the country. Wagonwheel Ranch, then, was his next objective.

CHAPTER 23

DUKE HARRINGTON

WAGONWHEEL RANCH APPEARED COMPLETELY deserted when Redding first glimpsed it from an Axblade ridge the second morning after Tondro's riders moved the stolen herd from its bed ground.

A faded Union Jack hung in one of the windows of the frame ranch house; there was no other visible sign of its foreign ownership. Its barns, corrals, and outbuildings were in good repair but on a far less pretentious scale than Crowfoot.

Deserted though Duke Harrington's headquarters appeared, Redding pulled up his horse well out of

176

gunshot range to size up Wagonwheel's layout. Some suspicion of danger was buzzing in his head. Long schooled to trouble, Redding was too much a realist to ignore the warnings of his primitive instincts.

In all probability the ranch was deserted; the Wagonwheel crew was probably busy on some far range with its fall beef gather. Tumbleweeds had blown across the lawned yard to bank against the front steps of the ranch house. No stock moved in the corrals or around the haystacks in the horse pasture. A rusty windmill idled on its wooden tower, its clutch out of gear, the sheet-iron tanks at its base half emptied by a month's evaporation.

Fifty miles to the south of where Redding now sat his saddle, Crowfoot's brand-blotted cattle now grazed peacefully on the southern limits of Duke Harrington's range. They had been moved up from the pass by night, Tondro being prudent enough to keep his Mexican drovers out of sight by day.

Yesterday's dawn had revealed the herd spreading over the grama-grass flats north of Wagonwheel's drift fence, segregated from the rest of Harrington's range by a deep, mile-wide arroyo which bisected the Wagonwheel graze laterally from the Axblade mountains to the Indian Reserve.

Any cruising brand inspector, covering this corner of the Territory, would see nothing amiss in cattle bearing the British syndicate's iron and grazing on Wagonwheel's south range.

Whatever plans Teague Darkin had for this portion of Joyce Melrose's beef, he had made certain, with Tondro's help, that only a scattering of Wagonwheel-branded steers would be found on Crowfoot's lease. And these could conceivably have strayed over the

177

mountains during the spring and summer months.

Daybreak yesterday had found Redding camped midway down the west slope of the Axblades. Tondro's crew had put the stolen herd onto Harrington's graze during the night. Then, their job done, Blaze Tondro and his *vaqueros* had vanished. To all outward appearances, Crowfoot's stolen herd had been feeding north of the Wagonwheel drift fence indefinitely.

Redding shrugged off Tondro's disappearance as of no immediate concern. The rustler crew would spend a day or two returning to Thunder Rock, on the east side of the Basin, probably covering most of that distance well below the Mexican border.

There was no mystery about Darkin's having called on Tondro for the manpower needed to get the herd off Joyce's lease. The Crowfoot foreman could not spare his own crew for the job without delaying the Crowfoot trail drive across the Basin on its way to Paloverde's railhead.

Tondro's willingness to work cattle not intended for his own illicit market outlets in Mexico was proof in itself of some close-knit teamwork existing between the rustler king and Teague Darkin.

Redding felt well pleased with the rewards of his trek to the Axblades these past three days. He had the evidence in his saddlebags now of Darkin's crooked work with a running iron during the past year. Better yet, he was now in a position to return to Trailfork to organize a posse under Sheriff Val Lennon, and plan their climactic strike on Tondro's stronghold.

That trap must not be sprung until Tondro and his men had had ample time to return to their hide-out; a scout would establish when to lead a posse into the Navajada wilderness.

With Joe Curtwright safely in boot hill now, there was little chance that Joyce's stolen cattle would ever be moved to the Indian Reservation and sold. The only job left undone, so far as Redding was concerned, was making contact with the mysterious Duke Harrington.

Now, looking down at Harrington's ranch, Redding got his first intimation that the Wagonwheel was not as deserted as it had appeared. Lennon's field glasses showed Redding a furtive movement of a window curtain in one wing of the main ranch house.

It was a small thing, an infinitesimal blur of motion, but no vagrant wind had stirred that curtain. It was held back for a good ten seconds and then released by hidden hands. The movement put a crawling tingle on Redding's skin as he realized he had been spotted and might at this moment be framed in a bushwhacker's gun sights.

But it was hardly likely, even if Harrington himself was here, that he would recognize anything hostile in Redding's appearance. His law badge was out of sight, pinned to his undershirt. Outwardly he was just a nondescript saddle tramp drifting down the mountain road which linked Wagonwheel with the Basin.

This British-owned ranch was better than a hundred miles by road from Trailfork and Crowfoot Ranch; another twenty miles removed from Tondro's bastion in the Navajadas.

Harrington would probably be out on the range, over-seeing his fall beef gather. Whoever was inside the house could probably be talked into revealing Harrington's present whereabouts.

Redding gigged the steeldust into a fox trot, ignoring the likelihood that he was under surveillance. He pulled up at the windmill tanks and let the horse drink. Then, dismounting with the stilted awkwardness of a man who had been many miles in saddle since daybreak, he rolled himself a cigarette while he took a seemingly casual look at the roundabout scene.

Finally he led his horse over to the hitchrack in front of the main gate and sent a tentative halloo toward the house. Empty echoes rebounded from the clapboard walls.

Redding half-hitched his reins around the chewed cottonwood tie bar and trailed his spurs leisurely through the gate and up a gravel path, kicking dry Russian thistles aside as he mounted the steps of the Texas-style gallery, which fronted the house.

As he rapped his knuckles on the front door, he thought he heard a furtive sound of motion inside. He knocked again, and waited, whistling a few bars of the "Cowboy's Lament."

Suddenly the window behind the faded Union Jack went up, with a suddenness that startled Redding's taut-keyed nerves. He turned without haste, to find himself being regarded by a wizened, egg-bald oldster who had a Remington .44 six-shooter thrust through the waistband of his bibless Levi's. The old man was leaning out the window, glaring at his visitor.

"If you're thinkin' of bracin' Wagonwheel for a job," this cadaverous-looking derelict called sourly, "you've drawed yoreself a blank, stranger. Wagonwheel's got a full crew, and roundup almost over, nohow."

Redding grinned, tonguing his cheek thoughtfully. This old gaffer was probably a roustabout left behind to watch after the place during the roundup. A crotchety old man who apparently scorned the traditions of Western hospitality, at least where drifting saddle tramps were concerned.

180

"If you're hongry, the woodpile is out back," snapped the roustabout. "Saddle bums work for their bait here."

Redding spoke for the first time. "I ain't looking for a handout, my friend. I'd like to talk to the owner of this outfit. You run this spread?"

Visibly flattered by this, the old man ducked his head inside, slammed the window shut, and a moment later unlocked the door and peered out at his visitor.

"This ranch," he said with a touch of arrogance, "is owned by the Albion Cattle Company of London, England, which same is five-six thousand mile from here."

Redding leaned against the doorjamb, casually inserting a toe of his Coffeyvilles against the threshold. "But I understand an hombre named Duke Harrington manages this outfit. Are you him?"

The roustabout scowled, undecided as to whether he was being hoorawed or not. "The Duke," said the old man finally, "draws pay for runnin' Wagonwheel, but he don't cotton to livin' in this hellhole jack-rabbit country. You'll most likely find him at the Palace Hotel, Market Street, Frisco, Californy, which same is a thousand-odd mile, from here—"

"All right, all right." Redding laughed. "But he ain't in California now. Not at roundup time."

A flush spread across the roustabout's seamed cheeks. He started to shut the door in Redding's face, when he found it blocked by the toe of the waddy's boot.

The roustabout made a clawing motion toward the gun at his belt; then checked the movement as he saw Redding drop a hand casually alongside his own holster.

"I tell yuh Harrington ain't here, stranger. You better scat afore I lose my temper."

181

At this instant a suave voice issued from somewhere inside the room at the roustabout's back. "Let the stranger in, Jinglebob. I'll see him."

The roustabout's reptilian eyes touched Redding briefly as he eased the pressure of the door on the rider's boot.

"Come in," Jinglebob growled, "but keep them fancy shootin' irons where they are."

As Jinglebob retreated behind the opening door, Redding stepped inside. For a moment he could see nothing inside the semidarkness which clotted the Wagonwheel house. Then he made out the vague shape of a spotted-horsehide divan extending at right angles from a lavastone fireplace. All the window shades were drawn against the heat of the day, making a shadowy grotto of this place.

Silhouetted against the hot glare of sunlight pouring through the doorway, Redding had the uncomfortable feeling that he had been out-maneuvered here.

He ducked his head to clear the lintel as he stepped inside, at once putting his back against the wall. Then he saw a man's tall shape limned indistinctly against the background of faded wallpaper across the room.

"Run up the shades, Jinglebob."

The man's voice carried a familiar timbre in Doug Redding's memory, one he could not immediately place.

"Did you hear me, Jinglebob?" snapped the voice. "I want Mr. Redding—alias George Blagg—to get his look at me."

Instinct sent the SPA detectives's hand toward the lowslung gun at his right flank. That movement was arrested by the dry metallic click of a gun hammer being notched to full cock across the room.

Old Jinglebob hobbled over to the window where he had first challenged Redding out it on the porch. He ran up the crinkled green blind to let a shimmering bar of sunlight flood the room.

A cold sensation struck Redding in the pit of his belly as he stared at the big brown coated man who held the six-gun on him. He had expected to find the dissipated, outcast son of British nobility standing there. Instead he was meeting the pale-green glitter of triumph in the eyes of Joyce Melrose's foreman, Teague Darkin.

"Your former range boss, Señor Blagg," sneered the Crowfoot foreman. "On Wagonwheel, however, I prefer to be called Duke Harrington."

CHAPTER 24

OLD BLOODSTAINS

PURE DESPAIR WAS A SEETHING SENSATION IN DOUG Redding. Accustomed to brushing close to death, accepting it as a hazard of his chosen work, the cattle detective knew he had never been closer to doom than at this moment.

"You're a man of many parts, Darkin," Redding said, groping his arms to hatbrim level, the breath running out of him in a long gust. "I won't say I'd guessed how the deck was stacked."

The outlaw-foreman showed his teeth in a taut smile which accentuated the rusty outline of his close-cropped mustache.

"A man of many parts, such as yourself, Redding? Jinglebob, take this man's guns. Our guest happens to be an operative in the pay of the Stockmen's Protective

183

Association."

The old roustabout approached Redding cautiously, as if he had been ordered to draw the fangs from a coiled snake.

"You told me you wanted to sleep till noon, Duke," whined the old man, reaching out gingerly to remove an ivory-stocked gun from Redding's near holster. "That's why I didn't wake you when I seen this buckaroo ridin' in."

Desperation put its wet ooze on Redding's skin. Another five seconds would see the Wagonwheel flunky in possession of his other gun. Yet to attempt a draw now would invite Teague Darkin's point-blank fire.

His moment of indecision was soon terminated by the feel of his second gun being lifted from leather. Jinglebob, taking no chance, crowded Redding's spine with the first Colt. With his prisoner disarmed, Jinglebob retreated quickly to stand with his back to the closed door.

"Well, Darkin," Redding said in a bleak monotone, "it looks like you've outfoxed me. I'll check the bet to you."

Teague Darkin—this man who, incredibly, was also playing the role of manager of this British-owned ranch—edged over to a circular mahogany table in mid-room and eased a hip against the polished curve of the wood. He holstered his gun now that old Jinglebob was covering their prisoner from the rear.

"We have things to talk over, my friend," Darkin said easily. "I tried to spare you the hazards of Lavarim Basin, you recall, the night you met my fiancée over at Paloverde."

Redding blinked. He was thinking back to how Tondro had held him prisoner at Thunder Rock Canyon

184

while his courier, Rafael rode to the Axblade graze to bring Darkin over to the mountain hide-out to identify him as an SPA detective.

Yet, at that time, Darkin had been ignorant of Redding's true identity. Jace Blackwine had not known that, or else he was bluffing, trying to collect a bounty from Tondro.

Redding was morally certain that Darkin had not known the truth about him at the time he hired "George Blagg" to work the Crowfoot roundup. He had first learned the truth from Joe Curtwright, most likely.

"Things to talk over?" Redding prompted, slowly lowering his aching arms "Such as what?"

Darkin reached in the pocket of his town coat for a cheroot, bit off the end, and thrust it between his teeth. His movements had a spurious aura of gentility which made Redding doubt that this man was actually a Britisher.

"You have seriously embarrassed my romance with Joyce," Darkin said, with only the thinnest note of malice touching his voice. "As a matter of fact, I would never have known she had any doubts as to the true circumstances back of her father's demise last spring had I not opened the Major's safe in her absence and discovered her correspondence with your Colonel Regis of the SPA in Sage City."

Redding said, "So that was why you and Blaze Tondro got wise that I was meeting Joyce at Paloverde that night."

"My friend Tondro, unfortunately, failed in his assignment to put you out of the way at the outset. I don't mind telling you I was no little disturbed to learn that the man he shot at the hotel that night was one of Blackwine's mustangers instead of the redoubtable

185

Douglas Redding."

There was a run of silence. Finally Redding said, "I had a little talk with another partner of yours, Darkin. Joe Curtwright, the Indian Agent. He tells me you bushwhacked Joyce's father." It was a shot in the dark, but it hit home.

For a moment Teague Darkin's outward mask was altered by Redding's disclosure. Then he shrugged. "Under the circumstances"—Darkin grinned—"I will not bother to call you a liar. It so happens that Joyce's father was a doomed man from the moment he took me on as his foreman. It was essential to my long-range plans that ownership of Crowfoot should fall into my hands. As long as the Major was alive, that was impossible."

Redding cut in. "But you murdered him because you were afraid he was wise to your rustling Crowfoot beef for rebranding with your Wagonwheel iron—and selling it to the government with Curtwright's connivance?"

Darkin shrugged. "The Major trusted me implicitly to the last, Redding. He thought his beef losses were due to Tondro's operations. I was careful to nourish that theory of his until the time was ripe to dispose of Major Melrose."

Redding's brain was busy. Ten feet separated him from the table where Darkin was leaning. He could cover that distance in two strides. The question was whether old Jinglebob would cut him down from behind if he made the move.

Stalling for time, knowing Darkin intended to murder him when it pleased his whim, Redding said, "You didn't have to murder the old man. Crowfoot would have been as good as yours as soon as Joyce became your wife."

186

Darkin's eyes flashed. "Joyce consented to our engagement to please her father, not because she loved me. I never had any serious belief that she would ever go through with the wedding."

Darkin moved away from the table, as if he had sensed the tension in Redding. Stooping, the Crowfoot foreman pulled a woolen Navaho rug off the floor, to reveal a brownish blot dyeing the wooden puncheons.

"Melrose stopped overnight at Wagonwheel on his way to the Indian Reservation last spring," Darkin explained. "He learned that night that the never-seen Duke Harrington was his own foreman. You see, Redding, I am really an Englishman. I am really Duke Harrington, although the title is a mere nickname."

Redding continued to stare at the stain on the floor. He knew without Darkin telling him that it was dried blood.

"I was too ambitious a man to exist on the meager remittances my family sent me from abroad," Darkin went on. "It was a good many years ago that I got tired of managing this ranch for my family's syndicate. So I went over to the Basin and took over the active management of Major Melrose's ranch, at a time when the old soldier was on his way to bankruptcy. Joyce was a pigtailed tomboy then."

Darkin paused.

"As I was saying, Major Melrose visited Wagonwheel on his way to talk to Curtwright about the Indian beef-issue business. Up until that night, when I chose to reveal myself, the only other persons who knew that Teague Darkin and Duke Harrington were one and the same man were my roustabout, old Jinglebob yonder, and Blaze Tondro."

Darkin gestured toward the stained floor boards.

"I told the Major who I was, The news stunned him. I shot him before he could recover himself. These stains are his blood."

"I guess I get the picture, Darkin."

"When Joyce called for a search, I brought the Major's body in, telling her I'd found I him over in the Navajadas, a victim of Blaze Tondro. The Trailfork coroner's inquest accepted my story without question, just as Joyce reported to Colonel Regis. Unluckily for Joyce, she kept your messages in the Major's safe. She did not know that I was in possession of the combination."

Redding curbed the mounting panic that flowed through every fiber of his being. Jinglebob had him covered from behind. These men were baiting him into a rash move.

Since the moment of entering this room, Redding knew he had been living on borrowed time. He saw the bright desire to kill kindling by degrees in Darkin's eyes now, knew Darkin planned to spill his blood at the same spot where Melrose had died.

"You haven't asked me yet," Redding said, patiently stalling for time now on the impossible chance that Jinglebob might relax his vigilance, "why I paid this visit to Wagonwheel."

Darkin blew a smoke ring at the ceiling. "I'm not particularly interested. The fact remains, Redding, that you have less than a minute to live."

Darkin yawned and lifted his gun from holster.

Redding braced himself for the point-blank shock of lead he knew was coming. Covered from two angles, there was no hope of grappling with Darkin. But he aimed to try it.

Darkin's thumb eared back his gun hammer.

"Redding," he said, as he lifted the gun for a point-blank aim, "it is strange that fate should decree that you would die under exactly the same circumstances as Major Mel—"

The Crowfoot *segundo* broke off as the door at Jinglebob's back suddenly slammed open, knocking the old roustabout headlong to the floor.

"Drop your gun, Teague!" A woman's voice laid its whiplash across this scene. "Don't make me kill you."

Redding thought, *I'm already dead. I'm hearing things!*

The voice belonged to Joyce Melrose.

CHAPTER 25

JINGLEBOB'S CONFESSION

TEAGUE DARKIN LIFTED HIS EYES FROM THE BUTTON on Redding's shirt he had mentally picked for his target.

Joyce stood crouched in the doorway above Jinglebob's sprawled form, a .25-3000 squirrel rifle held at hip level, its bore trained on Darkin's midriff with a rock-steady aim.

Redding, holding his frozen posture lest a movement from him might cause Darkin to squeeze trigger involuntarily, had to admire the steely insouciance of the outlaw before him.

Not so much as a muscle twitched on the foreman's handsome face. This sudden reversal of fortune meant Darkin's destruction, the evaporation of his dream of an outlaw empire. But his expression was that of a man glancing up at an annoying interruption.

Through the tail of his eye Darkin saw his

189

roustabout's preposterously bulging eyes take on a crafty glitter. The old man, in falling, had held onto Redding's guns. It was in Jinglebob's power to drive a slug into the cattle dick's back.

"No," Darkin said. "She means it."

Darkin lowered his gun. The Wagonwheel roustabout eased gun prongs to safety position and laid them gingerly on the floor. Then he reared back to a kneeling position, his back to the girl in the doorway, and raised his arms.

Doug Redding turned then, meeting Joyce's gaze. A grin touched his mouth corner, briefly, signifying the break of the intolerable tension in him.

Then, wheeling, he crossed the room in two quick strides and without warning drove a clubbed fist into Darkin's jaw with all the savagery at his command.

The blow snapped the Crowfoot *segundo's* head back with a spongy, popping sound so that for a moment his glazing eyes stared at the ceiling. Then his hip toppled against the hardwood table rim and his knees started to buckle.

Redding whipped across a left uppercut to Darkin's cheek which filled the room with the brutal, meaty sound of it, driving the big man to the floor.

His knuckles stinging, Redding stooped to jerk Darkin's gun from limp fingers. He prodded the fallen man briefly to uncover a hide-out gun under his right armpit. He tossed both weapons to the table and then turned to see Joyce Melrose lower her Winchester and take a faltering step toward him.

Redding suddenly remembered that Jinglebob still carried the Remington in the waistband of his pants. He strode in that direction, only to see the bald-headed oldster shake his head.

190

"You're calling the dance from here on out," Jinglebob said softly. "I'm settin' this one out."

Redding picked up his own guns and reached for the old-timer's Remington, jacked out the cylinder, and tossed the useless piece into a far corner of the room.

"Step over beside Darkin," Redding ordered, "and let's see you do a hog-tying job with that rope yonder."

Redding ignored Joyce, putting his full attention on the old man during the few moments it took Jinglebob to take down a rawhide *mecate* from a wall peg and truss the unconscious Darkin's legs at it knee and ankle, finishing the job by knotting the man's wrists together behind his back.

"Now, belly up to the wall yonder." Redding ordered, "and stand hitched. I'll fix you directly."

When Jinglebob had complied, Redding turned to the girl. She had leaned the .25-3000 against the wall; her face had gone chalk-white now that the strain of the scene was behind her, and she was trembling violently as Redding stepped forward and drew her into his arms.

He rubbed his stubbled chin across the glossy brown hair which tumbled from her cuffed-back Stetson, and his whisper was husky in her ear. "Miracles like this don't happen to a man often, Joyce. What brought you a hundred miles from Crowfoot to pull me out of a tight?"

She withdrew from his arms and sat down limply on the horsehide sofa. "It was no accident, my being here," she said. "I—I trailed Teague across the Basin. I thought maybe he was getting ready to skip the country—"

"Too bad for him he didn't."

"The other night when you left the ranch—I saw Teague and that Mexican come back, long after midnight. Teague left the ranch before daylight. I

191

saddled up and trailed him. He made a beeline for the North Gate and Wagonwheel."

Redding said incredulously, "But that was four-five days ago."

She tucked a wisp of hair under her Stetson. "I've been camped in a draw overlooking this ranch. I was afraid to show myself, but I had to know what business my foreman would have at Wagonwheel. Then I saw you ride in—and I was too far away to warn you that Teague was here."

A shudder wracked the girl as memories of this last grim hour overtook her in a sick green wave.

"I got here in time to—to see Teague showing you the spot where he shot Dad. The angle from the window was wrong for me to put a gun on that old man who had you covered. There was nothing left to do but kick the door in."

An overwhelming desire to seize this girl in his arms again, pour out his love to her, came to Redding. He thrust the impulse aside and turned to stalk over to where Jinglebob stood bellying a wall. The old man cranked his face around toward Redding, toothless gums working a cud of tobacco.

"I just work here, son. Take it easy on an old man."

Redding said gently, "I want to see Darkin's hole card. He claims he's Duke Harrington. He doesn't strike me as being an Englishman."

Jinglebob shook his head. "He ain't. You'll find the real Duke Harrington's bones rotting in the desert a good day's ride from here. Darkin knifed him in a brawl when he was a Wagonwheel cavvy wrangler, twenty-odd years back."

From across the room, Joyce Melrose said softly, "That must have been around the time Teague went to work for Dad."

"Yeah," Jinglebob said. "It wasn't hard, Darkin takin' over as the Duke. The Duke spent most of his time over in Californy, boozin' and gamblin' away his remittance checks. I was the only man on the spread then who even knew the real Harrington. I played along with Darkin for a split of his remittance *dinero*."

Redding said, "So Darkin got the idea of running Wagonwheel on the side?"

Jinglebob spat a brown gobbet of tobacco juice along the wallpaper. "He's got away with it all these years. An ambitious critter, that Darkin. Tied in with Blaze Tondro, shovin' stock acrost the border. And every year him and Curtwright got together on this deal to buy Wagonwheel beef for the Injuns. Strippin' said beef offen Major Melrose's west lease."

Redding said finally, "I think I can get you off with a light prison stretch, Jinglebob, if you tell the court what you've told me. You stand hitched for the time being."

Redding turned toward Darkin. The foreman had not moved. A rivulet of blood seeped from his battered jawbone. Redding checked the old man's roping job, not trusting Jinglebob, and then walked over to sit down beside Joyce.

"You want the whole story now," he asked, "or have you taken enough shocks for one day?"

She managed a vague smile. "When I opened that door I was mentally prepared to kill the man Dad wanted me to marry," she said. "You're working on this case because I called for you, Doug. I guess I'm entitled to an interim report."

Redding ran splayed fingers through his hair, marshaling the host of tangled facts in his head.

"You know the general situation already," he said

193

"Darkin had this undercover partnership with Blaze Tondro. It was Blaze who killed my brother Matt, or had I told you that?"

"No. Doug, I'm so terribly sorry—"

"It wasn't because Tondro got wise to Matt being a range detective. It was because Matt had fallen in love with Zedra Stiles—and Tondro has his eye on Zedra for himself."

He gave Joyce time to think that over; then he went on.

"By getting your father out of the picture, Darkin was ready to run Crowfoot as his own, giving Tondro control of a handy strip of border for his contraband running. As Duke Harrington, he could continue his deals with Curtwright, robbing Crowfoot, to lap up the graft from the Indian Reservation contracts."

"I heard you tell Teague that you had arrested that Indian Agent. Was that a bluff?"

"I was bluffing when I claimed Curtwright told me Darkin had murdered your father, Joyce. Curtwright committed suicide in Val Lennon's jail the next day."

She expelled a long breath. "Then you've just about finished your work in the Basin, haven't you?"

He grinned, hardly realizing he was nearing the end of what he intended to be his last deal behind an Association badge. "A couple of items left on the agenda, Joyce. The courts will deal with Darkin for your father's murder. The sheriff is getting a posse together to storm Tondro's hide-out in the Navajadas. Other than that—I'm free to tell you I love you."

Redding got to his feet and stepped to the door for a glance at the sun.

"We can reach Trailfork with our prisoners by tomorrow noon if you feel like traveling all night," he said.

Joyce stood up. "My horse is on picket in a draw half a mile from here. I walked down." She glanced at the bloodstain on the puncheons, and a deep shudder of anguish ran through her. "I can't get away from this place soon enough, Doug."

Redding glanced across the room at Jinglebob. "Ride herd on the old-timer," Redding ordered, "while I bring horses around. The quicker we turn Darkin over to Lennon the better."

CHAPTER 26

DEATH IN THE RAVINE

OUT AT THE WAGONWHEEL BARN REDDING FOUND two saddle horses. One, a line-back dun mare, he saddled for Jinglebob. The other was a Crowfoot pony, its saddle blanket still damp; probably Darkin had ridden to the south range to check on Tondro's herd. Looking back, Redding realized how close he must have come to beating Darkin to Wagonwheel this morning.

He led both horses back to the front gate, hitching them alongside his own gelding. When he reentered the house he found that Teague Darkin had regained his senses. The man sat propped against the table, his dazed stare fixed on Joyce. She sat on the divan with her Winchester covering old Jinglebob.

Although he believed the Wagonwheel roustabout would cause no trouble, Redding took the precaution of tying the oldster's wrists together with a length of pigging string.

"While I'm putting these buskies on their horses for the trip back to Trailfork," Redding said, "you might rustle up a sack of grub and some cooking-utensils from the kitchen, Joyce. We'll have to eat on the way."

Joyce joined Redding at the front gate, her arms laden with a grub sack, as Redding was tying his prisoners' legs together under their horses' barrels. In the distance she saw a smudge of dust lifting off the open range, marking the approach of three riders toward Wagonwheel.

From Redding's nod she knew the range detective had been watching that dust spiral as well.

"Probably some Wagonwheel men coming back from roundup," Joyce ventured shielding her eyes from the sun. "It's just as well we're getting out, Doug. Those riders might have objections to us kidnaping their boss."

Jinglebob laughed skeptically. "Darkin ain't known on this spread. Not that Wagonwheel is run by a band o' angels, not by a damn sight. Long riders with a price on their heads, some of 'em. Have to be, to shut their eyes to Wagonwheel's beef deals with Joe Curtwright."

Redding put the old man's remarks away in his head for future reference. He doubted if the British owners of this ranch had any knowledge of the rustling being engaged in by their American representatives. That angle could be cleared up in due time, after Blaze Tondro's rustler rule had been broken in Lavarim Basin.

The incoming riders were still several miles distant when Redding, with Joyce riding behind his cantle, vanished over the first ridge east of the ranch house. Beyond the brow of that rise they paused long enough for Joyce to visit her camp and return with her Crowfoot mount, a leggy palomino which she had raised from a foal.

Two miles farther on they picked up the Basin wagon road and followed it toward the cleft in the Axblade range known as the North Gate. Darkness overtook them as they were passing the summit, a vista of

Lavarim Basin's northern expanse visible to eastward.

It was ninety miles to Trailfork. Joyce was nearly spent, although she was making complaint. The mere ordeal of riding at the stirrup of her former fiancé, knowing the part she had contributed toward his eventual retribution on the gallows, was a severe strain on the girl.

"We'll give the horses an hour's rest," Redding suddenly announced, "while I rustle up some grub to tide us over."

The proximity of a creek near by, its wet murmurings making a welcome sound above the whispers of the night breeze in the piñon pines roundabout, prompted Redding to pull off the Basin road and lead his cavalcade down into the ravine where the stream burbled over its shallow rocky bed.

With Joyce helping with the unsaddling, Redding tied his two prisoners back to back against the trunk of a handy piñon and then went about the chore of watering their horses at the creek. There was an open park across the creek, fetlock-deep in lush bluestem grass, and there Redding tethered the four mounts.

When he waded back to the campground he found that Joyce had already rustled up enough deadfall wood for a fire and, drawing on her gunny sack of cooking-utensils and grub which she had picked up at the Wagonwheel kitchen, already had coffee on the coals.

Hunkering on his heels just outside the fire's glow, Redding harked back in memory to the campfire he had shared with Jace Blackwine's mustangers, a night when the smell of death had been blended with the aromatic wood smoke.

How different his situation tonight! Watching the girl's swift skill as she set about preparing a warm meal

197

for him and their prisoners, he thought, *There's a woman to ride the river with,* and he had a moment of wonderment as to whether the loss of this girl was not the uppermost penalty Teague Darkin had to ponder tonight as he stood roped to the piñon bole a dozen yards away, at the edge of the shuttering firelight.

Darkin had not opened his mouth during their ride up the North Gate grade. The man appeared to have accepted the inevitability of his situation, knowing he was lucky to be alive.

Redding was restless in his mind. A feeling that something was not as it should be destroyed the complete peacefulness of this firelight scene. That feeling persisted until, to satisfy it, he walked over to the piñon and made doubly certain that Darkin and old Jinglebob were securely tied.

He was returning from that job when a coyote's howl, deceptively near at hand, caused the saddle stock across the creek to snort their alarm and head up from their grazing.

A sudden splashing of hoofs in the creek told Redding that one of the saddlers had broken its picket rope or jerked up its pin. He saw the shape of the loose pony as it bolted along the platinum ripples of the creek where it spilled over a long incline of glacier-scoured granite; and Joyce Melrose, pouring coffee over by the fire, called out chidingly, "You haven't learned how to stake out a horse yet, cowboy?"

The runaway pony had vanished down the ravine now.

"It was your palomino, Joyce," he said, and ran over to where he had left his saddle. "I'll have to dab my loop on that renegade of yours. I'll be back before those spuds come to a boil."

Shouldering his saddle, Redding crossed the creek to where the remaining three horses, still spooked by the coyote's predatory call, returned to their grazing.

He saddled his steeldust gelding and mounted, took a long look across the creek to satisfy himself that it was safe to leave Joyce there for even so short an interval as he expected to be gone, and then put his gelding down the ravine.

He believed the palomino would not travel far before snagging its rope in the brush or stopping to graze. Fifty yards downstream, the heavy undergrowth of willows and dwarf cottonwoods began closing in behind him, shutting off his view of the camp.

He reined up for another look, mentally wondering at his nervousness in leaving the girl behind. At the moment she was pulling pine knots out of a deadfall log to replenish the fire. The upleap of flames revealed the motionless shapes of Teague Darkin and the Wagonwheel man, securely trussed to the piñon at the edge of the clearing.

Redding touched the steeldust's flanks with his rowels and pushed on into the total darkness of the ravine, concentrating his attention on locating the girl's runaway horse.

Back at the camp, Joyce Melrose tested the boiled potatoes with a tin fork, found them ready, and set them aside to cool. Her first inkling that all was not right came when she heard a horse whicker and blow its lips, from the direction of the North Gate road behind her; and her first reaction was to call Redding and tell him her palomino had somehow doubled back to the camp through the roundabout pines.

Turning, she saw a rider spur into the camp site from the road at the top of the ravine. Indistinct in the

199

firelight, the horseman reined up at the edge of the clearing to stare at Redding's two prisoners lashed to the piñon tree.

Joyce thought, *This is one of the Wagonwheelers we saw coming in from roundup this afternoon.* Then a shock of pure horror went through her as she heard Teague Darkin cry out, "Redding ain't here, Blaze— watch the girl! Watch the girl!"

Joyce opened her mouth to scream, thinking to warn Doug that somehow Blaze Tondro had trailed them here. But the cry froze in her throat as she saw a second and a third rider break out of the brush into the firelight and she saw the red ring of a rifle's muzzle slanting from one of their saddle pommels, aimed straight at her.

It was not the menace of that Winchester which turned Joyce's knees to water. The firelight shuttering on the first rider's face showed the scarred, ugly visage of the halfbreed Tondro, his black hair belted down the middle with a streak of white, like a skunk. Here, in the flesh, was the man whose name had filled her childhood nightmares.

Blaze Tondro dismounted. The two riders flanking his horse, Joyce now saw, were Mexicans, decked out in serapes and tall-crowned sombreros, flare-bottomed gaucho pants and gaudy jackets with gold-braided frogs.

The silence was broken once more by Teague Darkin, wrenching himself violently in his bonds. "Damn you, Tondro—if it was you that turned Joyce's palomino loose, why didn't you shoot Redding before he left?"

Tondro's beady eyes were fixed on Joyce's motionless figure. Her rifle was leaning against her saddle, ten feet away.

"What are you bellerin' about, Teague?" the rustler growled. "I turned no *caballo* loose. We just pulled off the road to scout this fire."

Darkin ground out an oath. "Cut me loose, you *cabrón!*" he shouted in Spanish. "Redding may be back any minute."

Ignoring Darkin, Blaze Tondro stalked across the camp ground to halt in front of Joyce. He flung a surly retort over his shoulder. "How did I know Redding was with you? The note O'Connor brought me said you'd nabbed Redding over at Crowfoot. You ought to count yourself lucky that I decided to collect our pay for that trail drive while I was in this part of the country. Otherwise I wouldn't have come back to Wagonwheel."

Through all this talk, Joyce Melrose had stood transfixed, knowing she would never be able to reach her saddle gun.

Now she saw Tondro suddenly reverse the rifle he was caging and poise the gunstock over his head.

She divined his purpose too late. She saw the chopping blow coming and gave vent to a scream which resounded across the ravine like the wail of a banshee. That scream was cut short by the sodden impact of butt plate on bone.

Joyce Melrose slumped like an axed tree, blood welling from her bruised temple. Tondro turned to see one of his Mexican henchmen, wielding a long-bladed *cuchilla*, slicing the ropes to release old Jinglebob and Darkin from the piñon.

Kicking free of his bonds, Darkin snatched a six-shooter from the Mexican's holster and turning to face Jinglebob, thrust the gun against the roustabout's belly and fired.

The old man fell back against the piñon trunk, and his legs gouged twin furrows through the leaf mold as he slid to a sitting position, his eyes holding their shock and anger as he toppled slowly over on his side.

"What in hell was that for?" demanded Tondro,

stunned by the ruthlessness of his *compañero's* action despite his own familiarity with violent death.

"On the way over the Pass tonight Redding let slip he knew it was me who cashed in Duke Harrington's chips," panted the Crowfoot foreman in a demented voice. "Only Jinglebob knew that. He sold me down the river while I was knocked out back at the ranch."

Darkin drove a kick into the fallen roustabout's ribs and then wheeled to face the others.

"Ramon! Pedro! Pitch a blanket on that fire. If Redding heard Joyce holler he'll be back and pick us off like sittin' ducks."

One of Tondro's men threw a saddle blanket over the campfire, shutting off the light. Darkin sprinted across the area and waded the shallow creek to reach the hobbled horses.

Tondro called out uncertainly, "What'll we do with your woman? She's bad medicine. Always has been. I say we ought to kill her."

Darkin's shout came back through the gloom of the ravine. "We're taking her with us back to Thunder Rock. She'll be my ace in the hole in case we don't nab Redding tonight."

CHAPTER 27

POSSEMEN RIDE

JOYCE'S CUT-OFF SCREAM CARRIED TO DOUG Redding's ears some hundred yards down the creek in a raveled, thin rope of sound which, in this tricky dark, he mistook for the screech of a panther that had scented the staked-out horses.

202

His attention at the moment was distracted by the business of tying his lariat to the headstall of the girl's palomino. The runaway mount had been blocked by an uprooted tree which had toppled into the creek from the north claybank.

Above the sluicing of water over the rocks, Redding could not be sure he had even heard the scream. He wasted time getting the palomino out of the tangle of water-logged brush, knowing the danger of the animal spooking and breaking a leg on the slippery boulders.

He was out of saddle, checking the frayed end of a broken picket rope dangling from the palomino's headstall, when the sharp crack of a gunshot drove its unmistakable echo down the ravine.

That could only mean trouble back at camp. Maybe Darkin or Jinglebob had somehow managed to loosen their ropes. Maybe Joyce had taken a shot at a panther stalking their livestock. Maybe—

Redding dropped the rope he had intended to use in leading the palomino back to camp and vaulted into saddle, putting his gelding up the slippery creek bed as hard as he could spur the animal in this tricky footing.

Before he got clear of the willow he saw the pink glow of Joyce's campfire suddenly wink out, as if the coals had been downed. It was only when he fought through the willows that his nostrils picked up a smudge of smoke and singed wool, and he knew that a saddle blanket had extinguished the fire.

He heard hoofs churning the river with great splashes, and a voice he recognized as Darkin's shouting.

A confused rush of noise hit Redding as he raked the steeldust with his spurs, snaking his Winchester out of its boot and levering a cartridge into the breech.

Fear was a retching sensation in his throat as he

realized that his prisoners had somehow gotten loose, that Joyce had uttered that scream. He remembered now how that scream had been cut off, and he had a sickening fear that she was dead.

The fire had charred a hole in the saddle blanket and a quick ribbon of orange flame leaped up, to give Redding a pinched-off glimpse of the mad activity going on up the ravine.

He spotted Blaze Tondro and a Mexican lifting Joyce's limp figure across a bare-backed horse, the one belonging to Jinglebob. Teague Darkin leaped astride that horse, getting an arm around the girl's body.

The fire glow ebbed when Redding was within fifty yards of the camp. But there was light enough for Redding to see Tondro and two other riders swinging into saddle to quit the clearing as Darkin, holding the girl ahead of him, sent his horse pounding up the ravine slope toward the Basin road.

Redding's horse stumbled, nearly throwing him. As it struggled to regain itself in the rush of water against its chest, Redding lifted his rifle to shoulder and drove a shot toward the last of the escaping riders. He saw a man's body lurch to the strike of his lucky bullet and pitch out of stirrups.

The horse under him regained its feet, and Redding lost precious time fighting it under control again. From the timber above the camp the darkness was broken by the nozzling sparks of gun flashes, and Redding knew by the whine and whip of lead bracketing him that Tondro and the others were shooting at the smudge of gun smoke which, catching the moonlight, showed them his location.

Darkness ran into the pit of the ravine as the moon edged into a fleecy nest of clouds. The campfire had ebbed under the smoldering blanket. Hoofs were pounding up the slope toward the road. Gun flashes continued to break the shadows up there as one of the riders held back to delay Redding's pursuit.

Redding was unaware that his horse had been struck by one of those fusilading slugs until, swinging out of the creek into the campfire's thick smudge, he felt the steeldust go down, a whimpering scream in its throttle.

He narrowly missed getting a leg caught under the falling horse as it toppled sideways into the turf. Jumping free, he swung his gun toward the road, then held his fire, knowing that without a definite target to draw down on, a random bullet might hit Joyce.

The moon slid momentarily from its cover, and a yell in Spanish, from high up the slope, told Redding that Blaze Tondro had seen him. "Redding is down—his horse is down."

As the moon faded again Redding saw a Mexican's sombreroed shape sky-lined on the Basin road up there. He fired at once, and through the confusing echoes of the shot he heard Teague Darkin shout, "Come on— we'll drift. He could hole up in that timber and pick us off like he did Ramon."

Redding groaned. Joyce's kidnapers were quitting this fight, withdrawing by way of North Gate. Hoofs were beating up sodden echoes, eastbound toward the Basin.

Desperation drove Redding at a slogging sprint across the clearing. He stumbled over the Mexican he had shot from saddle, but he knew the man was dead by the inertness of him, and he clawed his way through the whippy undergrowth until he reached the edge of the wagon road.

He flung himself belly down there, knowing how

Tondro worked, knowing the rustler might have held back to cover Darkin's getaway with the girl.

But that fast-ebbing rush of hoofbeats floating back on the breeze told its own story. Three horses. Tondro's and Darkin's, the latter carrying double, and the other *vaquero*. They had no stomach for the job of cornering Redding, even afoot, in timber where a fugitive could move at will without detection.

A crashing in the brush up the road toward the summit to Redding's left, made him spin around with rifle lifting. Then he relaxed as he saw a riderless pony, saddle leather flapping, bolt from the roadside chaparral and head out of sight toward Wagonwheel. That would be the dead Ramon's mount.

Redding came slowly to his feet, a sick despair blunting the fact that he wouldn't have to fight off heavy odds here in the North Gate tonight. A lucky bullet had left him afoot. His only hope of riding in pursuit depended on catching Joyce's palomino deeper down the ravine. That would take time, precious time. Joyce's kidnapers already had a long start.

He made his way down the slope toward the blood-red glare of the burning saddle blanket, which put its flickering glow over the black and scarlet edges of the campground.

At the edge of the brush he again stumbled over the Mexican's body. Redding's slug had drilled the *vaquero's* chest, passing completely through him. He thought bitterly, *Why couldn't that have been Tondro?*

Then he realized that Jinglebob was unaccounted for. Swinging toward the piñon, he caught sight of the oldster's sprawled body, blood guttering from a powder-burned hole punched through his shirt, belt-high.

Either Tondro or Darkin had shot the Wagonwheel

man. That was the gunshot Redding had heard, his first intimation that disaster had struck the camp during his absence.

A horse whickered from the grassy pocket across the creek, and Redding was surprised to see Darkin's horse still on hobble there. This, at least, was a break of luck; the outlaws had been in too much of a hurry to get away from the camp, before he returned, to unpicket the Crowfoot pony.

He waded the glassy run of the creek and led Darkin's mount back to where his steeldust had dropped, got his saddle free, and cinched it aboard the other mount. At least this spared him having to hunt down the palomino on foot.

Redding led the horse across the campground and knelt beside Jinglebob. He was startled to see the old man's rheumy eyes open, refracting the campfire light; Jinglebob's lips moved, and as Redding bent low he caught the man's expiring whisper.

"They're takin'—the Melrose girl—to Tondro's hide-out—in the Navajadas—son. Wish I could tell you—how to git thar."

A rush of thanksgiving welled through the cattle detective as he gripped the dying man's arm. "Thanks for tellin' me that, Jinglebob. I know where Tondro dens up. I've been there."

Something like a grin softened the tautness of the roustabout's lips. "Glad—glad. That's what—the Duke meant—when he said the girl would be his—ace in the hole—if they didn't tally you—tonight—"

Jinglebob's voice trailed off in a rattly exhalation, and Redding stood up, knowing the old man was across the Big Divide, wishing he could tarry here to give Jinglebob decent burial before the timber wolves were drawn here by the scent of spilled blood. But that was impossible.

He rode up to the Basin road, the dust and smell of the running horses still clinging to the night air. The wind off the Basin was in his favor; and when Redding reached the foot of the grade where the Basin flats began, he distinctly heard the distance-muted drumming of hoofs, headed southeast.

He reined up to let his horse have a breather and tried to reason this thing out. Somehow, Darkin had been rescued by Tondro and his Mexicans, who had apparently been the trio of riders Redding had mistaken for homeward-bound Wagonwheel punchers as they were leaving the ranch.

Armed with the knowledge old Jinglebob had given him with his last breath, Redding knew why Darkin had bothered to take Joyce Melrose with him in his last flight out of the Basin.

Joyce was the hostage Darkin would bargain with when the final showdown came at Tondro's hide-out in Thunder Rock gorge. It suddenly occurred to Redding that neither Tondro nor Darkin knew that their lair was no longer a secret. Redding had not mentioned, back at Wagonwheel, how he had trailed Clark O'Connor into the Navajadas the other day.

Darkin would feel safe in the refuge of Thunder Rock. He might choose to join Tondro in the border smuggling trade, now that he was forever cut off from Crowfoot and his alter-ego role as Duke Harrington.

As long as Joyce Melrose was alive, Darkin might try to win back Crowfoot as the ransom for her life.

Full daylight found Redding heading south on the Basin flats. He traced the tracks of the escaping trio to a line-camp shack with a Rafter B burned into its door and found evidence where the fugitives had pumped water in a trough for their horses.

Beyond this point, the trail became lost where Rafter B had driven a beef herd toward Paloverde.

At noon, the gaunt-faced lawman rested his horse at a chuck-wagon camp, where he wolfed down a meal; the cook's curious stare followed him as he headed south again, picking up a county road that would bring him to Trailfork.

Sundown was burning in the west when Redding reached his journey's end at Val Lennon's office in the Trailfork jail. It was a far different ending to this trek from North Gate than he had anticipated yesterday at this time.

The grizzled old sheriff met him at the door, grinning. "I got another prize specimen in my hoosegow to keep Joe Curtwright's cell occupied, son."

A wild irrational hope surged through the core of Redding's being. Was it possible that Lennon had stumbled across Tondro en route across the Basin?

"Who?"

"Clark O'Connor. Arrested him this mornin' just after he got back from the mountains. Claimed he'd been fishin'."

Anticlimax was like nausea in Redding. "Come inside, Sheriff," he said wearily. "I've got some bad news for you."

Night had come to Trailfork during the time it took Redding to recount Tondro's trail drive to Wagonwheel, his encounter with the so-called Duke Harrington, and Joyce's kidnaping.

"I figure they'll reach Thunder Rock sometime tonight," Redding wound up. "Whether Joyce survives

209

that trip I won't gamble on. The thing is, Sheriff, we've got to move out with a posse tonight."

Val Lennon's eyes took on a feverish glint. "I ain't been settin' on my haunches the past couple days," he said. "I got a thirty-man posse ready to drift. The town's middlin' full of cowpokes in from the beef gathers."

"*Bueno*. These thirty—you can count on 'em?"

"Picked 'em personal, son. Nary a Tondro spy in the bunch. Got 'em standin' by, waitin' for you to give the word."

Redding's look showed his disappointment. He had hoped to lead a posse of at least fifty riders into the Navajadas. Doc Stiles had said it would take two troops of cavalry to breach Tondro's defenses.

"Twelve of that bunch," Lennon went on hopefully, sensing Redding's doubts, "are storekeepers and bartenders here in town. Willin' to risk their hides to stamp Tondro out for good. They know Trailfork will die on the vine if they don't make this range fit for decent folks to live in." He paused. "If I had a month to work in I couldn't muster more than thirty men, son."

Redding got to his feet, fighting the weariness in him, but with Joyce Melrose's fate resting in his hands he knew he must keep driving himself to the limit of his endurance. "I'll go eat," he said. "I'll have to touch you for the loan of another horse, Sheriff. It was your pet steeldust that Tondro shot out from under me at North Gate last night."

The sheriff grinned. "You've about cleaned out my stable, son, but I know a good quarter horse I can borrow for you. Anything else you want attended to while you grab some grub?"

"I'd like to have four good stout lass ropes, each one fifty-sixty foot long, tied together and hung on my saddle, Val."

"You'll have 'em. When you takin' us out?"

"I'm not," Redding said. "I'll ride out to where the Sangre de Santos Creek crosses the Paloverde road. I want you and your deputies to leave town in twos and threes, like they were heading for their home bunkhouses. That way, if Tondro has any spies in town they won't get suspicious."

Lennon chewed his mustache. "You'll be waitin' at the Santos ford to guide us to Tondro's?"

"I'll meet you there at midnight, Sheriff. Be sure you have those ropes ready before I ride."

After Redding had left, Lennon felt a shiver of apprehension go through him. He had his doubts if any of them would live through this night ahead.

CHAPTER 28

OVER HELL'S RIM

WAITING AT SANGRE DE SANTOS CREEK FORD, DOUG Redding counted the posse riders who rode in from Trailfork, in pairs or singly. It was midnight sharp when Sheriff Val Lennon arrived, and Redding knew the strength he would pit against Tondro was complete.

"Only twenty-three men?" Redding asked sharply.

"Few of the boys lost their nerve," Lennon apologized, "so we're better off without 'em. Couple too drunk to ride on such short notice. Is the tally too short, son?"

The cattle detective did not show the disappointment he felt. "It's got to be tonight, Sheriff."

In the starlight, Redding recognized men he had seen

211

loafing on the gallery of the Emigrants' Tavern; a roulette croupier and a bartender from the Fandango. Less than half of these men were ranchers or cowhands. All were heavily armed—rifles, sidearms, shotguns.

"This is Doug Redding of the Protective, men," Lennon said. "Reckon you've got acquainted with him by now. You'll take his orders from here on out, not mine. Speak your piece, Doug."

Redding piled hands on saddle horn. Lennon had provided him with a chestnut quarter horse. From the pommel hung two hundred feet of lariats knotted together for Redding's undisclosed use.

They were waiting for him to speak, little realizing the long chain of events, of bloodshed and gun smoke and deadly risks which had brought Redding to this climactic hour.

"This won't be easy," he said. "Some of us won't return to the Basin. Each of you has got to believe in his own heart that this business is worth the price, or you don't belong here."

The gambler from the Fandango said, "We all got our reasons. I'm doin' this for Zedra and old Doc."

Redding nodded, touched by this loyalty to a woman whom many Trailforkers regarded as just another dance-hall jezebel. The sheriff had apparently revealed Zedra's secret to his posse riders, knowing the recruiting value of Doc Stiles's story.

"We should reach the approaches of Tondro's canyon an hour before daylight," Redding said, coming down to cases. "On the way there will be no smoking, no talking, no backing out. If any of you family men want to pull out, now is the time. No man will question your motives. I don't have to tell you Tondro won't cave without a lot of bloodshed."

Redding waited. No man spoke. Throats were cleared; bodies twisted in saddle, making the leather creak. Lennon had chosen his deputies well. Scared, most of them, but willing to ride into the jaws of whatever hell awaited them back in the brooding Navajada uplands, gambling on coming back."

" '*Stá bueono*," Redding said. "Let's ride."

Within twenty minutes the file of posse riders were following Redding into the canyon of Twelve Mile Creek. Soon the lifting pine-clad walls of granite swallowed them up, as they sloshed up the shallow stream as Clark O'Connor had done a few days ago.

At five-mile intervals Redding signaled halts, conserving horses and men alike for this assault on Tondro's bastion. The man hunters needed no urging to maintain a strict silence, knowing that danger might meet them head-on at any twisting of this rustler trail.

Dawn was a good two hours off when they reached the avalanche pile which filtered the waters of Twelve Mile Creek. Redding guided the party up the steep flank of this gorge and waited at its crest until the last riders had gathered around him. The moon was behind an overcast which dulled the landmarks hereabout; the crest of Thunder Rock Falls was a blurred nimbus at the box end of the canyon, too faint for the possemen to discern had Redding pointed it out.

Redding pointed to the black, mysterious gulf which marked Thunder Rock Canyon. "This mining road leads to the old shaft house where Tondro holes up," he whispered. "It's guarded around the clock by at least one sentry, but I think you'll get to the bottom of the gorge before sunrise, without any trouble."

Lennon spoke uneasily. "How about that escape tunnel you were tellin' me about, Doug?"

213

Redding said, "I'm leaving you here, to take care of that. The mine tunnel opens on the other side of the divide, I reckon, and probably on Mexican soil, out of your jurisdiction. I'll block that leak."

"Singlehanded? Don't be a fool!" someone objected.

"I'm carrying enough rope to let myself over the rimrock into Tondro's camp," Redding said. "It's got to be a one-man job. I'm the only one who knows the lay of the land over there."

Lennon stirred uneasily, aware that the SPA man was taking the brunt of the risks from here on.

"You move your men down into the canyon yonder, Sheriff," Redding went on. "Tondro won't be expecting you. Your risk will be taking his guard out of the play. When the guard spots you, he'll probably fire a shot to rouse the camp. The only way to do this thing is bull your way through and stampede Tondro's bunch into heading for their escape tunnel. I'll be there to meet 'em. And don't worry about me. One man can hold back an army, inside that tunnel."

Men nodded, getting the picture and not liking it. They were going to box Tondro's owlhoot legion against the dead end of the canyon, striking by surprise and showing no mercy. In that way they stood a chance to buffalo the rustlers into a mass surrender.

"Give me an hour before you head up the canyon," Redding said. "I want to do what I can to locate the two women who are up there, Zedra Stiles and Joyce Melrose. *Hasta la vista* and luck to you."

With that parting word, Doug Redding spurred away from the group and headed along the steep, brush-mottled slope of the mountain ridge which overlooked Thunder Rock Falls, the slope he had scouted a few days ago. Fifty feet away from the posse he was lost to

214

view.

Dawn was a pale-pink promise beyond the saw-toothed spires of the Navajada peaks when Redding reached the *rincon* where he had left his horse on his previous visit. He lifted the heavy coil of lariats he had tied together at the sheriff's office in Trailfork, hoisted it over his shoulder, and, carrying his Winchester, headed down the roof-steep declivity toward the sheer jump-off of the cliff.

Reaching the lava ledge, Redding paused to study the dim outlines of the shaft house below. The waterfall's thunder was an even roar on his eardrums; a restless vortex of wind currents carried the moist breath of the river to him.

He could make out no details, but lights glowed in the shaft house. That was bad. Lennon's possemen, even now making their way up the canyon toward Tondro's sentry post, had counted on the element of surprise in attacking this camp.

He worked his way along the rimrock with infinite caution, knowing death would be the price of a misstep, yet moving as rapidly as he dared, for daylight must not catch him at his work.

He estimated there was another half hour of darkness remaining when he rounded the box end of the gorge, approaching the glossy crest of the waterfall.

Fifty feet from the plunging cascade he selected a hardy jack pine, its roots thrusting deep into fissures of the rock, and tied one end of his rope coil securely to its trunk.

Approaching the rimrock on hands and knees, Redding dumped the remainder of the coil off into space. It plummeted down into the blackness and was lost to his view in the swirling mists from the falls.

He had tied four fifty-foot lariats together. That should give him rope to spare at the bottom.

Tondro's rustler camp was shrouded in a deep and brooding silence. Redding felt a moment's panic, wondering if Tondro and Darkin had brought Joyce here, as old Jinglebob had told him. If they had headed directly for Mexican soil instead, then Joyce was doomed.

He tied the Winchester around his shoulder with a makeshift sling created out of thongs he had cut from his saddle skirts. Seating himself on the dizzy edge of the chasm with his legs overhanging the rim, he gave his twin Colts a final checkup, thrusting cartridges into the empty chambers under the firing-pins.

All was in readiness. Redding got his secure grip on the hair rope which was the first of the four lariats he had knotted together. Some deep-rooted superstition caused him to reach under his shirt and rub the golden lizard ring he carried, slung around his neck, for luck.

Then, nudging the walnut stock of his rifle into better position over his back with an elbow, Redding swung his weight over the cliff's edge. He had no fears of the ropes not holding his hundred and eighty pounds. Each lariat had been designed to take the snap of a thousand-pound steer from its dallies on a saddle horn.

Dawn was beginning to gild the granite teeth of the divide as Redding kinked his left leg around the slender lifeline, to serve as a brake, and began his hand-over-hand descent of the rope.

The beetling overhang of the cliff prevented him from touching the granite wall with his toes. His palms would be blistered and bleeding by the time his boots touched solid bottom.

There would be no returning from Thunder Rock Canyon by this method. He had his last chip in the pot this time. All or nothing. It depended on how fate flipped the cards in the hour ahead.

CHAPTER 29

THUNDER ROCK SHOWDOWN

"THAT'LL FIX HER FOR THE TIME BEING, ZEDRA."

Doc Stiles put the finishing touches on the turban of bandage which girdled Joyce Melrose's head, having stitched the bloody welt on her skull where Tondro's rifle stock had clubbed her.

They were inside the partitioned cubicle in Tondro's shaft house which the outlaw had set aside, years ago, for the privacy of Zedra Stiles. Zedra knelt beside the bunk where Joyce lay now, holding the other girl's hands in hers.

Joyce had only the haziest recollection of their nightmarish flight across Lavarim Basin. She knew only in a vague way where she was now. Only the friendly presence of Zedra and her father kept her from hysteria.

The lantern hanging from a ceiling beam over the bunk flickered as the door of the cubicle opened and Teague Darkin, his jowls and chin covered with a two-day growth of stubble like fine rusty wire, entered the cubicle.

"I got to talk to Joyce—alone," Darkin gruffed at the old doctor. "It's a matter of life or death for all four of us, Doc. Tondro's given me an ultimatum to deliver to Joyce."

Stiles's rheumy eyes held a venomous glitter as he

217

said, "Miss Melrose needs rest, Darkin. I'll give you five minutes with her, no more."

Zedra gave Joyce's hand a reassuring squeeze and followed her father out of the room. Darkin regarded Joyce through eyes like burned-out coals, bespeaking his own exhaustion. The flight from North Gate had been as hard on him as it had on Joyce.

Joyce clutched the blanket about her and turned to the wall, flinching as Darkin touched her arm.

Darkin cleared his throat. "Joyce," he said in a rasping voice, "you got to talk to me. I know you hate my insides."

"We have nothing to talk about, Teague."

"This thing has passed out of my control, Joyce. Tondro has given me an ultimatum. Whether or not either of us lives to see daylight depends on you."

Joyce pulled herself to a sitting position on the bunk and turned to regard her erstwhile foreman with a loathing intensity she would have given a coiled rattlesnake.

"You ask me to help you—you, the beast who shot my father in cold blood! You made love to me only because you wanted my ranch as a rustling base for Tondro. And you think I would help you!"

Darkin licked his lips. "Tondro still wants Crowfoot," he said hopelessly. "You've got to become my wife if either of us leaves this place alive. It—it won't have to be a real marriage, Joyce. I realize I've forfeited your love. I—"

"You never had it, Teague. I accepted your ring because Dad set such store in you."

Darkin lowered his gaze. "I know, Joyce, I know. The thing is, you have your own life to think about. Unless you accept me on Tondro's terms, that half-breed will torture the both of us. And Zedra and Doc as well. That's how it stacks up, Joyce."

Joyce Melrose's lips twisted into an ugly caricature of a smile.

"Tondro can't touch Crowfoot unless I agree to marry you?"

A faint hope sprung alive in Darkin's eyes. "It is a small price to pay for the lives of four people."

The door opened, and the bearded face of Doc Stiles appeared there. "Your time's up, Darkin. Miss Melrose is in no shape to argue anything with you. If she wasn't made of whang leather and sawdust like her father before her, she wouldn't have survived the trip here."

Darkin stood up, staring down at Joyce with a slow desperation growing in his eyes. "Tondro's given me an hour to get your answer," he said hoarsely. "For God's sake don't let your hatred of me cause Doc and Zedra to lose their lives."

Darkin walked past Stiles into the blackness of the main shaft house, its walls confining the chorus of snoring from the Mexican renegades. The Crowfoot foreman stumbled over to the bunk Tondro had assigned to him. He saw Zedra step into the cubicle to join Joyce, saw the lantern go out.

Doc Stiles picked up his kit bag and spoke softly to the two women in the room. "I guess we'd all better make our peace with God. Tondro wasn't bluffing when he gave Darkin his orders."

The old doctor left the shaft house, feeling the need of fresh air. Stiles, so long a prisoner in this place that he could not be sure an outside world even existed, welcomed this coming dawn which he was sure, in his secret heart, would be the last he would ever see. The nearness of death's release had a paradoxical power to exalt his spirits now.

Doc Stiles's steps took him across the canyon floor toward the base of the waterfall. It was his habit to bathe in the crystal water of the vast pool to one side of the plunging cataract. That was his intention now as he stripped off his ragged coat and sat down on a rock to tug at his warped boots.

"Doc! Doc Stiles."

A voice was calling him, barely audible above the thunder of tumbling waters so near at hand. For a moment Stiles believed that his sanity had cracked, that his brain was playing him tricks. He twisted around, squinting through the half-light of the approaching dawn.

Then he caught sight of a tall chap-clad figure standing in front of the getaway tunnel which made its black oval against the base of the cliff, fifty feet from the waterfall. Staring at the apparition like a man in a trance, Stiles came jerkily to his feet.

"Doug Redding!" he gasped out. "It—it cannot be."

But it was true. The stock detective was no ghost, no figment of his imagination. Doug Redding stood waiting at the tunnel's mouth. By what miracle had he breached the heavy iron gates which Tondro had built inside that shaft?

Stiles stumbled his way up the sprawl of old mine tailings, half expecting Redding's shape to dissolve like a wisp of smoke. A moment later their hands met and clasped.

"Joyce Melrose—is she here, Doc?" Redding said harshly.

Staring off beyond Redding, Stiles's eyes spotted the thin spider web of knotted lariats dangling down the face of the cliff, from the rimrock a hundred and fifty feet above, and knew then how Redding had penetrated this outlaw citadel.

"Yes," Stiles panted. "She got in with Tondro and Teague Darkin not three hours ago."

"Is she all right?"

"Suffering the aftermath of a nasty concussion, but otherwise unhurt. She and my daughter are in the shaft house. What are you doing here, Redding? Are you committing suicide for that girl's sake?"

Redding pulled the old man into the shadowy interior of the tunnel mouth. "Listen, Doc," the detective said, and told the unbelieving oldster of Lennon's posse, even now coming up the canyon.

"It'll be sunrise in another ten minutes," Redding finished up, "and all hell will cut loose when Tondro's guards spot the posse riding in. I'm here to keep them from vamoosing through this escape tunnel. Is there any chance you can bring the two girls out here—get them somewhere out of range of ricocheting bullets?"

Stiles appeared incapable of speech. For a man so accustomed to living out his span without hope of freedom, Redding's words were too much for his tired mind to comprehend.

"Snap out of it, Doc!" Redding pleaded. "Time is running out. That posse will give Tondro's bunch no quarter. I can't have Joyce and your daughter killed during the fracas—"

Redding's words were cut off by a sudden spate of gunfire coming from a remote distance down the canyon, the sheer rock walls amplifying that shooting until it became an ear-numbing din.

"Sentries have spotted Lennon coming in," Redding yelled in the old man's ear. "I shaved this too fine."

The sound of gunfire tapered off, but close on its

221

heels there sounded a pandemonium of yells from the shaft house, muffled by the waterfall's unending roar, and Redding groaned his despair of getting Zedra and Joyce to safety as he saw a dozen half-clad Mexicans come tumbling out the shaft-house door, faces turned down the canyon whence the shooting had come.

The holocaust soon to erupt here was out of Redding's hands now. He heard Blaze Tondro's voice bawling orders, saw reason return to the panicked *vaqueros* as they ducked back into the shaft house like ants in a disturbed hill, emerging with rifles and gun belts as they headed toward the horse corral.

A great thunderbolt of sound rolled up the gorge, and Redding felt his scalp prickle as he visualized the hellfire old Val Lennon was leading his column of riders through.

Even as the thought took shape in his mind his pulses leaped to the dramatic spectacle of the Trailfork sheriff hammering into view around the near turn of the canyon trail, his law badge flashing in the first rays of the morning sun.

Empty saddles showed in that oncoming cavalcade of possemen, testimony to the brief and bitter fight which Tondro's guards had made against this surprise invasion of their fortress. But the posse had breached that blockade of hidden guns and were now carrying the fight into Thunder Rock itself.

A counterfire of guns crashed from the shaft house. Redding, waiting helplessly in the tunnel mouth with Doc Stiles at his side, saw Lennon and his men dive from horseback to take to the shelter of the brush and rocks, escaping the devastating fire which Tondro's trapped crew was pouring down the canyon.

There was no time now for Tondro's gang to mount

and ride to the defense of their sentries. The shaft-house doors swarmed with yelling men as Tondro sent his force out into the brush to shoot it out with the posse in hand-to-hand combat.

Redding thrust one of his Colt .45s into Doc Stiles's scraggy fist as the two of them bellied down on the rubbled floor of the escape tunnel. Any moment now, Redding knew Tondro would abandon his bastion and lead his disorganized horde of gunmen toward this tunnel and its escape route under the Navajadas.

The roar of the waterfall was lost under the continuous slam and crash of gunnery, where the pitched battle was raging in the rocks and brush where rustlers and possemen had taken cover. Crisscrossing lead laced the air, ricochets smearing gray streaks on the cliffs, punching holes in the shaft house.

And then, through the drifting gun smoke and the cacophony of battle sounds, Redding saw a blur of movement leaving the side of the shaft house which was out of sight of the battle.

Blaze Tondro and Teague Darkin, united now in the common peril facing this rustler bastion, were racing for the corral gates. An overwhelming urge to run out and head them off surged through Redding, but he held his place, knowing his job was to bar the escape tunnel when Tondro ordered his forces to retreat.

A moment later Tondro and the erstwhile Crowfoot foreman appeared from the horse barn, leading four unsaddled horses toward the side door of the shaft house. Redding knew then that Tondro was going to desert his men while they fought a rear-guard action to cover their leader's escape.

The shadows were still too thick alongside the near wall of the shaft house for Redding to see what was going on by the door where the horses waited, their reins held by Darkin.

But he had his answer in the next moment, when the four ponies bolted away from the building and headed at a dead run toward the maw of the escape tunnel where he and Doc Stiles were crouched, waiting.

CHAPTER 30

ROSTER OF THE DAMNED

"THEY GOT THE GIRLS WITH 'EM!"

Stiles's shout was true. The four horses were thundering abreast like a picture from the Apocalypse. Teague Darkin was on the left flank, leading Joyce Melrose's mount, her head bandage gleaming in the dawn's ruddy light. Tondro was on the extreme right, Zedra Stiles riding a stallion at his inside stirrup.

As they converged on the mouth of the escape tunnel Redding yelled in Stiles's ear, "Hold your fire, Doc!"

Redding came to his feet and lunged out into full view of the oncoming fugitives. Tondro at this moment was hipped around for a last glance at the pitched battle raging between his henchmen and Lennon's posse. But Teague Darkin spotted Redding's spread-legged figure blocking the entrance to the tunnel, and his frantic yell brought Tondro jerking around.

Darkin pulled his horse back, aiming to put Joyce between him and Redding's line of fire. With a cold laugh, Redding whipped gunstock to cheek, caught the Crowfoot foreman's shape in his gun sights, and squeezed off his shot.

He saw Darkin reel to the impact of lead tunneling his

224

midriff and slide off the rump of his horse, freeing Joyce's lead rope. Joyce screamed something Redding could not hear.

Events were moving too rapidly for Redding to grasp them coherently. He saw Teague Darkin come to his feet, saw the tongues of flame spit from the bores of Darkin's guns; and this time Redding took his time about aiming, and his second shot caught the outlaw between the ribs and put him out of the fight.

Tondro had reined up, not daring to ride closer to the spot where Redding was jerking the lever of his smoking Winchester. Doc Stiles stood beside him, arms hanging motionless at his sides, seemingly paralyzed by the violent action going on around him.

The rustler chief flung aside the lead rope of Zedra's horse. Taking advantage of Tondro's preoccupation, the girl he had held a prisoner to his will through the richest years of her life dived from horseback, was lost in the swirling dust.

With a wild yell, Tondro sent his horse hammering straight at the tunnel mouth, six-guns throwing their barrage of lead at the indomitable figure ahead of him.

Redding felt something like a lance of white-hot fire go through his body. His rifle sights were on Tondro, but the strength to pull trigger fled from his hand. The rifle sagged as another of Tondro's shots ripped the flesh of his right hip and whirled him half around.

He had a kaleidoscopic glimpse of Joyce Melrose running for the shelter of the cliff wall, having abandoned her horse; dim in the swirling dust clouds toward the shaft house was a writhing shape, vomiting blood, which was Teague Darkin.

Incredibly, Redding found himself toppling sideways, Doc Stiles grabbing him and going down on one knee

225

with him. Redding fell forward, his chin gouging the flinty earth.

Above him, Doc Stiles snapped out of his torpor at last and triggered a Colt. His bullet struck Tondro's oncoming horse in the chest, dropping it as if all four legs had been scythed off in one sweep.

Redding pulled his head off the dirt in time to see Tondro hurtling through space as his horse fell, to land at a zigzag run, six-guns blazing alternately, as if the loads in his Colts were inexhaustible.

Stiles was shooting at the oncoming figure of the man he had dreamed for eleven tortured years of killing, but his lead was going wild. Redding heard Doc's firing-pin click on a spent shell. The old man had failed him in this desperate moment.

Blood from an unfelt wound was trickling over Redding's face, clogging his eyelashes. Somehow he found the strength to lift his other six-gun from holster and lay his gun sights on the advancing Tondro. His ears did not hear the explosion of his .45, but he felt the recoil of the weapon on the crotch of his hand.

Like a dream in slow motion, he saw Tondro drop, his sombrero falling free to reveal the skunk stripe in his black head. Redding muttered aloud, "That squares your account, Matt."

Darkness was swirling around him. He saw Doc Stiles run out to where Tondro lay, reaching down to rip the man's shirt open and claw for the key to the iron gate in the escape tunnel which hung by a thong around Tondro's neck.

Stiles was screeching, like a crazy man in delirium, "You killed the hombre you called Blackie Fletcher because my daughter loved him, Tondro. Now you can die knowing that Blackie was a range dick the same as

226

his brother, Doug Redding!"

Those howled words were the last Blaze Tondro heard, short of the click of death's shutter over his senses. A few yards away, they were the last sounds that registered on Doug Redding's fast-fading intelligence.

Hot sunlight burned Redding's eyelids. Thunder Rock Canyon was strangely quiet; the gunfire and the yelling had ceased. He heard the boom of falling water, felt its coolness on his skin.

Doc Stiles's voice floated to him a as if through some long dark tunnel, but his words were meaningless. "He's coming around, Miss Melrose. He'll carry Tondro's scars as long as he lives, but he'll be walking before the geese fly north."

Doug Redding opened his eyes. Joyce's face seemed to be floating in a pink froth above him. He realized then that his head was pillowed in her lap.

He lowered his glance to see Zedra's father removing a probe from a mass of bullet-punctured flesh in his leg and wagging his head as he saw the telltale smear of black on the porcelain tip of the instrument which told the medico that his thrusting explorations had touched a bullet and not a fragment of bone.

"It's all right, Doug." Joyce's, whisper against his ear made sense for the first time. "The fight's over, and you've got nothing to worry about except getting well again."

Redding rolled his head to one side. He saw two of the Trailfork possemen, one of them the gambler from the Fandango, lugging a dead man out of the range of his vision. The corpse was that of Teague Darkin. It didn't seem real, any of this.

Then Sheriff Val Lennon, one arm in a bloody sling,

227

came into the range of his vision and squatted down to wink one rheumy eye at Redding. "Rallied around, eh, son?"

The wounded man managed a grin. "How'd it go, Sheriff?"

"A wipe-out. What few greasers we didn't leave for buzzard bait, back in the rocks yonder, my boys rounded up and dehorned. We aim to burn down the shaft house and dynamite that escape tunnel before we head back to the Basin, son."

Redding closed his eyes, feeling the soft swell of Joyce's breasts as she leaned over him, cradling his head in her arms. It was hard to realize that he had survived this shootout, that peace had come to the Lavarim country, and that Blaze Tondro and Teague Darkin and Joe Curtwright and all the rest were just names on a roster of the damned which Redding, one day, would put in his report to Colonel Regis—the last report he would make to the Protective before he turned in his star for keeps.

He heard Zedra's voice, and opened his eyes to see the girl his brother Matt had loved kneeling beside him helping her father remove a twisted blob of lead from his thigh.

The sunlight flashed from the golden lizard ring on Zedra's finger, the only memento she would have of her her lost love.

Redding saw tears glisten in the girl's eyes as she reached up a hand to where a great rip in his shirt exposed the ring he had carried as a good-luck talisman through this fight.

"I tried to show you—that ring—the night we met at the Fandango, Zedra." Redding spoke for the first time since he had returned to the land of the living. "I wish

Matt—could be here to see those rings—together again."

Zedra turned the loveliness of her smile upon him and said simply, "Those rings brought us luck, señor. That is how Matt would have wanted it. You—you'll take me to his grave on Mustang Mesa someday, *querido?*"

Dizziness swirled through Redding's head as Doc Stiles worked to stem the flow of blood from his bullet-shattered leg. "It's a—a promise Zedra. It'll be a shrine—for us both."

He lifted his eyes to meet the love and thanksgiving in Joyce's eyes.

"This ring—of mine," he said. "It was my father's—just like the one Matt gave to Zedra. I've always carried it—"

Joyce said, "I know, Doug. I know what it means to you."

Redding swallowed, suddenly drowsy, but knowing he must say something before the agony of his wounds made him pass out again. "That ring—I want you to have it, Joyce. And me with it."

He became aware that Joyce's head had come down to shield his face from the blinding glare of sunlight on the waterfall which made a silhouette of Doc Stiles, busy bandaging his leg now.

"I love you dearly, Doug. That is how it was always meant to be."

Her lips made a solid pressure on his as Redding surrendered to the ennui that was a gentle anesthesia on his senses; and he carried the warm promise of her kiss into his following dreams.

We hope that you enjoyed reading this
Sagebrush Large Print Western.
If you would like to read more Sagebrush titles,
ask your librarian or contact the Publishers:

United States and Canada

Thomas T. Beeler, *Publisher*
Post Office Box 659
Hampton Falls, New Hampshire 03844-0659
(800) 251-8726

United Kingdom, Eire, and
the Republic of South Africa

Isis Publishing Ltd
7 Centremead
Osney Mead
Oxford OX2 0ES England
(01865) 250333

Australia and New Zealand

Australian Large Print Audio & Video P/L
17 Mohr Street
Tullamarine, Victoria, 3043, Australia
1 800 335 364